THE ACTOR'S GUIDE TO
MURDER

THE ACTOR'S GUIDE TO
MURDER

Rick Copp

KENSINGTON BOOKS
http://www.kensingtonbooks.com

KENSINGTON BOOKS are published by

Kensington Publishing Corp.
850 Third Avenue
New York, NY 10022

All Kensington titles, imprints and distributed lines are available at special quantity discounts for bulk purchases for sales promotion, premiums, fund-raising, educational or institutional use.

Special book excerpts or customized printings can also be created to fit specific needs. For details, write or phone the office of the Kensington Special Sales Manager: Kensington Publishing Corp., 850 Third Avenue, New York, NY 10022. Attn. Special Sales Department. Phone: 1-800-221-2647.

Kensington and the K logo Reg. U.S. Pat. & TM Off.

Library of Congress Card Catalogue Number: 2003103755
ISBN 0-7582-0495-7

First Printing: November 2003
10 9 8 7 6 5 4 3 2 1

Printed in the United States of America

To Mom and Fred
For your love, support, and for never insisting I have something
to fall back on.

Acknowledgments

First and foremost, I would like to thank John Scognamiglio, who in addition to being a first rate editor, is also, I'm proud to say, a new friend.

I'd like to give special thanks to Joel Fields for being the first brave soul to read a very rough manuscript.

Thanks to all of the enthusiastic friends and family who read the many incarnations of this book and offered invaluable advice: Bennett Yellin, Marilyn Webber, Liz Friedman, Yvette Abatte, Lori Alley, Woody and Tuesdi Woodworth, Joe Dietl, David A. Goodman, Patricia Hyland, Craig Thornton, Sharon Killoran, Brian Levant, and my trusty Writers' Group, which includes Dana Baratta, Melissa Rosenberg, Dan Greenberger, Rob Wright, Allison Gibson, and especially Greg Stancl.

Thanks to Linda Steiner, Laurice and Chris Molinari, Mark Greenhalgh, Laura Simandl, Robert Waldron, Michael Irpino, Ben Zook, Mike Byrne, and Vincent Barra for their enduring love and support, and to Rob Simmons for being a constant source of inspiration.

Also, to my rocks at the William Morris Agency, Lanny Noveck, Cori Wellins, and Jim Engelhardt, my heartfelt gratitude.

And finally, thank you, Holly, Jessica, Megan, and Justin Simason for enriching my life every day.

Chapter One

I never would have gone to that *Smallville* audition if I had known my psychic would foresee the murder of someone I knew. On the other hand, homicides occur in Los Angeles every day, a network audition maybe once or twice a month. If you're lucky.

But there I was, sides in hand, running the lines over and over in my head. The casting director brought me in for the role of a teacher. *A teacher.* Hell, the kid who plays high school heartthrob/superhero Clark Kent looks thirty-five, so where does that put me? Unbelievable. They *always* used to cast me as a student. But now that lovable boyish exuberance that had won me so many youthful parts in television shows and commercials was disappearing faster than my once rock hard abs.

"Jarrod Jarvis?"

"Right here."

I took out my 8x10 glossy from the snappy leather briefcase my mother gave me last Christmas (her hint that it was time for me to get a real job), and handed it over to the casting director. She glanced at it, and then lit up as if reunited with a long lost relative.

"I'm Ellen. I loved you when I was a kid! I had your poster on my wall and everything!"

A major reason for the recent resurgence in my acting career is due to one indisputable fact. Most of the kids who watched me on television in the eighties are now in positions of power. It's a nostalgia thing, and there's no reason for me not to capitalize on it. I decided to make her day.

"Baby, don't even go there!"

It was the trademark line from my five years playing a bright, wisecracking, girl-obsessed troublemaker on the hit sitcom *Go to Your Room!* The writers trotted it out whenever my TV parents tried to blame me for some domestic crisis. It was printed on T-shirts and even mentioned in some book called *TV's Most Quotable Lines.* Okay, so it's not Pinter or even Neil Simon, but the show was what it was, which is probably the reason I never tearfully clutched an Emmy on national TV like Kristy McNichol.

Ellen exploded with laughter upon hearing my famous catchphrase. She could barely contain herself as she ushered me into the conference room.

Inside it was a different atmosphere altogether—three stone-faced producers and a fidgeting casting assistant tapping his foot behind a video camera. The walls of the room were peeling, the couch dusty and stained. As for the oppressive overhead lighting, well, let's just say every pore and pockmark on my face was ready for its close up, Mr. DeMille. Not an auspicious beginning.

Someone was eating Dorito chips from a big plastic fluorescent green bowl. They all stared at me blankly.

Ellen, who was so effusive and supportive up to that point, instantly changed masks. She was now playing the utmost serious professional, sliding my picture in front of the highest ranking producer in the middle, then retreating to the back of the room.

I was completely alone now.

The assistant started taping.

All I could hear was the whirring of the camera, and those damn Dorito chips. *Crunch, crunch, crunch.*

Ellen poked her head up from the back. "Anytime you're ready, Jarrod."

I had only gotten the sides by fax this morning, so I didn't have much time to prepare (a standard actor excuse that I've used shamelessly time and time again).

I wanted to throttle the guy eating the chips because it was throwing my concentration. How could I envision myself in a college lecture hall with Clark and his magazine cover friendly cohorts if all I could focus on was some idiot's annoying chewing?

I decided to use my anger and channel it for the scene. "Don't try to tell me I was seeing things, Kent. I know what I saw, and you were in the school parking lot lifting the rear bumper of that Saturn with your index finger."

I heard some mumbling from the back of the room. I presumed it was Ellen feeding me my cue line. Luckily, I already knew what came next.

"And yesterday, I swore I saw you run past my house at forty-five miles per hour. You're hiding something, you little scumbag, and I'm making it my personal mission to find out what it is!"

I was on a roll. I was making a meal of these lackluster lines. In my heart, I knew I had it in the bag.

"Thank you," said one of the producers as he picked up the next headshot.

I was only a third of the way through the scene. What was going on? I craned my neck to try and get some kind of explanation from my one ally Ellen, but she was already out the door to round up the next victim.

I picked up my briefcase and started out.

I couldn't help myself. I had to know. I turned back to the three Buddhas behind the table.

"Was it my reading?"

The big cheese in the middle looked at me. At first I thought he was going to verbally assault me. How dare a lowly actor speak to a producer unsolicited? But instead he cracked a smile and said, "Oh no. You're just too young."

I guess the day wasn't a total loss.

On my way out, I ran into Willard Ray Hornsby. Willard was auditioning for the same part. We were about the same age, but since Willard had prematurely graying hair, I thought he might have a pretty good shot at the role.

Willard and I had done a production of Agatha Christie's *Ten Little Indians* in Northridge (the epicenter of the big '94 earthquake) a few years back. The theatre was crumbling even before the trembler, but it was a nice space and we got several polite reviews in some of the better Valley weeklies.

"It's my birthday," Willard said as we hugged outside the casting office.

"Happy birthday!" I was embarrassed that I hadn't remembered. "What are you doing to celebrate?"

"Getting this part."

Willard was certainly more confident and focused than I had seen him in a long time. He too was a member of the Former Child Actor Club like myself, and the past decade had been one big dry spell for him.

"Wait for me, okay? I want to catch up!" he said as he squeezed my arm and boldly strode inside the lion's den.

Willard was born in Abilene, Texas. He would have stayed there if it weren't for his ambitious mother, Tamara Hornsby. In the early eighties, a movie company came to Abilene to shoot one of those cheesy psycho-motorist-stalks-nubile-young-hitchhiker TV movies called *Death Car in Texas* starring Charlene Tilton who, at the time, was riding the crest of her *Dallas* fame. Tamara yanked Willard out of school one day and dragged him to an open call for extras. Both mother and son were cast as patrons in a roadside diner where Charlene first appears, who played a perky coed on the way to her sophomore year at Texas A & M.

Tamara wasn't a shy local by any means. Before the second day of shooting was over, she was sleeping with the line producer and even managed to snare herself a small speaking role. By the time production wrapped, she was packing her bags and hauling her son out west to the land of fruits and nuts to live out her dream as a famous actress. Her emphasis was on famous, not actress.

She rented a small no-frills one-bedroom apartment on Cole Avenue and later enrolled Willard in Hollywood High, where we met. We were freshman lab partners when I wasn't off taping my series. Willard had acting aspirations as well, and if he was resentful of my success, he didn't show it.

He wasn't what you'd call leading man material. He was rather tall and gawky, his nose was long and bent, and his black hair was rather matted and oily, but he had these stunning green eyes that struck you dumb. Casting directors were quite taken with them and found him a lot of work as a geeky kid scientist or murderous mama's boy.

He never got a regular series role, and I could see that it bothered him.

We lost touch after high school, but a couple of years ago we ran into each other at a mutual friend's birthday party at Barney's Beanery, a hip and cheap Hollywood establishment where struggling actors with no money went to load up on carbs and liquor. Since then, we reconnected and became good friends if not best buds.

Willard claimed that he was destined to be unsuccessful in this lifetime because he had been a god in many other lifetimes. He had to learn humility. Whatever works, I say.

He was a big believer in past lives. In fact, he was convinced that we were sisters in seventeenth century Russia, where I was consumed with jealousy over his beauty, and smothered him with a pillow one night. He brought that up every time we had a fight. My boyfriend Charlie once said that since Willard could find no reason to be mad at me in this lifetime, he had to go back a few to justify his sometimes pissy behavior.

Willard bounded out of the conference room where I had bombed just five minutes earlier.

I was busy trying to figure out how I could make up for not remembering his birthday.

"I got it! I got the part!" Willard was ecstatic.

I was in shock. Not that he was cast and I wasn't, but that he was so confident going in that he would get it, and then he did. What was his secret? Was he reading a Deepak Chopra book I didn't know about?

Willard impulsively grabbed me by the arms and kissed me full on the mouth. It was the most obvious way for him to show me how excited he was. And it gave the other actors in the room an eyeful.

It was clear to me that Willard hadn't worked in a while, and this victory meant a lot to him. The fact that it was his birthday was icing on the cake (pardon the pun).

"I have a wardrobe fitting tomorrow and I start shooting on Monday," he said.

"Let me throw you a party tomorrow night. It'll be a combination birthday/congratulations party. I'll invite Laurette, a few people from class . . ."

Usually Willard was rather reclusive. In fact, I half expected him to decline my offer, but I got him on a good day. He was more than amenable to a celebration. We settled on eight o'clock at my house with an Italian theme (his favorite food and type of man).

Now all I had to do was break the news to Charlie. Fridays were always his night to order in Indian food and watch a DVD. I hated to break it to him that instead this week we would be blowing up helium balloons and moving all our living room furniture in the corner so we could have a makeshift dance floor.

But he would cave. He always did. He'd let me have a party because a party was what I needed right now. Socializing always improves an unemployed actor's spirits. Especially since most of the crowd who show up are actors who aren't working either. There's always safety in numbers.

Chapter Two

By the time I met my manager Laurette at Koo Koo Roo, she was arguing with a hulking Russian woman who could have been a linebacker for the Dallas Cowboys. There was a heated dispute over who had claimed the last available booth first. Despite the woman's formidable size, I knew she didn't stand a chance. Laurette was an extremely focused and tenacious woman, who was famous (at least in our circles) for getting what she wanted, whether it was a plum role for one of her clients, a boyfriend, money for her favorite charity, or a booth at a fast-food chicken restaurant.

Laurette's usual modus operandi was intimidating her adversaries with her imposing physical stature. She was a large woman, with hair stylishly coiffed and hands perfectly manicured. She dressed for success and carried her weight beautifully. Her confidence was infectious, her demeanor sweet but clearly in charge. I like to think a lot of smart men would take her any day over one of those stick-thin wispy women on *Friends*.

But today, she had nothing over this woman in size, so it would be up to her overpowering personality to save the day.

A lot of naysayers never thought Laurette's business would take off. Most of her clients were has-beens like me with tattered careers and no place else to go. She single-handedly capitalized on the nostalgia craze and found us all work, establishing herself as a manager as well. Laurette was like the mother hen in our circle of friends, taking care of everybody, making sure we were all happy. And that included securing a booth at Koo Koo Roo. She knew how much I hated sitting at the regular tables.

"There are at least twenty diners who had an unobstructed view of what happened, and they all saw *my* tray hit the table first," she said to the angry Russian woman. "Now, we can start polling them with the manager and let your vegetable soup get cold, or you can cut your losses and enjoy what's left of your lunch hour. What's it going to be, honey?"

Laurette said it all with a pleasant smile. And finally, the woman grabbed her tray of food and slumped away, defeated.

Laurette and I slid into the booth.

"So how did it go?" she asked.

"Not good. They didn't even let me get through the scene once. But Willard was there to audition too. He got the part."

"Willard? Hmmm." I could see Laurette's mind racing. Willard wasn't in her stable, and she was now focused on ways to get him there.

I grabbed some silverware off Laurette's tray and started poking at my boneless breast of chicken. Laurette and I met here for lunch because we were both attempting Dr. Atkins's High Protein Diet and healthwise, we could do much worse than Koo Koo Roo.

As I updated Laurette on my plans to throw Willard an impromptu birthday party at the house, I could see her thought process shift from Willard's current representation to the food in front of her. She didn't look happy. She gave me a conspiratorial look. I knew exactly where she was going.

"No. It's only been a day," I said. "We have to stick with this."

I followed her eyes to the glass case of side dishes. The macaroni and cheese was piping hot and calling to us.

I tried in vain to stop the inevitable. "We'll hate ourselves later."

"We can do an extra ten minutes on the treadmill."

That was all it took. We were both up at the counter ordering a large tub apiece.

"Besides," she said. "You're older now. Your future is character roles. You don't need to be in such great shape anymore."

That wasn't exactly what I needed to hear. In fact, after a crack like that, I needed that damn macaroni and cheese more than ever.

God, I missed the heady times of the eighties when I was on everybody's "Who's Hot" list. I was making four times as much money a week as my father, couldn't go to a mall without causing a stampede, and shared *Teen Beat* covers with Duran Duran. I loved every minute of it. Especially since it kept me so busy that I never had to honestly deal with my burgeoning homosexuality. My parents believed I collected all those *Teen Beat* magazines as keepsakes of my career. Ha! I just wanted to know what Simon Le Bon slept in every night.

Back then I was just foolish enough to believe it would last forever. But in the show's final season, the fun abruptly stopped. I was no longer cute enough for ABC's kid-friendly Friday night line-up. I had reached that awkward puberty stage. So the panicked producers brought in an adorable moppet for the family to adopt in order to spruce up ratings.

This was a major blow to morale, especially since the kid was a holy terror. One explanation for his irrational behavior was the fact his mother still breast-fed him at five years old!

This was also about the time our happy small screen family began falling apart. Our TV Dad plowed his Mercedes into a telephone pole and tried to flee the scene in order to avoid a Breathalyzer test. The twenty-five-year-old junkie who played my older brother was appearing less regularly due to his impending court trial on a date rape charge. But all of that paled in comparison to the *National Enquirer* printing photos of me kissing another male child star at the LA gay rodeo.

The network, in all its infinite wisdom, decided to pull the plug. That was 1985.

Essentially my career was dead. An innocent kiss amidst a bunch of gay guys in cowboy hats and spurs might seem harmless today, but back then it was as if I was a participant in the Manson family murders. Nobody took my calls.

I wasn't bitter. It was a different time in Hollywood. Rock Hudson had just died of AIDS. America was worried about Linda Evans's health because she had kissed Rock on the lips in a *Dynasty* episode. The thought of gay people was unsettling.

At first I tried to tell everyone we were just rehearsing for a Mart Crowley play. I buried the truth for as long as I could, but as we entered the nineties, and the Democrats won the White House, it became a little bit easier to stop pretending. And I finally had the opportunity to come into my own as a gay man out of the public eye.

My parents were petrified that I'd go the way of other child stars and hold up a video store or sue them for squandered residuals, but I didn't. In fact, on the Gary Coleman-Jodie Foster Post Child Star Meter, I was definitely closer to Jodie. I was pretty well adjusted.

My parents invested my earnings from the show well. In fact, we bought Intel at just the right time, and now I never have to work again. Don't hate me. That's just the way life works out sometimes.

As I hit my mid-twenties, that wretched acting bug bit me again. But this time it wasn't about fighting my way back into the spotlight. After spending several months in New York attending every Broadway and Off Broadway show on the boards, I developed a newfound respect for the craft of acting, something I had absolutely no understanding of when I was one of the highest paid actors on television. This time I could focus on the process instead of the fame, study with the best teachers, work with people I respected and admired.

It didn't quite work out that way. I wasn't opening at the Richard Rodgers Theatre playing Iago to James Earl Jones's Othello, but I did manage to reconnect with Laurette, my former high school beard/prom date, who was starting up her new talent management business. She quickly secured me a few plum parts on a handful of hit shows. One of the more memorable roles was a tour de force performance in *Touched by an Angel* as a paraplegic teenager who hears the word of God through his Nintendo game.

Laurette fished her wallet out of her purse and turned to me. "So my afternoon is clear and you have no more auditions until Monday. Want to go see a movie?"

"No, I have an appointment I want to keep."

"What?" she asked as she paid for our side dishes. I could tell her interest was peaked. We talked every morning to meticulously go over our schedules, and this was something she didn't know about.

I dreaded telling her. "It's . . . um . . . I'm seeing . . . Isis."

"Oh God!"

"It's been a year. I think it's time."

Isis was my Egyptian psychic. It's not like Laurette didn't believe in psychics. She just didn't relish the idea of me listening to what another woman had to say.

"Just be careful, Jarrod," she offered. "You tend to give her readings a little too much power."

I was armed and ready for this one. I only had to list all the predictions that had come true over the last few years—the sudden resurgence in my career, my solid relationship with Charlie, and my high blood pressure. She even saw another soul joining our family, and two months later Charlie brought home our Pekinese Snickers.

I didn't care what anybody said. Isis was good.

"Look, she does have talent, especially when she told me my entire family should be institutionalized," Laurette said. "I know she can see things. But you pay attention to her every word, and then you run out and make it all happen. No wonder she loves you so much."

"There's nothing wrong with making things happen if you like what she says."

Laurette knew she wasn't going to win this one, so she stopped trying. She decided to direct her attention to the macaroni and cheese.

"I don't have much to ask her today," I said. "I want to talk mostly about my career, and why it's become so important to me again."

"I can answer that one. You miss being the center of attention."

"What do you mean?"

"All your life you were the center of attention, especially when you were a kid. Now outside of our little clique, nobody much cares. You're trying to recapture the glory."

How dare my best friend offer up such a simplistic, ridiculous, completely insensitive theory? Of course she was absolutely right. I couldn't even begin to argue with her.

"Actually I could care less *why* it's become important again. I just want to know if I'm going to get a guest part on *ER* or something."

Laurette nodded. I knew she felt bad for not finding more work for me, but she was trying her best. And she had other clients to think about. We polished off the macaroni and cheese.

"What time are you meeting Isis?"

"I've got an hour."

I knew exactly what was on her mind, so I beat her to it.

"Frozen yogurt?"

She grabbed her purse and hauled me out the door.

After I left Laurette at Baskin Robbins arguing with the sales clerk over the pitiful amount of Butterfingers pieces he put in her fat free yogurt, I drove over to Isis's apartment complex in West Hollywood.

I parked on Harper Avenue, a quiet, tree-lined street built up with an endless row of weathered three story buildings packed with struggling actors, directors and musicians. You could smell the desperation in the air.

I crossed the street to one of the newer freshly painted buildings, stopped outside a gate and rang the bell.

After I was buzzed in, I headed up to the second floor and knocked on the door.

Isis opened the door and gave me a hug. She was about thirty-five, tiny, thin, with big brown eyes and a warm, relaxed smile.

Her apartment was small and cramped, but she had worked hard to make it feel cozy. There was nothing subtle in her decoration—the furniture was thrift shop chic with lots of frilly print pillows flung about that she had brought back from her family's home in Cairo. The walls were filled with religiously themed portraits, her favorite being Christ on the cross. I had to position myself so I was facing away from that one. I could never feel comfortable asking her if I needed toys to enhance my sex life with Charlie while Jesus stared at me.

She offered me a drink from a large jug of water. I declined.

If you looked around the room, you would notice that every item in the place, from paper towels to cat food, was huge. Not just family size. More like small country size. She obviously bought in bulk. She liked to brag about how much money she saved every week with her thrifty way of shopping. Isis spent the first twenty years of her life in Egypt. I often wondered how difficult those years must have been for her without a Price Club card.

We sat across from each other on the floor, her coffee table between us. She dealt a few cards, rolled some crystals in her hand, and closed her eyes. This was my favorite part. The start of a psychic reading was always so full of pomp and circumstance, as if the universe was about to throw a party and you're the honored guest. It's all about *you*, and as an actor, I can attest that it doesn't get much better than that.

She asked me to give her the first three numbers between one and nine that came to mind. I did. She asked for three more. I gave her three more. She rubbed the crystals harder. Her eyes remained closed.

I was beginning to worry. By this point in a reading Isis's eyes usually popped open and she was off and rolling. But today her face contorted into a mask of distress. I shifted uncomfortably. What was going on?

She dropped the crystals. The sharp sound startled me. Without opening her eyes, she flipped over a card. It was the "Death" card. Okay, I wasn't going to panic. I had been to enough psychics to know the "Death" card didn't necessarily mean you're going to die. It could mean the death of a relationship, or the death of your fears, or even the end of a certain phase in your life.

Isis finally opened her eyes and fixed them upon me. She had a very serious expression on her face. Now I was worried. Normally at this point she would be prattling on about how this year was going to be a year of upheaval and transition, how I was going to clean house to prepare for my new cycle. But none of that came. She was gearing up to tell me something, and I wasn't sure I wanted to hear it. I couldn't stand the suspense anymore.

"What? What is it?"

"There's going to be a death. I don't know how else to say it."

"Who? My boyfriend? My dog? Me? Who?"

"I'm not sure. But it's someone close to you." She swallowed hard, and shook her head as if trying to rid her mind of the disturbing images. Her voice cracked as she spoke. "A murder. I see someone murdered."

Isis threw a hand over her mouth and fell back.

Suddenly it didn't seem appropriate to ask if I was going to get a juicy part on *Judging Amy*.

Chapter Three

I was still dizzy from the shock of Isis's revelations as I gripped the steering wheel of my BMW and navigated my way along the winding streets high up in the Hollywood Hills.

My first thought was Charlie, my boyfriend of three years. Could Isis mean Charlie? After all, Charlie was a detective with the LAPD. He was always putting himself in danger. Every night I arrived home before he did, my mind raced with the agonizing possibilities. What case was he working on? Thanks to my sometimes chronic self-absorption, I couldn't remember.

I fumbled for the cell phone and quickly punched the speed dial. I got his office voice mail. I left a brief message. I didn't want to panic him.

"Omigod! Call me as soon as you get this! Isis said someone close to me was going to die, and I'm freaking out that it might be you! Call me! Call me! Call me! Oh by the way, we're having about fifteen people over tomorrow night for Willard Hornsby's birthday. Sorry."

I clicked off. What if it was Charlie? Or what if it was Laurette, or Ellen the casting director, or Willard, or Isis herself? But then again, it could be Dolores the sweet natured checkout lady at the

Beachwood Market where I shopped, or Kamil, the handsome hairy-chested Turkish mechanic who always smiled and waved when I pumped gas at the Mobil station. Or God forbid . . . Snickers!

I tapped the garage door opener that was clipped onto my sun visor as I swerved up to a cottage-like English Tudor home on a hillside. The door croaked and strained as it lifted up, and I gunned the car inside. There was no time to waste.

One of my fears was instantly allayed however, as I reached for the house key that led into the kitchen and heard the familiar sound of a jangling dog tag. Snickers was fine. I heaved a sigh of relief.

I bent down to give her a pat as I came in and went straight over to the phone to check the messages on our answering machine. There were none. At least for the time being there was no bad news for me. Everyone was apparently alive and kicking. I would feel a lot better, though, once I knew Charlie was safely back in his office after a day of fighting crime.

Charlie and I met on a fateful night three years earlier. I was visiting my friend Michelle from acting class in her small house on Gardner just off funky, grunge-influenced Melrose Avenue. We were celebrating the completion of her studies to convert to Catholicism (I don't judge, I just support) and had indulged in far too many jello shots, as Catholics old and new are prone to do. We were trying to control our hysterical fits of laughter (I'm sure one of us said something funny, but who can really remember after that many jello shots?), but a neighbor in the vicinity couldn't sleep because of our racket and called the cops.

A few minutes later, standing there in the window was a six-foot-two, strapping young man with dancing, playful hazel eyes, short-cropped hair, and an engaging, charismatic smile that should come with a warning for causing severe heart palpitations.

Of course I discovered the smile later. At the time, he wasn't smiling. He was supposed to be giving us a stern warning.

Through my blurry haze, I asked if he and his partner wanted to come in and join us. Michelle, for some odd reason, thought the idea of that was even funnier than anything we had said before. She toppled over on the couch, howling.

Charlie's partner was all business, but Charlie confided that they had received a call that a wild raucous party was in full swing. He had expected sixty or seventy people, not two obnoxiously loud out of work actors with too much time and liquor on their hands.

There was an instant chemistry. I wasn't even sure he was gay, but I knew he was mine. I quickly scanned for a wedding ring, and smiled when I didn't see one. Michelle and I apologized profusely, and promised to keep the noise in check.

Charlie nodded and headed back to the patrol car with his partner. I thought he winked at me when he turned to leave, but I couldn't be sure. Michelle was positive he did.

Well, I was about to drop the whole thing and mix up another batch of jello shots when I thought I heard a prowler. Michelle was certain that it was just her cat Mustafa banging a crumpled up piece of paper around in the next room. Still, why take chances?

I scooped up the phone and called the police. I specifically requested the nice officer who had paid us a visit earlier. Charlie was back in ten minutes. I followed him outside as he checked the immediate area for any signs of trespassing. I had no time to lose. By the time his sweep was over, I found out he was from Michigan, had just turned thirty, was about to get promoted to detective, lived in Silverlake (LA's second biggest gay neighborhood), and was recently divorced. From a woman.

Some people take years to realize they're gay. I knew when I was ten, right about the time John Stamos joined *General Hospital.*

I stopped short of asking him out. I was so taken with him, I had never seriously considered the possibility he would say no. Now it was all I could think about. But if I let him leave without asking, I'd have to call him again and risk stalking charges.

Luckily the stars were on my side.

"So I'm off duty after this," he said. "You know a place where I can get some breakfast?"

I shrugged. "There's a diner in the mini-mall around the corner. I was thinking about grabbing a bite there myself."

And that was that. We'd been together ever since.

Charlie had never seen an episode of *Go to Your Room!* until after we started dating. He never dreamed he would be sharing his life with an actor, let alone a former child star. The only reason he ever came to Los Angeles in the first place was to follow his new wife, who had gotten a job at the LA Coroner's office.

The wife dumped him two months after Charlie uprooted his life to move with her, and he came out of the closet three weeks later. It turned out to be the best thing that ever happened to him. I thank her every day, because I believe it was the Universe's way of forcing Charlie to confront his issues, and getting us closer together so we could finally meet. It was destiny.

And besides, Isis had told me six months earlier the man of my dreams was going to come into my life as an authority figure. I figured a cop was close enough. He had arrived to protect and serve. Charlie wasn't a big believer in psychic phenomena but he tolerated my relationship with Isis.

The thought of Isis snapped me back to reality. Her prediction was still gnawing at me. I had never seen her so intense, so disturbed. Usually I prefaced every reading by telling her to withhold any truly horrific premonitions. I just didn't want to know if my chain-smoking Aunt Sadie was going to succumb to throat cancer. But I had forgotten to lay the ground rules this time. I was too concerned with questions about my career. And for that, I was now obsessing over which person in my life was about to expire.

Isis wasn't perfect. She never batted a thousand, but she always came pretty damn close. Now the question was, who could she be talking about? My parents in Vero Beach, Florida? My sister in Bar Harbor, Maine? Mr. Reilly, my sexy high school creative writing teacher on whom I had a terrible crush? The name of every person I had ever come in contact with in my whole life was rushing through my head.

I heard the garage door creak open again. I exhaled a deep breath.

Charlie was home. Snickers jumped to her feet and scurried over to the door to greet him. She ran in circles, unable to contain her excitement. I felt like joining her.

The door to the garage swung open and Charlie sauntered in. Both Snickers and I hurled ourselves at him. He was completely taken by surprise.

"Whoa! What's all this?"

"You're alive! We're just so happy you're alive!"

"Me too," he said, eyeing me suspiciously, the way Ricky Ricardo used to look at Lucy. "What have you been up to?"

"Didn't you get my message?"

"No." He still had that suspicious look. It was time to fess up. "I went to see Isis today . . ."

"Oh no . . ." Charlie threw his hands up. He didn't want to hear it, but I was already on a roll.

"She said someone close to me was going to be murdered."

This stopped him briefly as he opened the fridge to grab a bottle of Miller Lite. He didn't want to give any credence to Isis's psychic gifts, but couldn't help himself.

"So you thought it was *me*?"

"Well, look at the line of work you're in. It's certainly plausible that you could die unexpectedly, get shot by a perp or something. I mean you don't have to be a fan of *NYPD Blue* to know all the possible storylines."

"I'm fine." He brushed his soft lips against my cheek. That always shut me up, and he knew it. "So what are we doing about dinner?"

"Um, actually, there was two parts to the message you didn't get. It's Willard Hornsby's birthday, so I offered to throw him a party . . . tomorrow night . . ." I started talking faster when I saw the irritation on his face. "Only fifteen people or so. And I can call Susan at LA Spice and have her cater. You like Susan's food. It's just that I feel we owe Willard. He gave us a breadmaker last Christmas and all we got him was *All About Eve* on DVD."

"That's what he wanted."

"I know . . . but a breadmaker! I went to Macy's and saw how much it cost. A lot more than that DVD."

"Prices don't matter. It's the thought that . . ."

"Bullshit. *Everybody* notices. Especially in Hollywood."

"It's just that I was looking forward to just kicking back . . ."

"I know."

"Watching a movie . . ."

"I know."

"Ordering Indian food . . ."

"I know."

Charlie knew it was a done deal, and I was just letting him vent until he finished his beer. Once he got it all off his chest and wandered away to take a shower, I was off and running with party preparations.

I had no auditions the following day, so I was able to throw myself into the role of party host. Susan and her crack catering team showed up at six o'clock and took over the house. Susan loved working at my place. It had a fabulous open kitchen and lots of charm.

Mr. Bone, an architect, built the house in 1928. He died shortly thereafter, but I was convinced his spirit still roamed the hallways since Snickers had a tendency to bark at nothing, just air. I always assumed she was saying hello to Mr. Bone. The alternative was that my dog had troubling psychological problems. And a ghost haunting my house was a much more colorful story than a schizophrenic Pekinese.

After an exhaustive title search, I couldn't find one single famous person who ever lived in the house. Not one, not even a cheesy seventies sitcom star like Joyce DeWitt. Nobody! Charlie would tell people that *I* was the first famous person to live in it. That was sweet of him, but I still wanted to brag that I slept in the same bedroom as Humphrey Bogart or Charlie Chaplin or, hell, Erik Estrada!

I spent the previous night and the following morning calling up everybody on my short list to make sure they could make it. Remarkably, almost everybody could. I'm sure the fact that LA Spice was catering helped clear a lot of calendars.

I called Willard last to confirm his arrival at eight. He seemed genuinely excited that I was going to all this trouble just for him, but the fact was I loved throwing parties, ever since Isis told me I was a good host and I had the perfect home for entertaining. Charlie loved hearing that one.

Susan and her catering staff buzzed around spreading linens and heating up hors d'oeuvres. Laurette was the first guest to arrive. She and I liked to sample all the food without the pressure of other guests racing ahead of us to load up on all the best morsels.

Around seven, more people arrived. I had invited Willard's mother Tamara and her husband Spiro, but they were dining with a studio bigwig at Morton's. Birthday or not, Tamara had her Hollywood social life to think about.

We all crowded in the living room to greet the birthday boy. He called and said he was running a little late, so we waited . . . and waited . . . and waited.

By ten, guests started to make excuses and leave. I had now left five messages on Willard's answering machine.

And my stomach was churning with dread.

All I could think about was Isis and her prediction. Charlie tried assuring me that Willard was fine, but even he knew his words were hollow. Something must have happened to him. We had spoken by phone at seven-fifteen. He was going to take a quick bath and head over.

Charlie and I jumped into the BMW and sped down the curving, shadowy streets of the Hollywood Hills that spilled onto Sunset Boulevard with its massive billboards and bright lights. We zipped through the plush greenery of Beverly Hills before swerving off a side street into Brentwood towards Willard's house.

Charlie, behind the wheel, kept eyeing me.

My body kept shaking so he turned on the heat. But I wasn't cold. It was nerves.

As we pulled up to the small stucco house on the corner, I was surprised to see all the lights on. Willard was home.

We got out of the car, and walked up the path to the front door. It was open. A Macy Gray CD wafted out from the kitchen. We saw an open bottle of wine and two half empty glasses sitting on the coffee table as we poked our heads inside. Charlie told me to go back and wait by the car, but of course, I stayed right on his heels.

"Willard?" I called out as my eyes darted about the room.

Charlie checked the den. There was no sign of him. On his way back, Charlie slipped on some water that had spilled on the floor. He caught his balance, and then headed towards the back bed-rooms.

I noticed that the glass door leading to the yard was open a crack. The breeze from outside ruffled a stack of magazines on an end table. I heard Charlie calling for Willard as he checked all the rooms in the back of the house. I stepped outside onto the patio, looked around, and then froze in my tracks.

"Charlie! Charlie, come quick!"

I raced over to the edge of Willard's small lap pool. There, float-ing face down, was a lifeless body. I jumped into the water, still yelling for Charlie, and turned the body over. Willard Ray Hornsby's face stared up at me, his eyes empty, his mouth agape, the life inside of him completely drained out. It was just as Isis had predicted.

Chapter Four

Whoever said it never rains in Southern California wasn't at Willard Ray Hornsby's funeral at Forest Lawn Cemetery that bitter Monday morning three days after his untimely death.

Charlie and I stood huddled underneath my bent, rusty-handled umbrella (who ever thinks to buy a new one in Los Angeles?), straining to hear the minister's eulogy through the whipping, violent winds and torrential downpour. As our group stood, just a small cluster in the vast lawn of endless headstones, the minister tried as best he could to project through the inclement weather, but it was a hopeless cause.

After a while, I focused on watching the small, intimate crowd of mourners gathered to pay their respects. I knew most of the faces, including Laurette, of course, and a few actors from Willard's scene study class.

And then there was Willard's mother Tamara, whose main concern at the moment was the state of her hair. She kept clutching it, fearful it was all going to come tumbling down from the top of her head. She was close enough to the minister to actually hear what he was saying, but it didn't interest her much. She was so preoccupied with her damn hair.

After Tamara packed up her young son and headed west in the eighties to make her mark, she never did anything of note except for playing a background babe in a James Bond movie. This led to a few television roles, but it was her marriage to an up-and-coming studio executive that finally got her in the right circles. She played it up for all it was worth—parties, Aspen ski weekends, charity balls with the other wives of the rich and powerful.

The fact that her new husband had no room in his life for a step-son didn't matter. She was on her way. Willard was treated like a puppy that had just peed in her favorite Joan & David's. She even forgot to invite him to Thanksgiving one year. Judd Nelson got his place at the table instead.

Of course, all good things must come to an end, and Tamara's husband of eight years dumped her for a pretty young thing who was about to make her mark in a big screen version of *The Perils of Penelope Pitstop*.

Tamara didn't have to play the scorned divorcée for long. She used her contacts to secure an invitation to a political fundraiser hosted by Warren Beatty. Since Annette Bening already had him wrapped up, she set her sights on recently widowed media mogul Stan Schulberg. Stan was eighty-two-years-old but looked seventy-six if he was a day. He was one of those legendary men who bought and sold TV networks as a sport. He had billions, and Tamara se-duced him shamelessly. By the time she squeezed a marriage pro-posal out of him, he was already hospitalized with pneumonia. His terrified children and rightful heirs to his fortune did everything in their power to delay the nuptials, but Tamara wasted no time in dressing up the ICU room with flowers and calling in a rabbi for an emergency service. And there, before two registered nurses serving as witnesses and to monitor the respirator, Tamara and Stan were married.

She forgot to invite Willard.

Within two weeks, Stan Schulberg was dead and Tamara's savvy lawyers secured her a half a billion dollars from the estate faster than you can say Anna Nicole Smith.

Standing next to Tamara near the coffin was her boy toy, excuse me, husband Spiro Spiridakis. Spiro was a six-foot tall, sculpted Greek God whose primarily role in Tamara's life was to share her bed and help spend all that money. While Tamara was pushing fifty-five, Spiro wasn't more than thirty. He looked twenty. But when you don't work, and can spend your day working out at the gym and getting herbal face treatments, that's not such an impressive accomplishment. Both Tamara and Spiro looked bored and put out by this whole funeral affair. Tamara kept dabbing her eyes with a handkerchief, but I would bet my entire life savings that the only moisture on her face was a direct result of the rain.

Spiro kept checking his watch, sighing, then staring blankly at the minister. He was probably running late for a shiatsu massage at the Burke Williams Spa in West Hollywood.

Finally, the minister wrapped things up with a rather impersonal tribute to Willard's life. From what I could make out through the rain, it was a standard issue tribute, nothing particularly related to Willard's actual life, just a perfunctory "Boy, will we miss him," and then a final prayer.

I didn't blame the minister. He didn't know Willard. He only had Tamara to rely on, and needless to say, none of his friends were ever consulted. If Tamara had put as much effort into her son's eulogy as she did into her hair, the poor minister would have at least had a fighting chance to make some minor impact on the gathered mourners.

Before the minister was able to close his Bible, Tamara and Spiro scurried off towards their parked limousine.

The rain was subsiding, and the crowd quietly began to disperse. I stared at Willard's coffin, so full of questions, so confused as to what actually happened.

After Charlie and the cops combed the premises for any signs of foul play, Willard's death had been ruled an accident. According to a preliminary coroner's report, Willard's alcohol level was off the charts, and apparently in his drunken stupor, he tripped over something on his patio, fell into the pool and drowned.

Charlie said that when the police broke the news of her son's death to Tamara, she closed her eyes, shook her head, and said, "It was only a matter of time, I suppose." Then she launched into a sad story of how her son couldn't cope with Hollywood's constant rejection, how he dulled the pain of his battered self-esteem with booze, how his story was one more cautionary tale for those starry-eyed youngsters who wanted to scrape together their last few dollars and migrate to Hollywood to make it as the next Tom Cruise or Julia Roberts.

It was all so neat and tidy. Tamara had all the answers. But she didn't know squat. Not a clue where her son's head was at emotionally. As far as I knew, they hadn't spoken in a while. And from my own run in with Willard the day before he died, he was in an ecstatic state, completely full of hope and enthusiasm. He had just gotten cast in a juicy guest-starring role on *Smallville*. For any out of work actor, a crumb like that would keep your spirits up for months.

More questions gnawed at me about this tragedy. There were a couple of empty tequila bottles found near the body. If he was drinking hard liquor on the night he died, then why was there an open bottle of wine and two glasses on his coffee table? Who else had been there that night?

And Willard didn't even like tequila. Whenever we went out for margaritas, he would order the fruit-flavored ones because peach and strawberry usually drowned out the sharp taste of Jose Cuervo. Even more disturbing was the fact that I had just talked to him a few hours earlier. He was alert, happy, and anxious to get to the party. How on earth did he have time to go from that to bitter, drunk, and accident-prone? I hated myself for obsessing about details. Now was the time to grieve. But I couldn't help myself. The nagging details and unanswered questions were cropping up and consuming me.

Charlie watched me glare at Tamara and Spiro as a few mourners stopped to offer their condolences. Charlie was getting nervous. He was afraid I was about to do something to embarrass him. And as usual, he was right.

"I'll be right back."

"Jarrod, don't . . ."

"I'm just going to tell Willard's mother how sorry I am."

Charlie sighed. He knew that was a bald-faced lie. He knew I couldn't stand Tamara or her steroid popping lover boy. And he knew that I wouldn't be happy until I let them know it.

I charged down the hill towards the limousine. Tamara and Spiro had managed to shake off the few stragglers who tried offering comfort and were now focused on disappearing into the safety of their car. If they had only moved a little faster.

"Mrs. Schulberg?"

She turned to face me. There was a hint of recognition in her eyes, but it took her a moment to process who I was.

"Jarrod," she said finally. "I'm so glad you were able to come. I know how much you meant to Willard."

"I thought the world of him too. I still can't believe it."

She wanted so desperately to get in that limo with Spiro and speed away, but for appearances' sake, she had to go through the motions.

"Yes," she said, letting out a deep breath. "Such a tragedy."

"I just can't understand how this happened."

"Willard had a lot of problems, Jarrod. So he drank. Quite a bit, I'm afraid."

"What kind of problems do you think he had?"

She hadn't expected this. She was hoping the Cliff Notes explanation of her son's death would satisfy me and send me on my way. She was wrong.

"He was unhappy. He couldn't get work as an actor, and I know that bothered him. Relationships never seemed to work out. He couldn't catch a break. I used to see such hopelessness in his eyes. Sometimes I think he was looking for a way out . . . some way to stop the pain . . ."

"He got a part the day before he died," I said. "A good one. We were both up for it and he got it. I hadn't seen him that happy in a long time."

Tamara fixed her gaze upon me. She was either embarrassed to be so out of touch with her son or she was hiding something. Her eyes pleaded with me to stop this assault and retreat. No such luck.

"Did you know it was his birthday last week?"

"Yes. The police told me some friends were throwing him a party and he didn't show up," she said, her voice quivering for maximum effect. "That's when someone found him."

"I did. I was the one who found him."

She kept staring at me, trying to figure out what I wanted from her. She fumbled for words, anything to say. "You may not know this, Jarrod, but he was also very depressed about getting older."

I shrugged. "Didn't seem to bother him last week. But you know him a lot better than I do. You're his mother."

She nodded, her face tight, and she locked me with her gaze once again. She knew my comment was bubbling over with sarcasm and it pissed her off. She decided not to respond and started to turn away when I piped in again.

"I'm just confused, Mrs. Schulberg. All these things you're saying about Willard, his hopeless state of mind, how he drank too much, I never saw any of that."

Tamara looked at Spiro, who shifted uncomfortably, his eyes darting back and forth. He offered her no help. She stared at me, her face frozen in a mask of calm. Underneath I was sure was another story.

"Perhaps you didn't know him as well as you thought," she said.

"How well did *you* really know him?"

"He was my son. I loved him. But I won't lie to you. We weren't as close as I wanted to be. I begged him to come visit me more often."

I felt it coming. I knew I should have kept my mouth shut, but I just couldn't resist.

"Unless you only have one extra place at the Thanksgiving table, and Judd Nelson's already agreed to come."

She bristled, surprised I even knew about that. But she wasn't going to give me any further ammunition I could use against her later.

"That was completely inappropriate," she said.

"I think your son's death is completely inappropriate."

Spiro finally stepped in. He moved in front of Tamara, his body physically shielding her from any more of my comments. The first thing I noticed was his open shirt and bronzed chest, the thick, black hair matted against it from the rain. The jerk didn't even have the decency to wear a tie to the funeral.

His cold, dark eyes bore into me. "Leave it alone."

He tried intimidating me by moving up close, hovering over me. And it worked. I didn't want to mess with him. But I'm also an actor, and it wasn't hard to make it look like I was unimpressed by his bulk.

Why I was antagonizing these two was beyond me. Perhaps I was overcome by grief and anger, and they were the easiest targets, given how they had both treated Willard when he was alive. Or perhaps there was something else at work. Something driving me forward to sort out the devastating events of the last few days that wasn't yet clear to me.

I arched my back and glared at them with a hard, unflinching stare overflowing with contempt. "I want you to know that I don't buy any of the bullshit you two are dishing out."

I figured that was it. Spiro was going to beat me to a pulp. My eyes flickered down to see his hand rising up in a fist, ready to strike. But then, I heard a comforting, familiar voice.

"Ready to go, Jarrod?"

It was Charlie. Like a guardian angel, he was right there behind me. And his presence deflated Spiro's immediate plans to mark up my face.

Tamara was quite flustered at this point, and was back to playing with her hair. This had all been too much for her. "Please, Jarrod, just let Willard rest in peace."

"That's what I want too, Mrs. Schulberg. But right now, something tells me he can't."

Her mouth dropped open at the insinuation. Spiro took her by the arm, and guided her to the limo. He ushered her inside, climbed in behind her and slammed the door shut. The car roared away.

I stood there with Charlie. I had no idea what possessed me to confront a dead man's mother like that on the day of her own son's funeral. I certainly wasn't proud of it. But as I watched the limo disappear in the cloudy haze, the wind kicked up again and the rain beat down once more, and I became convinced that it was Willard Ray Hornsby's restless spirit urging me forward to find out what really happened on the night of his thirtieth birthday party.

Chapter Five

I suppose if Charlie had some 8 x 10 photos made up of his handsome face and started driving around town to auditions, I might feel a little threatened. It's never a good idea to compete with your boyfriend. So I understood why Charlie was upset that I wanted to painstakingly examine the facts surrounding Willard Ray Hornsby's untimely death.

Acting was my business. Crime was his.

And since his fellow LAPD detectives had already ruled that Willard's drowning was an accident, there was no point in either of us poking our noses into the matter any further. If only it were that easy for me to let something go.

I still had too many questions. And it certainly didn't help that I was an obsessed conspiracy theorist, or as Charlie sometimes referred to me, "conspiracy nut." All depends on your point of view, I suppose. I was also replaying my psychic reading from Isis over and over in my mind. She didn't say a close friend was going to drown accidentally. She said a close friend was going to be murdered. And she was spot on most of the time with her predictions. But given the skeptics, Charlie included, it wouldn't have helped to bring up that little tidbit as proof it was a homicide.

I've always been fascinated by the possibility of foul play. And when you have a bunch of actors for friends who live to create their own drama, it can become an obsessive pursuit. There was that cruise to Catalina we took one Thanksgiving weekend to recreate the mysterious drowning of Natalie Wood. Charlie had assumed we were just going to kick back, stuff ourselves with turkey, and play the Silver Screen Edition of Trivial Pursuit, but that was before I cast him in the role of Christopher Walken and myself as Robert Wagner. Laurette gave a memorable turn as the doomed Natalie.

So it came as no surprise that I was like our beloved Snickers with a new rawhide bone. I just couldn't let it go.

As we climbed into bed the night after the funeral, I couldn't help myself. "Willard's house isn't cordoned off with yellow police tape or anything, is it?"

Charlie stopped after taking his shirt off and stared at me. "No. It's not a crime scene. Why?"

"Just curious."

"I don't want you going over there."

"I've got a busy day tomorrow. I couldn't go even if I wanted to," I said as I fluffed my pillows and slipped underneath the massive goose down comforter.

Our bedroom was a serene periwinkle blue with soft lighting and a big comfortable bed you could get lost in. It was my favorite room in the house, not just for the obvious reasons, but because I felt safe in here, like I was cocooned away from the pressures of real life.

Our house was inverted, so the bedrooms were downstairs from the upper floor, which had the kitchen, living room, den and dining room. Built against a hillside, the structure looked out onto a stone courtyard and a cluster of giant bamboo trees and a small trickling waterfall that added to the peacefulness of the property. One felt far away from the bustling expanse of Los Angeles, yet downtown Hollywood was only a short five-minute drive down a hill.

Our home was an escape from the rest of the world, but on this night, the one person I needed to escape from was on the other side of the bed. And he wasn't going to cut me any slack.

"I don't believe you," he said. "I think you want to find some evidence that suggests Willard's death wasn't an accident, and that his mother had something to do with it because you don't like her."

He was absolutely right, though I loathed admitting it. So I didn't. Feigning indignation was far more satisfying. "How can you say that? What's happened between us? When did you stop trusting me?" As thick as I was laying it on, I knew it was useless. Charlie knew me too well.

He sighed. "I want you to promise you're not going to go over to that house tomorrow and stir up any trouble."

Checkmate. The "p" word. Charlie was a pro when it came to mining feelings of guilt. Actors rarely felt guilt over anything, but I did. And when the man I shared my life with made me promise, I was hard-pressed to break it without a consuming sense of dread, and he knew it. What he didn't know was that in my mind, I *wasn't* going over to Willard's house to "stir up trouble," I was going over there simply for my own sense of closure. To walk through his house before saying goodbye to him for the last time. And if for some bizarre, unexpected reason, a clue turned up that led to some answers, then so be it. It may have been a questionable technicality, but I was desperate.

Luckily at that moment, Snickers scuttled into the room, leapt up on the bed, and snuggled in the crook of my arm. It allowed me to avert my eyes from Charlie when I said, "I promise."

Charlie seemed satisfied. He gave me a soft kiss on the mouth, then rolled over and went to sleep. I tried ignoring the pangs that stabbed me in the stomach. Those incessant guilt pangs that kept reminding me of how I had just lied to my boyfriend. But for me, I had to know the truth. The circumstances just didn't add up in my mind. And in my naiveté, I actually believed that nothing could go wrong and Charlie would never have to find out anything.

I picked up Laurette at her office in Glendale and we drove over the 405 freeway towards Brentwood the following morning. I didn't want to go back to Willard's house alone, and I knew Laurette's curious nature would get the best of her, and that she would want to go with me.

The promise of lunch at the Cheesecake Factory once we were finished sealed the deal. That was one promise I had no problem keeping. Our Dr. Atkins's diets were apparently history, though neither of us was willing to say it out loud just yet.

"Maybe if I got you more auditions, you wouldn't get so obsessed about stuff like this," Laurette said as we exited the freeway, and turned onto Sunset, heading towards Brentwood. Laurette was big on blaming herself for everything, and she was very concerned that this whole Willard business was going to drive a wedge between Charlie and me.

"First of all, I'm not obsessed. I just feel I owe it to Willard."

Laurette gave me that look that said, "We both know you're obsessed, but in the interest of being a supportive friend, I'll just nod encouragingly."

Willard had always wanted to live in Brentwood. It was where Marilyn Monroe lived. He had adored Marilyn. He wasn't even born in 1962 when she died of a pill overdose, or perhaps by the hand of one of the Kennedys (we've already established I'm a conspiracy theorist), but there was something about her tragic life that spoke to him. In fact, Willard's house was only a few blocks away from the house where Marilyn died. He always had this need to be close to her. His bookshelves were lined with biographies of her life, and his most prized possession was a signed poster from *Some Like It Hot*. I remembered the day he took all the residual money he made from a recurring role on *Who's the Boss?* playing one of Alyssa

Milano's boyfriends and outbid everybody for it at a celebrity auction. And now in a cruel twist of fate, Willard, like his heroine, had died at home alone in Brentwood, with the strange circumstances still a mystery.

I parked the car at the curb outside Willard's home. The immaculate tree-lined street was quiet, except for a lone elderly gardener a few houses down trimming a hedge with his clippers.

Laurette climbed out of the passenger's side, and joined me as we headed up the walk to the front door. She was starting to have second thoughts.

"This isn't breaking and entering or anything like that, is it?"

"Of course not," I lied. "Willard was a friend."

Laurette's eyes flickered back and forth, checking to make sure no one was watching us. The gardener down the block was immersed in his work, and never even looked up as I marched up to the door and jiggled the knob. It was locked.

"Let's try around back."

Before Laurette could protest, I stepped down off the small porch, and pried open a chipped, weathered wooden side gate. I slipped through, and Laurette, not wanting to be left behind alone, followed close on my heels.

We found ourselves in the backyard. Except for a few chirping birds and a skittish squirrel that ambled up a tree as we approached, the area was still, almost like a painting. The morning breeze stirred up a few leaves as we both stared at the small lap pool.

"Is that where you found him?" Laurette asked, her voice tense.

I nodded. It had been almost a week since the night I stumbled across Willard's limp and lifeless body, but the image was as strong in my mind as if I were seeing it for the first time. I couldn't shake it, which probably explained my need to push ahead and prove there was more to his death than a simple trip over some patio furniture and a headfirst dive into this tiny pool.

Laurette was starting to panic. She checked her watch, and looked at me with pleading eyes. "It's already eleven-thirty. You know how crowded the Cheesecake Factory gets at lunchtime. If we don't head over there soon, we'll never get a table."

"I just want to check things out inside."

I sauntered over to the sliding glass door that led into Willard's living room and pulled on the handle. It was locked too. Then I noticed a small window leading into a downstairs bathroom that was cracked open. I had been on the Atkins Diet just long enough to convince myself that I could squeeze through it.

I waded through some bushes to get to it, grabbed the sill, and hoisted myself up. I could hear Laurette's hushed, urgent voice behind me. "What are you doing? Stop it! Don't do that!" But it was too late. I was already half way inside. There was no going back now.

Photos of Marilyn during various stages of her career adorned the small, spotless bathroom. I paused long enough to look at one candid moment from the set of her last film, *The Misfits*, that Willard had put in an expensive silver frame and placed lovingly next to a medicine cabinet mirror. There was sadness in her eyes, a sense of hopelessness. So much vulnerability captured in the briefest of moments. I wondered if I was fooling myself. Maybe Willard's mother Tamara was right. Maybe he had given up on life, and was slowly killing himself with booze. Maybe I was chasing answers that didn't exist. After all, he worshipped Marilyn, and Marilyn suffered a similar tragic demise. Maybe all of this was exactly what Willard wanted.

Or maybe that's exactly what someone wanted everybody to think.

I left the bathroom, and crossed into the living room, where I spotted Laurette pacing nervously outside the sliding glass door. I flipped the latch on the inside handle and pulled it open. She plowed inside, and slammed the door shut behind her.

"I'm a wreck. Just do what you came here to do, and let's get the hell out of here."

The police had already combed the house from top to bottom and found nothing out of the ordinary. Everything seemed to be exactly the same as the night Charlie and I had last been here. I assumed Tamara and Spiro had yet to scour the place for anything of value.

I started in the kitchen, checking all the drawers, but found only some spare keys, a few take out menus, assorted corkscrews and kitchenware.

Laurette yanked open the refrigerator and found a wheel of Brie cheese. She sniffed it.

"I wonder if this is still good."

I smiled. Food always became an overriding obsession when we were nervous. Or sad. Or happy. Or excited. Food was just an overriding obsession, come to think of it.

As Laurette shut the refrigerator door, she stopped to look at the wide array of magnets that decorated the massive Amana fridge. Most of them were miniature posters of Marilyn's films including *The Seven-Year Itch*, *Gentlemen Prefer Blondes*, and *How to Marry A Millionaire*. There were a few other movie classics and vintage stars represented, but Marilyn dominated. It was then that my eye caught something: a small slip of paper sticking out of the bottom of the refridgerator. It must have been stuck to the fridge with a magnet, and somehow fallen off. I bent down, used my index finger to slide it out from underneath the grate, and blew the dust off it. It was a check drawn from Willard's Wells Fargo account, and made out to someone named Terry Duran.

"You know a Terry Duran?" I asked Laurette.

She shook her head. I looked at the amount. Five hundred dollars. I decided to look for more clues upstairs. Laurette had no intention of separating herself from me, so she gamely followed.

Willard's bedroom was small and cozy, and on his night table I found a couple of books with interesting titles . . . *Finding True Love in a Man Eat Man World: The Intelligent Guide to Gay Dating*,

Romance, and Eternal Love and *Living Well: The Gay Man's Essential Health Guide*. Tucked away inside the health guide was a receipt from A Different Light, an independent bookstore specializing in gay and lesbian books, located in the heart of West Hollywood. The books had been purchased on the day he died, probably as a birthday present to himself. Why would Willard bother to buy a couple of self-help titles if he was so hell bent on drinking himself to death? Tamara's convenient and easy summary of her son's state of mind felt more off the mark every minute.

Laurette had finally given in, and was now at Willard's desk, firing up his Dell notebook computer. Luckily Willard had his password automatically stored for convenience, so she had no trouble hacking her way into his AOL Internet account. She was flying through his e-mail for anything suspicious, but most of the unread mail was just advertising offers of sex and work-at-home business opportunities.

I poured over a stack of magazines by Willard's bedside. He was a voracious reader, consuming a host of pop culture weeklies and monthlies, subscribing to everything from *People* to *Rolling Stone* to *U.S. News and World Report*. Most hadn't even been thumbed through yet. There were also a few local gay-related rags, including *Frontiers*, which had an entire section in the back devoted to ads for mostly unlicensed body work specialists, which if one were to read between the lines meant hustlers.

I flipped through the magazine to a page that had been earmarked, and studied the black and white photos of various men, all shapes and sizes, ages and persuasions. One photo in the center had been circled with a black Sharpie pen.

He was young, probably in his mid-twenties, stripped to the waist, his smooth, toned chest glistening. There was a tattoo of an eagle on his left bicep. And because he was probably an aspiring actor who didn't want this side work to come back and bite him in the ass some day, his face was blurred. The caption underneath read, "You'll soar to new heights when my soothing hands work their magic on you. Call Eli today for an experience your body will never forget." This was followed by a pager number and the best hours to call.

I tore the page out of the magazine, folded it up and slipped it in my pocket.

Laurette looked up at me from the computer, her face a ghostly white. "You might want to come look at this."

I crossed over and peered over her shoulder. On the screen was one of those animated e-mail special occasion cards you can order on-line. Cute furry bunnies exploding with birthday cheer accompanied by a musical ditty designed to brighten your day. This was a bit different. It was the cartoon image of a man lying prone in a coffin with words dancing above him.

Happy Birthday . . . I hope it's your last.

The coffin then slammed shut and there was a sick cackling laugh that trailed off. The image just kept repeating itself over and over, until I reached over and clicked on the exit bar. Neither of us wanted to see it again. The e-mail address from where the card was sent was just a list of random numbers using a Hotmail account. I jotted it down.

Laurette closed the notebook computer and stood up. "Okay, I'm ready to leave. How about you?"

I had to agree. The ominous birthday greeting had shaken us both up.

As we headed back down the stairs, I heard a noise coming from the kitchen. I grabbed Laurette's arm, stopping her. Someone else was in the house.

Laurette slowly began to hyperventilate as I guided her back up to the second floor, and down the hall to Willard's bedroom. We ducked inside, and gently closed the door, hoping whoever was there wouldn't come upstairs. We were wrong. There was a thunderous clomping on the staircase. Whoever it was had heard us and was moving fast, heading straight for us. And from the sound of it, there was more than one person. Maybe three or four.

I grabbed Laurette's hand and pulled her inside the bedroom closet. We pushed ourselves up against the back wall, hurriedly arranging the hanging clothes in front of us as cover. Outside, we heard the bedroom door bang open, and the scuffling of feet across the floor.

We both held our breath.

I couldn't make out what the muffled voices were saying, but after a brief exchange, there was more banging and clomping before they left the bedroom and headed back down the hall.

Both Laurette and I let out deep sighs of relief. We hadn't been discovered.

But then, out of nowhere, a loud incessant beeping pierced the air, startling both of us. It was relentless and coming from inside the closet. It took us both a second to realize it was Laurette's cell phone. She frantically fumbled for it as it kept ringing and ringing. I swear she had the volume jacked up to full blast. When she finally got her hands on the phone, she dropped it, allowing another few earsplitting rings to escape.

After what seemed like an eternity, she managed to pick it up, flip it open, and whisper, "Hello?"

I pressed my ear against the closet door to try and hear if the clomping feet were coming back our way, but I couldn't make out anything above Laurette's urgent, panicked voice.

"What do you mean he didn't show up? I spent a whole week of my life getting him that Safeway grand opening!"

Laurette lowered the phone, and hissed, "Gary Coleman's being a prima donna again!"

It was as if she had suddenly forgotten where we were and who might be just outside the door. That was Laurette. Work always came first. But at that moment, my eyes fell to the floor where I saw shadows lurking outside the crack in the bottom of the closet door. The mystery guests had come back, and this time they were certain someone else was in the house with them.

My mind raced. I searched the closet for some kind of weapon; a shoe, an umbrella, anything. But there was nothing. Laurette dropped her phone, and let out a tiny audible gasp as someone outside jig-gled the door handle. Before I could grab it from the inside, some-one wrenched it wide open, and pushed the clothes apart to reveal our hiding place.

A harsh light washed over us.

Laurette squealed and closed her eyes, expecting the worst.

And I looked into the angry eyes of four female uniformed cops, guns drawn and aimed straight at me.

Chapter Six

Charlie and I love watching *Oz*, that brutal soap opera set in a maximum-security prison on HBO. It's guilt-free TV. Because it's critically acclaimed, we don't have to feel sleazy watching all the full frontal male nudity.

But after spending an afternoon in the LA County Jail, I didn't care if I ever saw another episode again. The smelly, pot-bellied, dirty-faced lowlifes squeezed into my cell looked nothing like the tanned, buffed, adorable actors who populated prison on TV. Once again, pop culture distorted my view of reality, and as I huddled in a corner, praying to God that nobody talked to me, any dark fantasies I may have once harbored about incarceration evaporated forever.

The stench of urine permeated the air as a muttering, wild-eyed, scraggly-faced man walked up and down the length of the dank, bare cement cell in front of me. I couldn't make out what he was saying, but like everybody else in the cell that day, I'm sure he was protesting his innocence. This was not how I expected things to turn out when I hijacked Laurette and set out to search Willard Ray Hornsby's Brentwood home.

Apparently the elderly gardener down the block from Willard's house wasn't as focused on his hedge clipping as Laurette and I originally thought. The minute we entered the house, he was on the phone to the police. The four women cops who showed up refused to listen to our harried explanations, and promptly placed us both under arrest for breaking and entering. Laurette, who was convinced she might actually be a lesbian after a string of bad choices in men, realized on this day that she was indeed a full-fledged heterosexual when she was roughly frisked down for weapons by the four butch officers.

After carting us downtown in the back of a squad car, we were fingerprinted, photographed, and ultimately separated. As two of the officers led Laurette away, she finally broke down and started sobbing. All of this had just been too much for her, and I felt rotten about it. This was totally my fault, and as I sat on the hard bench in this cold, cramped cell, I knew Laurette would find some way to pay me back for the emotionally debilitating trauma I had put her through.

I closed my eyes, imagining this was just another audition, that the muttering, crazy man in front of me was just another aspiring actor running his lines, and that the corrections officer standing guard outside the cell was the casting director waiting to escort me inside to face more producers.

"Jarrod Jarvis?"

See, it was time for me to breeze into the conference room and face the bigwigs. Just like always. I had done this a thousand times. And in my mind I felt this time I was going to nail it.

Snapping out of my fantasy, I looked up to see the stern-faced guard, his massive, fleshy arms folded in front of him, his eyes judging me.

With disdain in his voice he said, "I guess you're free to go."

I didn't know what his problem was. He kept his eye trained on me as he inserted a key into a lock on the cell door. I felt like he wanted to tell me that in his mind two hours in a holding cell wasn't nearly enough to teach me a hard lesson.

Who was this guy to judge me? How would he know anything

about me in the first place? When the steel bars slid open, and I stepped out into the hall, I suddenly understood. The guard did know the whole story, because there, standing just a few feet behind him, was Charlie.

He turned to the guard and nodded. "Thanks, Ned."

I smiled sweetly and said to Charlie, "Would you believe I'm just researching a role?"

Charlie never cracked a smile. I knew I was in major trouble.

The drive home from jail was interminable. Laurette sputtered the endless details of her time served in jail, and how close she came to becoming the bitch of a bank robber who bore a remarkable resemblance to Faye Dunaway, post-*Mommie Dearest*. Laurette was determined to talk non-stop the entire trip, if only to cover up the thick tension in the car.

My BMW had been impounded, and I wasn't going to be able to get it back until the following day, so we all piled into Charlie's Ford Explorer, and swung onto the Hollywood Freeway North to head back to the house.

Charlie kept his eyes fixed on the road, never wavering even to glance at Laurette through the rearview mirror as she chattered away. Laurette's days as a budding Nancy Drew were over. I knew I wouldn't be able to count on her help anymore. This ordeal had shaken her up, and she was happy to return to the boring day-to-day business of managing has-beens. And I also knew she would never again fall for a promise of lunch at the Cheesecake Factory.

I, on the other hand, was only spurred on more by our search of Willard's house. There were so many more questions now. I wanted to know who Terry Duran was and why Willard was paying him five hundred dollars. I wanted to find out more about the *Frontiers* ad for the hustler with the eagle tattoo and what his connection to Willard was. And most importantly, I wanted to find out who had sent Willard that grotesque animated birthday greeting on-line.

Laurette finally ran out of things to say as we roared up Beachwood Drive, the Hollywood sign glistening in the sunlight before us. We drove the rest of the way in uneasy silence.

Charlie pulled the Explorer inside the garage, and we all silently slid out of the car, averting any eye contact with each other. Snickers, oblivious to the tension at first, scampered eagerly over to greet us as we entered the kitchen.

"Laurette, why don't you stay for dinner? I'll make pasta," I said hopefully.

"Can't. I have my therapist tonight, and obviously after the day I've had, it's going to be a slam-bang, action-packed session. Wouldn't miss it for the world." She whipped out her cell phone and called a cab before I could stop her.

"Don't call a cab. I'll drive you there. I'll even wait outside until you're finished, and then I'll take you home."

Laurette knew exactly what I was doing. Avoiding the inevitable. I've never been good at facing problems head on. I prefer to step over them, let them grow and fester until they get so big, I don't have any choice but to deal with them because they're staring me straight in the face (I never claimed to be emotionally healthy).

Charlie was biding his time, waiting to get me alone, so he could lay into me, and I wanted nothing more than to escape his wrath. This was much bigger than Lucy trying to pull the wool over Ricky's eyes. I had embarrassed him at work, put him in an awkward position with the force.

Charlie already had a tough enough time of it because he was openly gay. He had been ridiculed, passed over for promotion, frozen out by some of the more homophobic officers. Everything he achieved took double the effort because a lot of officers were rooting against him. But Charlie was nothing if not determined, and through sheer bravado and hard work, he had earned the respect of even the most hateful cops in his division. Still, it was an uphill battle, and he didn't need the news of his boyfriend getting arrested to spread through out the department.

To make matters worse, there were the crime reporters who pored over every arrest report. There would definitely be a red flag when they came across my name, given my notoriety as a former child star. By next week at this time, my mug shot would probably be splashed across the front page of every tabloid from the *Enquirer* to the *Globe*. I might even find myself in Leno's monologue or in Dave's Top Ten List. I would be yet another sad statistic of what happens to child stars when the work dries up and nobody wants us anymore. I would be one more cautionary tale about the dark, seamy underbelly of show business. People would shake their heads in a mix of disgust and pity.

I was convinced that all of this was racing through Charlie's mind as well. Laurette was nervously nursing a Pepsi One, and heaved a huge sigh of relief when she saw the green-checkered cab pull up out front. She gave us both a quick peck on the cheek, patted Snickers on the head, and made her escape.

And I was left alone with Charlie.

"I'm sorry." It was all I could think of to say.

"You *promised*, Jarrod."

"I know, but when we were over at Willard's house, I found a few things that might . . ."

He cut me off. "I don't care! I already went through the house! I found nothing, absolutely nothing, to suggest foul play! Willard's death was an accident! When are you going to accept that?"

His ego was bruised. He had combed Willard's house the night we found his body, and turned up nothing. He couldn't get his mind around me doubting his skills as a detective. But what was I going to tell him and his police cronies? I know this is a murder because my psychic medium says so? Probably not the best way to go.

"Why are you doing this, huh? Laurette can't get you any auditions, so now you want to be a detective?" he said, his face flushed with anger. "You hoping to crack come big case wide open, get a few headlines so some producer gets the bright idea to cast you as the new Columbo?"

46

"You know that's not true."

"Then why? What is it?"

"Willard was my friend."

Charlie took a deep breath. He knew he had his opening, and he took it. "There's something else going on here, Jarrod. And I think we both know what it is."

I swallowed hard. My face was flushed, my hands trembling. I knew what he was trying to get at, and it infuriated me, mostly because he was right on target. I had spent an entire afternoon in a jail cell working it through my mind, but that didn't mean I was ready to talk about it. We were both fully aware that the can of worms we were about to open was enough to supply a three-month fishing expedition in the North Atlantic.

Charlie stood his ground, staring at me, waiting to discuss the real reason behind my latest obsession.

But I couldn't. I just wasn't ready. I was too confused, too focused on the tiny clues I had uncovered that day.

The thought of tearing open the heart of our relationship and examining it into the wee hours of the morning was just too excruciating. I wished I could be as open, forthright, and fair minded as Charlie. He deserved that. And sometimes I was. But right now, he was getting the moody Jarrod who refused to deal with the real issues. The former child star Jarrod who could be bratty and shallow and terrified to face the raw emotions that would surely bubble to the surface.

No, I had to get out of there. Now.

"You can think what you want," I seethed. "But I'm not playing this game with you tonight."

I whipped around and started for the garage before I realized my car was still impounded. So I turned around again, marched past Charlie and a confused Snickers, and headed straight out the front door. I walked down our narrow street hoping there weren't any skunks or snakes out tonight. Skunks I could handle. Snakes scared me to death.

Our street spilled out onto Beachwood Drive, and I hiked down the road towards downtown Hollywood where I would eventually join the lost starry-eyed teenage runaways, the strung-out drug pushers and the camera-laden tourists snapping pictures of Lassie's star on the Walk of Fame.

I had no idea where I was going. I just knew that escaping the confrontation back home was what mattered now.

The past would come back to haunt me soon enough.

Chapter Seven

I don't know how long I walked along the grimy, littered streets of Hollywood Boulevard towards the restored glitz and glitter of the newly built Hollywood & Highland Center, new home to the Academy Awards and the recently refurbished Mann Chinese Theatre. But when my feet finally started to throb in pain, I caught a cab home.

I had cooled down considerably at this point, but my resolve to press on with this wild obsession had not diminished. I knew Charlie had a right to be angry. Maybe if I was fixated on someone else's death, he might have been more tolerant. But this was Willard Ray Hornsby. And Willard Ray Hornsby was the other child star I shared the front pages of the tabloids with all those years ago when we were caught kissing at the gay rodeo.

When we were teenagers, Willard and I had spent a lot of time together signing autographs at malls and making guest appearances on *Super Password*. We shared a common bond. We were both struggling to find ourselves amidst the hoopla and fanfare of TV fame and fortune. We were also both hiding our true selves from the world, and when we both realized that, we became closer than ever.

Yes, we slept together. We were a couple of horny teenagers, groping and slobbering one another with kisses, finding solace in the fact that we were both experiencing the same strange feelings. And at the time we were conditioned to believe they were unnatural feelings. It was an intensely private affair, one we decided to hide from the world.

Our curiosity about others like us finally got the best of us, and we started making mistakes, the biggest one being our impulsive decision to make a surprise appearance at the rodeo. That's when an enterprising photographer captured our brief, spontaneous public display of affection. That one picture made an indelible impression on the American public, as well as on all our friends and family.

Willard and I would forever be inextricably linked.

His mother Tamara hated me for it. She was convinced I had led her only son down a forbidden path, and there was no going back.

When Charlie and I started dating, I shared all of this with him in the interest of full disclosure. As always, he was sensitive and understanding and even encouraged me to keep up my friendship with Willard.

In retrospect, this may have been a mistake. Charlie was watching his other half doggedly pursue leads like some bereaved but fiercely strong-minded widow in a Lifetime TV movie. Willard had only been dead a week, and I'm sure Charlie didn't expect me to put his death into some final perspective after such a brief period of time, but it surely must have hurt him on some visceral level to see all of my old feelings for Willard reemerge after such a long time.

During the last years of his life, Willard and I were close, but our bond wasn't nearly as strong as it had been when we were kids. Months would go by without us talking on the phone, having lunch, or even running into each other at an audition. We were friends, but it wasn't the kind of friendship that would merit such an outpouring of emotion and determination.

There had to be something else at work, something driving me forward and causing me to question all the evidence and speculation beyond my surreal attachment to the deceased.

When I stood over Willard's floating, lifeless body, there had been a brief moment where I saw myself lying there, face down in the pool. It made me shudder. Could that be me? I saw so much of myself in Willard. We had traveled on parallel paths for years. And it chilled me to the bone.

There are no guarantees in life. What if Charlie left me? What if I couldn't get work? What if I sunk into a depression? All of those things could happen, and send me spiraling down into the depths of former child star hell. It was a fear that ripped through me like a bullet. And that's why I wasn't being sensitive to Charlie, why I didn't believe the police theory that it was an accident, why I was willing to risk more jail time to dissect all the events leading up to my discovery of the body. Because if Isis was wrong and it wasn't murder, if Willard really couldn't handle life without fame, money, and a high Q rating, and all of those losses led him down a path of self destruction, then it could also happen to me. And I wasn't ready to accept that, for him or for me.

When the cab pulled up to the house, I could tell Charlie had already gone to bed. I let myself in, and quietly made my way through the house towards the stairs that led down to the bedrooms. Snickers dashed in circles, barely able to contain herself, as if I had just returned from a yearlong trip around the globe. Dogs don't have any real concept of time. I had only been gone a few hours.

I opened the bedroom door and poked my head in to check on Charlie. He was bundled up in the comforter, and I could only make out a bit of his hair on the pillow. He was asleep. Or at least pretending to be.

I closed the door, and headed back upstairs where I mixed myself an apple martini and settled down in the den with Snickers on my lap to watch *The O'Reilly Factor*, a spirited chat fest that was always good for a few laughs. Host Bill O'Reilly's panel was arguing over another military build up proposal, but in my mind, I imagined them debating the inevitable tabloid coverage of my arrest. Since I was caught breaking into Willard's home, I was sure the photos of us smooching would once again surface for further public consumption. And who knows? By this time next week, Bill O'Reilly and his talking heads could very well be discussing my recent misfortune.

I hoped my enormous ego was blowing this incident out of proportion and no one would really care, or even devote much print to it. But I knew my fears had merit, having dealt with the media on many occasions.

I drifted off to sleep on the couch, and awoke the next morning to find Charlie already gone. I combed the kitchen for a note, but he hadn't left one. He was still mad at me for storming out.

After walking Snickers around the neighborhood and brewing some coffee, I searched through the pants I had worn the day before and found the items I had lifted from Willard's house. I unfolded the check that was made out to a "Terry Duran" and studied it. I was surprised the police had never found this, but since they were so convinced Willard's death was an accident, it probably never crossed their minds this could be a clue.

On the check's memo line, in plain view, Willard had scribbled "trainer." How did I miss this? Willard himself was telling me exactly who Terry Duran was. Yes, it could mean "corporate trainer" or "horse trainer", but this was Los Angeles, and here it could only mean one thing: personal trainer. Terry Duran was probably a young buffed stud Willard hired to help get him into shape. I pulled out the yellow pages and started calling every gym listed that was in a reasonable radius to Willard's house in Brentwood. Finally, after calling about fourteen, I hit pay dirt.

"Hello. Custom Fitness. May I help you?" asked a cheery, relentlessly upbeat voice that can only be heard in LA.

"I'm looking for a Terry Duran."

"She's not in yet. Can I take a message?"

Terry Duran was a woman. I hated myself for assuming Willard would want a male trainer he could drool over. Then again, I understood his logic. With a woman, he could stay focused on his lifting and pumping without any unnecessary distractions.

"When do you expect her to come in?"

I heard a rustling of pages as the receptionist checked the schedule.

"She's got a client at ten, but she does have a slot open at eleven if you'd like to make an appointment."

"No thanks," I said and hung up. If I hurried, I could pick up my car at the impound yard, and make it over to the west side before ten.

By the time I filled out all the paper work and inspected every inch of the car for any new dents, it was going on ten-thirty. I raced down Wilshire Boulevard, grateful that the morning rush hour was finally tapering off. I was hoping to catch Terry Duran before she finished up with her morning client and left the gym for parts unknown.

Turning onto San Vicente Boulevard, I searched for a space to park. It was prime shopping time in the business district of Brentwood, and all the wives (and a few husbands) of studio executives and Hollywood powerbrokers were out in full force. I finally found a space, managed to squeeze my BMW boat into it, and plunked a few quarters in the meter to buy myself enough time. Across the street, just above a small independent bookshop, was Custom Fitness.

After climbing the stairs to the top floor, I found myself out of breath. This was probably how they convinced you to join. You felt so out of shape from the walk up, you were compelled to hand over your Visa card for a lifetime membership.

The gym was quiet. Only one or two clients were working out with trainers. It was clean, sunny, and had a friendly atmosphere. On the Stairmaster was Marlee Matlin, the hearing impaired actress who won an Oscar for *Children of a Lesser God*. Since then, she has spent her entire career as the "go to girl" for any deaf female parts. I figured if she worked out here, then the place had an upscale clientele. There was a heavy man, his gray t-shirt drenched in sweat, reading *Variety* as he huffed and puffed on the treadmill, and two more men in the back near a weight rack. One, toned and tanned, spotted the other one who was far more pasty and flabby as he strained to lift a barbell.

I was afraid Terry Duran had already left when the door to the women's locker room flung open, and a tall, imposing woman, around thirty years old, came out. She was lean, in good shape, but there was a hardness about her, her demeanor vaguely masculine. She had Julia Roberts hair, curly auburn locks that flowed down to her shoulders in a tousled mane. She wore a purple sports bra and black spandex shorts that accentuated the curves of her perfectly formed butt. This girl had it going on.

Marlee Matlin smiled and waved at her as the woman grabbed a bag from behind the reception counter, and headed towards the door.

The exhausted man on the treadmill looked up from his *Variety* and managed to wheeze, "Bye, Terry." Bingo.

I met her at the door. "Terry Duran?"

She looked up at me and smiled. "Yes."

"My name is Jarrod Jarvis."

Her eyes twinkled as she cocked her head and looked me up and down from head to toe. "I know who you are. So are you going to say it for me?"

I sighed. I hated doing it. But I wanted to pump her for information so I didn't have much of a choice. I struck my impish stance, wagged my finger in her face, and said, "Baby, don't even go there!"

She roared, and I have to admit, there was a small part of me that found satisfaction in bringing such joy to people with those five stupid words. Though I knew if one day I cured cancer or walked on Mars, it would still be those words that I would be remembered for. They would be engraved on my tombstone.

Terry was having a ball, repeating the phrase over and over. I decided to press my advantage. "I'm a friend of Willard Ray Hornsby."

She stopped laughing. "Willard, huh? Well, when you see him, tell him he missed three appointments last week, and I have a rule. If you don't give me a twenty-four hour cancellation notice, you still have to pay for the session."

She didn't know. And now I had to be the one to tell her. "Terry, I'm sorry, but Willard's dead."

She froze and just stared at me, not sure if she heard me right. I continued. "He had been drinking. The police say he tripped over something in his backyard and fell into the pool. He drowned."

Her eyes welled up with tears. "I . . . I can't believe it . . ."

I pulled out the check and handed it to her. "I found this in his house."

She looked at it a moment, and wiped the tears away from her face. "Willard knew I was always having money trouble. Sometimes he'd pay three months in advance when I had rent due."

She broke down sobbing. The other gym patrons watched us curiously. I didn't know what I should do. Hug her? Leave her alone? I still had questions to ask.

Terry shook her head. "God, and I was so mad at him for standing me up last week and wasting my time. If I had only known . . ."

"Terry, I found a birthday card someone e-mailed to him."

"Last week was his birthday? I had no idea . . ." Her voice trailed off.

"It was a threatening note. You saw Willard a couple times a week. Did he ever mention anyone who might have had it in for him?"

"No. Everybody around here loved Willard. I mean, sometimes the trainers would give him a hard time because he'd show up with a box of donuts and hand them out to everybody, but it was funny.

Nobody got seriously mad." She grimaced as she started putting everything together. "Are you saying someone murdered Willard?"

"I have no proof of that. But things just don't add up for me, and I'm trying to figure it all out."

She opened her bag, fished through it, and then produced a card. It had her name, address, phone and pager numer, and e-mail address. "If you need any help, call me. Please. I adored Willard. He was so . . ." Her eyes welled up again. "Excuse me."

Terry Duran fled out the door, and I was left to face the hostile glares of the gym clients who watched the scene, and blamed me for Terry's shattered state. I decided it was best I get out of there.

As I walked down the street towards my car, I thought about Terry Duran. Was it an act? I had no clues to suggest it was, but this was LA, a town filled with wannabe actors who could more or less pull off a convincing performance. If she was as fond of Willard as she said she was, why didn't she call to check up on him when he didn't show up for the second or even third training session? There were no messages from her found on his answering machine. Then again, their relationship was strictly trainer-client, so it wasn't her job to follow up and find out why Willard was standing her up. She had other clients to train and money hassles to deal with. Which spoke to a lack of motive. Terry Duran desperately needed Willard and his generous checks in advance. Why would she ever jeopardize losing a cash cow like that, if her financial difficulties were as severe as she suggested? It seemed to me at the moment that Terry Duran was not on Willard's enemies list. So I decided to look elsewhere for answers. And I was going to start with the shirtless young buck with the eagle tattoo in the *Frontiers* ad.

Chapter Eight

I pulled onto Wilshire, and stopped at the first Starbuck's I came across. I was craving a hazelnut café latte, and I figured a jolt of caffeine would keep my energy level up as I followed my trail of clues.

As I waited for my coffee, my eyes fell to the basket full of sandwiches on display, and I ached to snatch them all up, everything from the mouth watering turkey pesto to the spicy cajun chicken. Laurette and I hadn't discussed our diet in days, so I felt safe in assuming it was history. I grabbed the turkey and a bag of sea salt kettle chips and watched hungrily, my mouth watering, as the chipper clerk rang it all up. Then I settled down at a corner table, pulled out my cell phone, and checked my messages. One from Laurette, curious to know if Charlie and I had made up, another from Laurette asking me if I had lunch plans (she never did get to the Cheesecake Factory and it was driving her insane), and one from my dentist confirming my six month cleaning appointment for tomorrow. None from Charlie.

I wondered if I should just break down and call him? Both of us could be annoyingly stubborn. I decided to give him some more time to see the error of his ways and rush home to beg my forgiveness.

I dug the *Frontiers* ad out of my pocket as I dove into my sandwich, and studied the image of the tattooed kid again. I couldn't be sure Willard even knew him. Maybe he had just ripped the ad out of the magazine and left it by his bedside in order to jumpstart a wet dream after he fell asleep. But I would never know for sure if I didn't call the pager number listed in the ad. After a moment of hesitation, I put down my sandwich and punched in the number. The voice mail message was brief.

"Hi, this is Eli. Please leave your name and number and I'll get back to you as soon as possible. Serious calls only, please." After the beep, I rattled off my name (I decided to use "Brandon," as a tribute to Jason Priestley's ten loyal years on *Beverly Hills 90210*) and my cell number and hung up. Then I tore open my bag of chips and started in on those as I waited and watched a crowd of City National Bank employees from next door pour in for a quick pre-lunch caffeine fix. I sometimes forgot that there were people in LA who were not connected to the entertainment business. What did they talk about? The weather? It never changed. I found the whole idea of "non pros" inside the city limits fascinating.

Within five minutes, my cell phone was clanging, and I fumbled through my mess of plastic, half eaten sandwich, and empty potato chip bag to find it.

"Hello?"

"Hey, Brandon, this is Eli."

I paused. I had no idea how to go about this. I had never called "a massage therapist" through a *Frontiers* ad before. I didn't know the etiquette.

He decided to help me along. "You looking to get a massage today?"

"Um, sure."

Another pause. He must have been used to dealing with frightened, blithering idiots, because he wasted no time in bailing me out again.

"You want to come here, or would you prefer I come to you? It's seventy-five dollars in, a hundred dollars out."

"I'll come to you."

"Great. I'm up in Laurel Canyon. 8842 Lookout Mountain Avenue. You know how to find it?"

"I have a Thomas Guide." I never left home without my handy LA County street guide for just such occasions.

"It's a brown ranch-style house on the left just past East Horseshoe Canyon Road. You can't miss it. Come around back. I'm in the guesthouse. You want to come, say, around one?"

An hour from now. Plenty of time to get worked up into a complete panic.

"Um, sure." Now I was repeating myself. I always did that when I was nervous.

"Looking forward to meeting you, Brandon," he said, an inviting tone in his voice. It was hard not to be intrigued.

"Um, me too." At least I was now adding a bit of variety to my monotone responses. I pressed the "End Call" button and sat back in my hard wooden chair at Starbuck's. What did I think I was doing? One fight with my boyfriend and suddenly I was driving up to some remote house in the hills to get an erotic massage from a tattooed hustler! I kept telling myself I was only doing this for Willard.

I looked at the photo of Eli in the ad again. I would've killed for those rippled abs.

After polishing off my sandwich, I jumped behind the wheel of the BMW again, and tore off down Wilshire, turning onto Crescent Heights Boulevard, and followed the stream of midday traffic up through West Hollywood, past the looming billboards of the Sunset

Strip, and onto the calm rustic ambience of Laurel Canyon. As I made a left onto Lookout Mountain Avenue, all evidence of city life evaporated.

Like my own home in Beachwood Canyon, this was an escape from the bustle of LA life, and there was a peaceful silence that fell over the whole area. It's hard not to feel a bit vulnerable when you're up in the hills, all by yourself. Although houses populated both sides of the streets, an overwhelming sense of fear and loneliness washed over me. Here I was, driving up to a secluded house to meet someone I knew nothing about. It didn't seem like the smartest move, but I had come too far already to turn back now.

I slowed down when I spotted the brown ranch-style house in the distance, just past East Horseshoe Canyon as Eli promised. I pulled over close to a hillside, got out, and walked the rest of the way. I noticed that nobody else in the neighborhood appeared to be around to hear me yelling if anything went wrong. Then I chuckled to myself. Once again I was being overly dramatic and paranoid. Besides, I took a scene combat class once where the teacher told me I was a natural fighter, so I wasn't worried about defending myself if the need arose.

I walked around to the back of the house as instructed. It was a beautiful home with impeccable landscaping, probably owned by an aging, successful film or music executive who was lucky enough to possess that reliable gay decorating gene that he used to express himself. The entire property was immaculate and well kept. My cynical side assumed Eli was probably well kept too.

There was a lap pool similar to Willard's in back just to the right of a small, quaint guesthouse, a miniature version of the main house. My stomach started flip-flopping as I rapped on the thick wooden door. Just then it dawned on me how stupid I had been. What if he recognized me from TV? I had used the name "Brandon." My whole plan was falling apart at the seams, and I hadn't even met him yet.

The door opened.

Eli's ad didn't do him justice. He was around twenty-two years old, with a tight, lean body and handsome face. It looked as if his nose had once been broken, probably in a bar brawl, which gave him a dangerous quality that was a complete turn-on. He wore tattered gray sweat pants and a form-fitting navy blue tank top. He greeted me with a warm smile.

"Hi, Brandon. Come on in."

He waved me inside, and after a split second of indecision, I crossed the threshold into the unknown. He shut the door behind me, and the flip-flopping in my stomach got worse. Was I just new at this undercover work, or were my instincts screaming to tell me something?

There were movie posters on the wall. *Rebel Without a Cause*, *East of Eden*, and *Giant*. All James Dean movies. There were a couple of books on acting strewn across a small wooden chest that served as a coffee table. So far this guy was a walking cliché. A massage table was set up in the middle of the room, a white sheet thrown over it, with a headrest in front. As I took in the scene, I suddenly felt a pair of big, solid hands caressing my shoulders.

"So," Eli whispered in my ear from behind, "what are you looking for today?"

I took a long deep breath before answering in a squeaky, nellie voice that surprised even me. "Um, anything. I'm not sure. Whatever."

"Okay, why don't you get undressed and lie down on the table? I'll take care of the rest."

It took every urge not to run screaming into the hills. But I was on a mission, and I was prepared to make any sacrifice necessary, even if that included showing him my flabby stomach and the gross zit I spotted this morning on my right butt cheek. I slowly unbuttoned my favorite Tommy Hilfiger short-sleeve shirt, taking my time to fold it and place it on the arm of his couch, and then I unhooked my belt buckle, slipping out of my Ralph Lauren jeans. He watched me, smiling. This was unbearable.

I instinctively turned away as I slid off my Joe Boxer briefs. And that was it. I was buck naked. I could hear him moving behind me, and then I felt the palm of his hand touching the small of my back as he guided me over to the table. I climbed onto it, my face in the headrest. After a moment, I felt warm oil on my back, and then his hands kneading it into my pores.

"You're a little tight. Just relax."

Of course I was a little tight. I was a complete wreck. If he was expecting to give me more than a massage, Charlie would never forgive me. Even in the name of finding the truth. I had to act fast before we went too far down this road.

"So we have a friend in common," I said, injecting as much casual confidence in my voice as I could muster.

"Oh, really?" I knew he was curious. His strokes were more tentative.

"Willard Hornsby."

His grip on my shoulders tightened. A sharp pain ripped through my body. I howled in pain. Finally, he let go.

"Sorry. You have a lot of tension stored up. Just trying to get rid of it." I felt more oil drizzling down my back, and then he continued. "I don't know this guy you're talking about. Wally did you say?"

"Willard. Hornsby. I thought you knew him."

"Nope. Never heard of him."

"I found your ad in his house."

He chuckled. "There are a lot of guys in this town who have my ad. And I have a lot of clients who don't give me their real names . . ." He paused for effect. "*Brandon*."

"Willard's dead."

"I'm sorry to hear that."

"I'm trying to figure out how it happened."

"You don't know?"

"The police say it was an accidental drowning. I think there's another side to the story they're just not seeing yet."

"So you're like playing detective? Checking out all the leads?"

"I'm the Sherlock Holmes of West Hollywood."

"Cool. And this guy had my ad, so I'm a suspect? What a trip. I've never been a murder suspect before. How cool."

I couldn't tell if he was genuinely excited or playing it up for my benefit. But then, out of the blue, I got the break that made this whole field trip worthwhile.

"Well, let me know how it all turns out. I love a good whodunit. Was it Colonel Mustard with the candlestick in the conservatory? Who killed Willard Ray Hornsby?"

He had just hung himself. And I relished in pointing it out. "Funny. I never mentioned that Willard's middle name was Ray. He only allowed people who were close to him to refer to his full name."

Eli abruptly stopped massaging my back.

There was a long, eerie silence.

Finally, I turned over and looked up at him. The warm smile was gone. He was biting his lip, his bent nose flaring, his dark coal eyes suddenly menacing. My flip-flopping stomach acted up again. I had been so hell bent on catching Eli in a lie that I never stopped to think what I would do after I actually did.

His eyes bore into me. "I think we're done here. You better go."

It sounded like a marvelous idea. I jumped off the table and started scrounging about for my clothes. He never took those dangerous, livid eyes off me as I hurriedly threw on my pants. I didn't bother buttoning up my shirt or threading the belt back through my Ralph Lauren pre-washed jeans. I just wanted to get the hell out of there.

At the door, I turned to face him. He just stood there, rage in his face, his fists clenched. He hated himself for screwing up, and he hated me for calling him on it.

"I'm not accusing you of anything. I just want to know what happened to Willard."

"Get out of here." His voice was low, threatening. He didn't have to tell me twice. I did an about face, and marched out the door.

As I crossed the lawn towards the gate that led to the street, my stomach was going crazy, flip flopping wildly as if my instincts were trying to jar me awake, warn me of impending peril.

By the time my brain started to catch up, it was too late.

A powerful force slammed into me, causing me to lose my balance. I toppled over into the swimming pool, and slammed into the cement bottom shoulder first at the shallow end. By the time I surfaced to catch my breath, I sensed someone else in the pool with me, splashing violently towards me.

A pair of big, strong hands grabbed me by the hair and dunked me under, holding me there. I flailed about in a confused, dazed state. What was happening? Only when I tasted the bitter chlorinated water as it flooded my lungs did the stark realization finally hit me.

Eli the tattooed hustler was going to drown me.

Chapter Nine

As he held my head under the water, I knew it would only be a matter of moments before I swallowed enough water and succumbed.

I flapped my arms wildly, reaching out for anything that might help me. I felt Eli's gray sweat pants, and managed to grab a fistful of material, and pull myself closer to him. Then, I shot my hand out and, snatched a hold of his balls, and squeezed as hard as I could.

His grip on my head loosened, and I was able to pop my head above the water's surface, gasping and sputtering, the cool air pouring into my lungs, offering me a respite from impending death.

I wiped the sopping wet strands of hair out of my eyes, and saw Eli, a pained look on his face, staring at me, fury rising once again.

In obvious pain but with his adrenaline pumping, he lunged at me, his hands encircling my throat as we flew back against the hard cement side of the pool. He got up close to my face. So close I could smell the western omelet he had for breakfast on his breath. Why I was thinking of food at such a time as this defies explanation, but as he was choking me and I started to lose consciousness, I couldn't help myself. It was the only thing I could focus on.

I clutched his steel arms with my hands and tried to pry them off me, but it was hopeless. He was a lot younger, a lot stronger, and a lot madder. I must have set off an internal rage with my questions, and it was driving him forward, determined to kill me.

I tried going for the groin again with my knee, but he anticipated it, and pinned me against the side of the pool with his body, his legs jammed up against mine, as he squeezed harder and harder. I felt my eyes retreating up into the back of my head, as images of Charlie in a dark suit at my own funeral took over. I kept asking myself, "Why didn't we make up before this? Why didn't I tell him how much I loved him? And why aren't there more people here to mourn me?" And then there was blackness.

I heard voices in Spanish as my eyes fluttered open to see three Mexican men staring down at me. Two were in their thirties, had potbellies, mustaches, and wore Lakers t-shirts and ball caps. The third was much younger, early twenties, wiry, and with the whitest teeth I'd ever seen. He smiled as I came to, and then gently lifted my head, helping me to sit up.

I coughed up some water, and tried to get my bearings. I was still in the backyard of the house in Laurel Canyon. Eli was nowhere to be seen.

I asked the men what had happened, and the younger one, who spoke English well, told me they were gardeners for the property, and arrived to find Eli rescuing me.

I jerked my head and said, "He said he was rescuing me?" Apparently, when the gardeners happened upon the scene, Eli pulled my unconscious body from the water and told them I had fallen into the pool, and couldn't swim, and he jumped in to help me.

"Where is Eli now?"

"He went to get help," the younger man said.

They helped me to my feet, and despite a woozy feeling in my head, I felt well enough to drive home. The men were apprehensive about letting me go in my condition.

"Don't you want to wait for Eli to come back with a doctor?"

I smiled. "Somehow I don't think he'll be coming back with anybody."

I thanked them for staying with me, and making sure I was all right. Yesterday, a gardener was responsible for the police arresting me and throwing my ass in jail. Today, three more gardeners were responsible for saving my life. Strange how it all evens out.

I walked back down the road to my car, and found a slip of paper tucked underneath the windshield wiper. At first I thought it was a Handyman's advertisement or a Chinese take-out menu, but when I picked it up and unfolded it I knew it was a note from Eli. "*Leave it alone or next time I'll finish the job.*" Why was everybody telling me to leave it alone? First Spiro at Willard's funeral and now this two-bit hustler with the eagle tattoo. And what were they talking about? Leave what alone? In their panic to get rid of me, they were all but showing me their cards.

All these threats just confirmed in my mind that there was more to Willard's drowning than just an unfortunate trip over a lawn chair. Didn't these clowns realize that the more they warned me to stay away, the more I'd be determined to find out what the real deal was? I also found it interesting that I nearly suffered a similar fate as my dear departed friend Willard—drowning in a pool. Maybe this was Eli's modus operandi, and there just weren't any gardeners to show up and save Willard on the night of his birthday party.

Eli's note was right out of a bad B movie, or at best an episode of *Barnaby Jones*. The whole thing just pissed me off. How dumb was he to leave a hand-written threatening note? If Eli thought he had succeeded in scaring me off, he was sadly mistaken. In fact, if I could patch things up with Charlie, I knew he would be enormously helpful in scaring the hell out of Eli. But that would also mean telling Charlie everything. And I wasn't sure I had the guts to come clean about my impromptu visit to a hustler's bungalow.

As I drove down Laurel Canyon and across Franklin to Beachwood Drive, I stopped at the small market just past the gates to Hollywood Land. Nestled in the canyon just below the famous Hollywood sign was a tiny village with a café, novelty shop, hair salon, and realtor's office. It was like a small town where people waved as they drove by, residents had their names engraved on stones in a small park just outside the cafe, and tourists stopped for directions on their journey to get as close to the sign as possible for a photo op. This was a haven for artists, musicians, writers, and actors. A hideaway far from the disappointments and rejections of the company town below. I adored this neighborhood. Charlie and I lived just up the street from the village and had a charge account at the market.

I parked the car and hurried into the store for a few items. I figured I would make Charlie's favorite dish, baked ziti, for dinner. He said it was his favorite, but since it was the only thing I knew how to cook, I figured that it was just his kind heart making me feel useful.

I grabbed a scuffed plastic yellow shopping basket and raced up and down the aisles, grabbing various ingredients. I noticed the line at the checkout counter growing, and Bill, the sweet-natured owner, was short-staffed today, so I hurried up the last aisle, tossing a small bottle of oregano into the basket, before getting in line.

There must have been five or six people waiting ahead of me as I browsed the magazine rack to pass the time. And that's when I saw it. On the cover of the *National Enquirer*. My mug shot. Splashed right there on the front page. The headlines blared, "The Tragic Saga of Another Fallen Child Star!" My arrest must have hit the wires just as the tabloids went to press.

I stared dumbly at the rack stuffed with copies. My eyes fell to the *Star* one rack below the *Enquirer*. They were a little more creative. Prison bars superimposed over a publicity photo of me when

I was a scrub-faced cherubic twelve-year-old with the caption, "Baby, don't even go there!" Underneath that it read, "80s sitcom star does go . . . straight to jail!" My arrest was everywhere. Pretty soon the legitimate wire services would pick it up, and I'd be another footnote in Hollywood lore.

A tired-looking woman unloaded her cart in front of me, holding the hand of her hyperactive nine-year-old daughter. The girl looked at me, then looked at the rack of tabloids. Her eyes grew to the size of saucers.

"Mommy, look, it's him! It's him!"

The woman stopped, a tub of cottage cheese in her hand, and followed her daughter's gaze to the mug shot on the cover of the *Enquirer*, and then glanced back up at me. She tried to hide her surprise, but she was no Meryl Streep in the acting department.

I dropped my basket full of baked ziti ingredients and fled the market.

I felt the world closing in on me. Willard's death had barely merited a brief blurb in *Entertainment Weekly*. My arrest at his house was front-page news. This was only the beginning of an avalanche of sordid deeds they would surely pin on me, whether they were true or not.

I jumped in the BMW and roared off, glimpsing back to see the mother and daughter, the check-out clerk, the bag boy, and yes, even Bill, the sweet-natured owner, all standing at the front of the store, watching me speed away. How could I ever show my face in there again?

I felt as if my head was spinning like Linda Blair's in *The Exorcist* as I parked the car in the garage, and stumbled through the door leading to the kitchen.

Snickers, tail wagging, tongue flapping, was at her usual post to greet me as I hurried to the pantry and grabbed the nearest bottle of blue Smirnoff vodka. Then I sifted through the fridge for any mixer I could find—club soda, juice, tonic, anything. It was bare. Ice would have to serve as my mixer.

Snickers stared up at me, her excited eyes dancing. As I swallowed a gulp of the vodka and began to relax a bit, I looked down at her. Dogs are God's gift to the human race. You can be splashed across the papers, trumpeted as a has-been screw up with an arrest record, and a dog will still look at you as if you're the most perfect, most important being in her entire world. Of course, the fact that a dog depends on you to feed her and take her out to do her business could have something to do with this unconditional love and devotion, but at that moment I was in no mood to question my dog's motives.

I poured myself another vodka and hurled it down my throat. I usually don't drink much, especially since Charlie never touches the stuff. But stress can often break down your will power, and today, stress was consuming me.

The phone snapped me out of my mental spiral, and I snatched it up when I saw Laurette's name on my caller I.D.

"Have you seen the tabloids?" I said.

"Have I seen them? Honey, they're everywhere! My phone's been ringing off the hook all morning."

"How did they find out? How did they get my mug shot so fast?"

"Please. If it can happen to Pee Wee Herman, it can happen to you. Just be glad they didn't nail you for jerking off in a porno theatre. The point is I'm getting offers."

"Offers? What kind of offers?"

"Commercials. Guest spots. Talk shows. The whole town's buzzing about your arrest. This could be the break we've been waiting for."

"I don't want to be a novelty act. I want to get hired because I'm a good actor."

"We've got heat, Jarrod. Let's not waste it. Prove to the world you can act later. Now we won't get a *West Wing* or *Will and Grace* off this, but I did hear from *Mysteries and Scandals* and *TV Guide:*

The Truth Behind the Rumors. They both want to do pieces. I called Ricki's people, and though she loved watching you when she was a kid, she doesn't feel it would be appropriate to have you on the show."

"Why not?"

"She's got kids now. She's worried about role models. Doesn't want to glamorize your crimes by putting you on her show."

"Crimes? When did I commit more than one?"

"The *Globe* is coming out with a story about some incident when you were eighteen and cracked up your car in a drunk driving accident."

"Yes. But it was the other driver who was drunk, not me."

"Like that matters. They're a tabloid, for god's sakes. I know this is tough, getting arrested and all . . ."

"Yes. I'm sure you understand. You were arrested too!"

"But I'm not a former child star. Nobody cares that I was there. They just said you were with 'a platonic gal pal'. Nothing more."

I poured a third vodka. Laurette was usually more sensitive and supportive than this, but she was seeing an upswing in business, so there was no reasoning with her.

"I really think we need to strategize," Laurette said. "Go through the offers. See which ones make the most sense."

"None of them. I'm not going out on the talk shows as a circus sideshow. When you get a legitimate offer, call me."

"Jerry Springer isn't legitimate?"

"Listen, Laurette, I don't want to talk about this anymore. I've had a tough day all around. It started with a hustler trying to drown me in a lap pool."

There was a long pause on the other end. I could actually hear Laurette processing this latest information.

"Okay, got the headline. Now I want to hear the story."

"I called the guy in the ad."

"What ad? What are you talking about?"

"The ad we found in Willard's bedroom . . ."

I heard the garage door open. Snickers began running in circles. Charlie was home.

"Laurette, I have to go."

"Wait, you can't just hang up."

I hung up just in time. Charlie walked in, gave me a careful, considered smile, then bent down as Snickers rolled over and spread her legs. He scratched her belly, and she closed her eyes, in complete ecstasy. I was jealous. I wanted my belly scratched, but I wasn't sure where I stood with Charlie at the moment.

He reached into his back pocket and pulled out some folded pages that had been stapled. We sized each other up for an awkward moment, both of us too stubborn to make the first move. Then, he stepped forward, took me in his arms, and whispered in my ear, "I love you."

That was all it took. I hugged him as tight as I could, so relieved we weren't fighting anymore. There was a trust between us. No matter how bad things got, no matter how mad we left the other, there was enough love there to get us over the hurdles. And I knew I would be testing that love and trust again and again in the days to come. But right now, it was about my favorite part of being in a relationship. Making up. Damn. Why did I have to run out of the store without those baked ziti ingredients? Now I had nothing to show him how much I cared.

"I brought a peace offering," he said.

He handed me the folded pages. I opened them to see an official looking document from police headquarters. It was Willard Ray Hornsby's autopsy report.

Chapter Ten

There was only one person from whom Charlie could have gotten his hands on an autopsy report. And that was Susie Chan, his ex-wife. Susie worked in the L.A. Coroner's Office, and was on a meteoric rise. I kept seeing her name pop up in the *Times*, as she seemed to be the first stop for the media whenever they needed a quote. A couple of high profile murder cases had thrust her into the spotlight, and Susie, ambitious by nature, basked in the attention.

I tried to mask my jealousy of Susie. After all, Charlie had long proclaimed his preference for men. But still, they had dated for almost ten years and been married for two. There was a lot of history between them. And they had long put aside any hurt feelings and grudges, and occasionally met for dinner to discuss police work and their respective personal lives.

I was never invited.

It just about drove me mad. In Charlie's mind, he believed it would make me feel uncomfortable. So I tried not to make an issue out of it. But I'm an actor; we make issues out of everything.

"I didn't know you were going to see Susie."

Charlie knew where I was going, and put an immediate stop to it.

"I called her to get a copy of the report. For you. As a peace offering. End of story."

"I wasn't making an issue out of it."

"Oh no. Not you." I always enjoyed a little well-timed sarcasm, but never from my boyfriend. And the cross look on my face encouraged Charlie to choose another tack.

He took my hands in his, looked me straight in the eye, and said, "I was just trying to do something nice. Because I love you and I'm sorry for what I said last night. So please, just take a look."

I opened the report and scanned the contents. Despite my beloved boyfriend's claims he had secured a copy of Willard's autopsy out of his blind devotion to me, this was clearly a maneuver designed to give himself the upper hand. Because as I perused the pages, Charlie was anxious for me to get to the report's conclusion where at the bottom of the page, in bold black letters, blared the words, "Cause of Death: Drowning by accident."

When I started reading other parts of the report, he leaned over and pointed to it just in case I had missed it.

"Look at that. According to Susie's conclusions, Willard's death was an accident after all."

"What does she know? She believed you were straight for twelve years."

Charlie didn't like that one. But he decided to ignore it for the sake of the truce.

He shrugged. "It was an accident, Jarrod. End of story."

Charlie always wanted to get to the end of the story. He made a habit of flipping to the last page of a mystery novel first to see who committed the crime. I preferred to prolong the drama, which again, speaks to my life as an actor. I always pored over every word, searching for any key detail that might shed some light on the characters and situation.

There certainly were no bruises or contusions on Willard's body, nothing to suggest a struggle of any kind. Maybe I was going overboard in my quest to turn his death into an Agatha Christie potboiler. Maybe he just did a Dick Van Dyke pratfall over a piece of lawn furniture and fell into the pool. But if he didn't hit his head on the bottom, why did he drown? If he were conscious, he wouldn't have just given up and swallowed all that water. And if he were suicidal, couldn't he have just gulped a fist full of sleeping pills and chased it down with a Diet Coke?

And what about Spiro and Eli? Both men were so determined for me to drop my inquiries, to be on my way, docile and satisfied by the police and coroner's findings.

Something in the report caught my eye. A small detail near the end of Susie's findings. I looked up at Charlie.

"It says here there were traces of soap found in Willard's lungs."

"So?"

"If he drowned in the pool, why would there be soap in his lungs?"

"I don't know, Jarrod. Maybe he washed his face earlier, and accidentally swallowed a few Irish Spring suds. Susie has to put everything she finds in the report. If she thought it was significant, she would have said so."

"Okay, you win." I closed the report and handed it back to Charlie. He looked enormously relieved. I was finally giving up my career as a detective.

By now, you know me well enough to surmise that I was simply appeasing him for the moment.

Charlie decided to take full advantage of the truce and backed me up against the kitchen counter. He pressed his body into mine. Then he kissed me sweetly on the lips.

"I love you," he whispered.

"Uh huh." Man, he was good when he tried.

I grabbed the back of Charlie's head and pulled him towards me. Our lips devoured each other, and he tore open the buttons on my shirt, and slipped his hand inside. He caressed my chest, and the nipples grew hard. Our hips clasped together like two magnets, and both of us could feel the other's bulging excitement. I wrapped my arms around his neck as he worked my belt, unhooking it finally, and thrusting open my pants.

He stopped long enough to pull off his t-shirt and I slid my hands down his back and stroked it with my fingers. This always drove him mad. No lovemaking session ever went by without him begging for me to scratch his back. All I could think about at the moment, however, was how I had clipped my nails that morning, so I didn't have much traction. Still, he didn't seem to notice as he lifted me up on the counter, yanked down my Joe Boxer under-shorts, and took a pause before lunging down and burying his head in my lap. I threw my head back, banging it hard against the cupboards. It stung like hell, but the euphoric sensation down south dulled the pain.

I opened my eyes long enough to see Snickers, lying a few feet away on her stomach, looking up at us with an innocent, sweet face. She never seemed to like watching her two daddies engage in such physical, animalistic behavior, but then again, she could never bring herself to leave the room either.

I was getting close to climax. I clutched a fist full of Charlie's hair as his head bobbed up and down, now at a frantic pace. Small, intense breaths escaped from my mouth.

Yes. Yes. Yes.

The phone rang. Neither of us stopped. We had both long put our priorities in order. Nothing could ever be more important than late-afternoon oral sex.

The machine picked up. I heard my cheery voice say, "Hi, Jarrod and Charlie aren't in right now . . ." Charlie's voice took over. "So leave your name and number and we'll call you back." Right before the beep, Snickers barked on the tape. I remember wanting the whole family involved in the making of the outgoing message. Sometimes I scared myself with just how gay we could be.

Charlie kept pumping right through the beep, and my short breaths had turned into glorious gratified moans. I was close. So close. Any second now I would explode with a flurry of fanfare.

That was when Laurette's sharp voice pierced the air. "It's me. I can't stand the suspense anymore. Why did the hustler try drowning you in a pool today? Call me."

Click.

Charlie stopped, stood up, and wiped his mouth with his forearm. I leaned back, and banged my head against the cupboard again.

Charlie's eyes betrayed no sympathy. "What's she talking about? What hustler?"

"Oh, didn't I mention that when you came in?"

Charlie was in no mood for games. And I was so worked up from our spur-of-the-moment lovemaking session, I could scarcely catch my breath.

I finally gave up and explained what had happened today at the house in Laurel Canyon. Charlie instantly scooped up the phone, called the station, and ordered a patrol car to pick up Eli. He was going to haul this kid's ass downtown and shake him up a bit for trying to do away with his boyfriend. Charlie slammed down the phone, and headed for the garage.

I still sat on the kitchen counter, my pants down around my knees, a numb expression on my face. "Aren't we going to finish what we started?"

Charlie turned and looked back at me. His face said it all, and it was a big fat no.

I figured now that he was in a foul mood, it might be a good idea to share everything about my day. Pile it all on now and save potential grief later. "By the way, I'm on the cover of at least two tabloids today."

"I know. Two of the dispatchers were reading copies at lunch. It was hard to miss you." It must have been embarrassing for Charlie. I couldn't imagine the ribbing he took, but he never complained about it before, and he wasn't about to start now.

He opened the door to the garage, and stood there for a moment. "You coming?"

I hopped down from the kitchen counter, and, frustrated, pulled my pants up and zipped the fly as I followed him out the door.

Chapter Eleven

By the time Charlie and I reached the station, Eli had already been apprehended, dragged downtown, and tossed inside an interrogation room with a two-way mirror. Say what you want about television's portrayal of cops, but some of the details they never fail to get right. Charlie told me to wait outside as he charged into the room to confront my attacker.

I stood there, feeling alone and vulnerable, pretending that the cops and desk sergeants and dispatchers weren't stealing glances my way. A few smiled, recognition in their faces, either from watching me on TV or having just read about me in the tabloids. A few more looked, but there was no fondness or sense of nostalgia in their eyes. It was pure contempt. I was a living, breathing reminder that their fellow detective Charlie Peters was a "faggot." The legacy of a Chief of Police during the eighties and early nineties, who was a notorious racist and homophobe, and whose militaristic, unfeeling approach to law enforcement had led to the riots of '92 was still strong after all these years inside the L.A.P.D.

I wandered over to the two-way mirror that looked into the interrogation room to hear the conversation between Charlie and Eli the tattooed hustler. There was a small, rusty speaker just below the glass that allowed me to listen in.

I heard Charlie's deep, commanding voice. "So you deny trying to drown Jarrod Jarvis?"

"He was trespassing. I thought he was a burglar or something."

"He says you attacked him after he started asking questions about Willard Ray Hornsby."

"Look, I told him and I'll tell you, I don't know who that is."

"So when you thought Mr. Jarvis was a burglar, you still took the time to answer a few of his questions?"

Eli paused. He wasn't the brightest bulb in the chandelier by any stretch of the imagination.

Charlie, in full Sipowicz mode now, yanked a photo out of his shirt pocket, and slapped it down on the table in front of Eli.

"You sure you don't recognize him? This may be your last chance to come clean."

It was obvious Eli hadn't read even one of those acting books I saw on his coffee table. His performance was awful. "Oh, yeah, I remember him now. I'm not good with names, but faces, faces I know."

Charlie sat down, pulled his chair up close to Eli. "How do you know him?"

"He was a client. I give massages."

"Just massages?"

"Yes."

Charlie's steely hazel eyes ripped into Eli, forcing him to shift in his chair and start to fidget. He looked away, and I could tell he was desperately trying to get his story in order. Charlie didn't speak. He waited. And he would wait all night until Eli broke.

"Sometimes I give a little more. It depends on what they're willing to pay."

"And was Willard willing to pay for more?"

Eli nodded. He knew he had just admitted to being a prostitute, and wanted to be careful not to completely incriminate himself, but again, this was no brain surgeon, and the longer he sat there, the more inclined he was to talk.

Charlie could see that Eli was nervous, getting more restless, and just wanted to get the hell out of there. So he changed his demeanor, decided to play the good cop for a few minutes.

"Can I get you something to drink, Eli? Water? Soda?"

"No. Are you going to charge me with something?"

"Well, if we wanted to, we sure could. You just confessed to receiving money for sexual favors, and then there's the alleged attempted murder on Mr. Jarvis, but if you level with me, we might be able to work something out."

"I wasn't going to kill Mr. Jarvis, I just freaked out. He thought I had something to do with his friend's murder."

"If you're innocent, why would you go crazy like that?"

"Because I know the cops. And they look at someone like me, and they figure, yeah, he's the guy. The hustler was over at his house a couple of times. He had to have done it."

"Did you?"

"No!"

"But you did go over to his house?"

"Yeah, sometimes he'd call . . . for a massage. I'd go over, give him what he wanted, and leave."

"What else can you tell me?"

"Nothing."

"Are you into water sports, Eli?"

Eli's body tensed up. "No. Why would you ask me something like that?"

"It just seems like an awfully big coincidence that Willard died face down in his lap pool, and you tried drowning Mr. Jarvis in your landlord's pool just today."

"I didn't kill Willard!"

"When was the last time Willard called you?"

"A week ago, maybe two. I don't remember."

"Was it Friday, April 26?"

"I said I don't remember."

"Do you remember where you were that night?"

Eli stopped. He wiped his runny nose with a bare forearm, and thought hard. Then a smile crept across his face and his eyes lit up.

"Yeah, yeah, I remember where I was."

"Where?"

"San Francisco. I have a friend up there. He's got a bar in the Castro, and sometimes I go up there to dance."

"Dance?"

"Yeah, on top of the bar, in front of a bunch of guys. They stuff dollar bills in my jockstrap if I shimmy a lot in front of them."

"Charming."

"Pays the bills. And I bet if you go up there, you'll find plenty of old farts who were there that night. They'll definitely remember me."

Charlie stood up, wandered over to the two-way mirror and stared out at me. He knew I was there, and the expression on his face told me he was tired. Tired of pursuing a murder case that for all we knew wasn't even a murder. I had been with him long enough to know what was going through his mind.

If Eli were telling the truth about San Francisco, it would put him hundreds of miles away from the scene. And it's quite possible, given his simple mind and current line of work that he did panic when I questioned him about Willard. He was afraid I was going to turn him into the police for his hustling activities, and that they would pin a murder on him for the mere fact that Willard was one of his johns.

Charlie came out of the interrogation room, and walked over to me. There was hope in his eyes, hope that I would drop this matter altogether so we could put this all behind us and move on with our lives.

I instantly poked a hole in his balloon and deflated any hopes he had. "If he's so bad with names, why did he remember that Willard's middle name was Ray?"

"Jarrod, please, he's got an airtight alibi."

"If it checks out. He's not telling us everything. If he didn't kill Willard, he knows who did."

"We don't have any proof that *anyone* killed Willard."

I thought about bringing up Isis's prediction, but again, probably not the best course of action to rally the troops.

Charlie sighed. "I'm going to book him for assault. Unless you really believe he was trying to kill you."

"No. Let him go. I don't want to press charges."

Charlie nodded. "Okay. Your choice. Give me a few minutes to wrap things up here, and then we'll go home and finish what we started."

I didn't want Eli rotting in some jail cell for a simple assault. I was determined to put him under surveillance. I was confident that Eli the tattooed hustler was the key that would eventually unlock the door to the facts surrounding Willard's death.

Isis told me that someone close to me was going to be murdered, not die accidentally. No, I was far from finished. But Charlie didn't have to know that. At least not yet.

Chapter Twelve

Laurette called me a few times over the next couple of days, imploring me to reconsider the sudden flood of offers that had poured into her office. But I refused. I was much too busy tracking the movements of Eli to take the time to humiliate myself in an exclusive interview on *Access Hollywood* in front of a national television audience.

Eli wasn't going out much, except for a pack of cigarettes and a six-pack of Budweiser once a day around noon.

I sat in my car, parked just down the street from the Laurel Canyon house, and watched as several nervous looking men of various ages, shapes, and sizes arrived throughout the day for Eli's "special" massage session. They were spaced out enough so there was no chance of any of them running into each other. I spent hour after hour in the car, playing every Madonna CD ever made, calling any friend I could think of to "catch up" on my Motorola Elite cell phone, counting the number of trees that lined the street.

If only I knew how to wire tap. I could actually know what was going on inside the guesthouse instead of who comes and goes. But I had no Impossible Missions Force at my disposal, so I had to make due.

A short, stout man with a piggish face hurried out the driveway. His cheeks were flushed and his eyes darted back and forth to make sure he wasn't seen leaving. He was probably married and this was the only way he knew how to deal with the yearnings and desires he had undoubtedly suppressed since childhood. I saw him go inside about an hour earlier, and despite the quality time he had spent with Eli, he looked just as tense and scared as he did when he arrived. It was as if he expected to run into his minister or a Rotary Club buddy on this quiet, remote street.

Ten minutes later, I finally got some real action. The garage door opened, and I could see Eli, dressed in a pair of jeans, leather cowboy boots, and a see-through netted shirt, don a black motorcycle helmet and climb onto a Harley Davidson. After a few kick starts, the bike roared to life and Eli sped off down the road. I was so excited that something was actually happening after days of interminable boredom that I barely managed to start the car and squeal off in hot pursuit before he disappeared around a bend.

I kept a safe distance from Eli as we rolled with traffic down Laurel Canyon, passing Sunset Boulevard and the massive Virgin Megastore Complex, where the street turned into Crescent Heights Boulevard and carried us south towards the Beverly Center, a giant indoor mall constructed in the eighties, packed with shops, theatres, and restaurants. Eli weaved in and out of traffic, ignoring the cars that had to stop short to avoid sideswiping him.

I detested motorcycles in heavy traffic because they assumed they had the right of way, the right of everything. They were too impatient to obey simple traffic laws, and I had to fight off that ever-growing L.A. commuter condition the media referred to as "road rage." Sometimes I wanted to just ram into the tail of one, and give him a good scare. But that was just me.

The light turned yellow, and Eli shot forward, zipping through the intersection, as it turned red. I got stuck behind an elderly woman in a Honda Civic, who didn't dare drive over five miles per hour. Just ahead, Eli roared up the ramp into the five story Beverly

Center parking structure. Maybe he was just going shopping, but I had to be sure.

When the light finally turned green and mercifully the elderly woman in front of me turned onto a side street, I sped up and made a fast turn onto the ramp and up into the mall.

I stopped at the gate, rolled down the window, and heard a cheery mechanical voice say, "Please take the ticket." I would love to know whom exactly they recruit to be these irritating authority voices.

I yanked the ticket out of the slot and raced up to find an available space. After parking and taking the escalator up several more levels to reach the long line of department stores and specialty shops, I knew I had to be careful not to be seen. Eli would know immediately that I was following him, and any chance of finding out anything useful would go up in smoke.

I had no idea where Eli had parked his motorcycle or which store he was in, but I kept walking, scanning the sparse midday crowd. He could have been anywhere. If he had disappeared into Bloomingdale's or Macy's, it would be impossible to find him.

I was hoping to spot him in one of the smaller stores, like Structure or Eddie Bauer. But I had no such luck.

Satisfied he wasn't anywhere on the first level, I took the escalator up until I reached the top level that housed a food court, movie theatres, and a Brentano's bookstore, among other shops. The food court was nearly empty, and I figured Eli didn't read much, so I chose not to scout out the bookstore just yet.

And then I saw him. He was standing in line to buy a movie ticket, his left arm hooked around his motorcycle helmet, holding it against his waist.

I rushed over to the line, and stood just a few people behind him. At one point he turned his head, and I was afraid he might see me, so I looked away, pretending I recognized someone. I strained to hear what movie he was going inside to see. It was an action movie starring rap star Ja Rule. Whatever tickles your fancy. He bypassed the concession counter (something I could never do) and disappeared down the hall of doors that led into the various features.

After buying a ticket for the same movie, I stopped to buy a large tub of popcorn and some candy. Real investigators wouldn't think to do this. Their focus is on the person they're staking out, but detective or not, I can't go into a movie without a medium popcorn and a super size box of Junior Mints.

I walked down to the purple door where I saw Eli enter, and waited until the previews started and the lights faded to blackness before daring to sneak inside.

There were only three other people in the theatre besides Eli and myself. The screen was the size of a postage stamp. The Sony flat screen HDTV Charlie and I had in our den was bigger than this one. The theatre owners at this complex seemed more concerned with quantity rather than quality, and it may have explained the low turn out, even for the middle of a weekday. I slipped in a back row seat and watched Eli who sat off to the side about three rows down in an aisle seat. He kept glancing back. Afraid he would see me, I ducked my face behind the tub of popcorn. He was waiting for someone.

As the previews ended, the THX digital sound advertisement blasted through the tiny theatre, and the movie finally started to unspool on the screen in front of us.

Eli slouched down in his seat, folded his arms, and stopped looking back. I kept my eyes on him, but at this point he actually seemed interested in the movie. There was a violent drug bust in the opening scene, lots of cops screaming, "Freeze, motherfucker!" And Ja Rule himself, making a spectacular entrance on a crane, with an Uzi cradled in his arm, mowing down the bad guys in a spray of bullets.

During the mayhem, light streamed into the theatre as the door in the back opened. A man entered, walked directly down the aisle to where Eli was sitting and slid in the aisle seat in the row directly behind him. The man whispered something in Eli's ear, and then I saw him slip a white envelope through the crack between two seats. Eli nonchalantly took the envelope and stuffed it into his jeans pocket.

I kept hoping the glow from the screen might illuminate the mystery man's face, but the scene in the film was at night so it was too dark to see much of anything.

After a minute, the man behind Eli got up, and walked back up the aisle of the theatre. At that second, the scene on screen cut to a bright gloriously sunny day, and the light from the screen lit up the man walking past me. It was Spiro, the chiseled Greek God boy toy of Willard Hornsby's mother, Tamara!

Spiro disappeared out the door. Eli kept watching the movie. He wasn't going anywhere. I dropped my tub of popcorn and raced outside the theater to see Spiro heading for the escalator.

I followed him down to the second level of stores, where he checked his watch, and then sat down on a bench. Concerned that I was out in the open for him to see, I darted into an H2O, home to a myriad of face creams, shampoos, and various other skin products. I was watching to make sure he hadn't spotted me when a familiar voice startled me from behind.

"Jarrod?"

I knew who it was. But I turned around anyway and feigned complete surprise.

"Tamara, imagine running into you here."

Where else would she be but a store that specialized in skin products designed to preserve everlasting youth? This woman was fighting age every step of the way. I grabbed an armful of bath gels and body oils off the shelves as if I had actually come in here to shop.

"It's good to see you." She hugged me, as if our altercation at the funeral had never happened. I was startled, half-expecting her to plunge a knife in my back while her arms were around me.

"So how are you doing?" I said.

"I miss him terribly." She let go, her eyes downcast.

There was a twinge of sincerity in her voice. This wasn't the Tamara I knew at all. This was almost, dare I say, a grieving mother. I had such a strong, disapproving opinion of Willard's mother that it was disconcerting to see her now so vulnerable, so anguished. What had happened since the last time I saw her?

She looked back up at me, her eyes brimming with tears. "I know you have certain ideas about me, and frankly, some of them are true, but I did love my son. I thought you should know that."

Either she was a better actress than I thought or she was speaking from the heart. I had always assumed she didn't have one.

"I've been meaning to call you," she said, wiping the tears away from her face with a handkerchief. "At the funeral, you asked me if Willard was in therapy, and I said I didn't know."

I nodded, remembering.

"Well," she said, "He was. The therapist called me when he read about Willard's death in the papers. He was very saddened by the whole thing."

"Do you remember his name?"

"Vito Wilde. He has an office on Manchester and Sepulveda, near the airport. Call him yourself. He'll tell you about Willard's state of mind." She took my hand, and squeezed it. "He told me Willard was deeply depressed, and was dealing with a lot of issues. So you see, Jarrod, I was right."

Just because Willard was seeing a therapist didn't necessarily prove he was unhappy enough to drink himself to death. I also could have pointed out that the root of all those issues he was dealing with was probably standing right in front of me. But accusing Tamara of being a terrible mother wouldn't have done either of us any good. So for the moment, I told her what she wanted to hear. "Yes, I guess you were right after all."

"Dr. Wilde didn't get into any specifics, but he did say there was something eating away at Willard. My guess is he got mixed up with another pill popping lowlife who took advantage . . ."

A beefy hand encircled Tamara's arm, physically pulling her away from me. It was Spiro. He had spotted the two of us chatting from the bench outside the store, and decided it was time to intervene.

He spoke firmly into her ear. "Time to go, honey. We're going to be late."

She nodded, and then gave me an apologetic look.

"It was nice seeing you, Jarrod."

"Same here," I replied as I watched Spiro spirit his wife away. As they retreated towards the elevator that would carry them down to the parking structure, I caught a glimpse of Eli, the white envelope sticking out of his pocket, ambling past H2O. I couldn't resist shaking him up a bit.

"Hey, Eli!"

He looked up, confused, and searched the mall until his eyes settled on where I was standing. I held up a couple of small bottles. "They have a lot of aromatherapy oils in here that some of your massage clients might enjoy."

He stared at me in shock. What the hell was I doing there? He didn't answer. He just fingered the envelope in his back pocket, quickly looked away, and stalked off in the other direction, as far away from me as possible.

Chapter Thirteen

It took me a few days, but I managed to get an appointment with Dr. Vito Wilde. I told him I was having trouble getting over the death of a close friend, and needed to talk to someone. Luckily, I had made the minimum amount of money during the year from a few small acting gigs to keep my health plan with the Screen Actors Guild in good standing. They agreed to cover eighty percent of the cost. The rest I pilfered from the house repairs fund Charlie and I kept at Bank of America.

Despite the sizable nest egg I earned as a child star, I was hopeless with money. So it was with great relief that I handed over the financial reigns to my better half. He handled everything. I never had to worry about bills, which allowed me more time in the day to go to auditions and, of course, solve crimes. The downside I soon discovered was that Charlie kept a meticulous ledger of all our expenditures down to the last penny. Once my wallet was empty for the week, I had to find new and creative ways to come up with cash. A small withdrawal from a minor account like house repairs was probably my best bet. It wouldn't even be a blip on Charlie's radar.

In the heavy morning traffic it took me a solid hour to get to Wilde's office. It was a hot, steaming day and my nerves were frazzled. I still had no idea how I was going to go wheedle information about Willard out of the good doctor. Therapists are notorious for their discretion and personal code of ethics. Dr. Wilde and his kind could never fit into my loose lipped group of friends.

I pulled the Beamer into a vast parking lot that was home to a large strip mall with stores ranging from Staples Office Supplies to a Vons supermarket, both of which dwarfed a small brick building with a small, weathered, chipped sign that read, "Los Angeles Counseling Services". I also made note of a Del Taco just south of the lot, since I had discovered that investigating works up an enormous appetite.

I rode the elevator to the second floor, and entered through a door that led to a small waiting room. On the wall was a row of switchers with instructions to flip the one next to your doctor's name to alert him that you had arrived.

I then sat down and started browsing through a *People* magazine article about a woman using DNA evidence to prove her husband's infidelities. It warmed my heart to learn there were other people in the world just as obsessive as I am.

The door to the inner office finally opened, and Dr. Vito Wilde stepped out to greet me. He was younger than I had expected, probably around thirty-five, and tall, massively tall, over six and a half feet. He was barrel chested, with a round face, mostly covered by a neatly trimmed beard and wire-rimmed glasses. His shirt-sleeves were rolled up revealing thick, hairy forearms. He held out his hand and I shook it.

In the gay subculture, Dr. Wilde would be what we call a bear—big hairy men who enjoy the company of other big hairy men. Ask any bear you come across, and he'll tell you, it's not just a look, it's an attitude, a way of life. And with the growing acceptance of alternative lifestyles, their numbers are growing. They converge at festivals and convention weekends all over the world. I wasn't sure if Vito had any connection to a Bear organization, or if he was even gay, but the minute he opened his mouth, my suspicions were confirmed.

"Hello, Jarrod, please come in."

For such a hearty man, his soft, gentle, effeminate voice was a dead giveaway. If I closed my eyes, I would swear I was talking to Laura Bush. As he led me back to his private office, he turned and said, "It's been pretty hectic around here today. I'm trying to catch up. I just got back from San Francisco."

"There on business?"

"No. I went up for the Folsom Street Fair."

Bingo. Folsom Street Fair was a famous gay-sponsored weekend long festival for leather lovers. Bears were drawn to it like a camp-ground barbecue. So far I was batting a thousand. But unfortunately I wasn't there to do a profile on Dr. Wilde. I was there to trick him into talking about Willard.

He led me into a comfortable room with an overstuffed couch and lots of fluffy pillows for maximum comfort. I sat down, sinking into the cushions, and grabbing one of the pillows to clutch in front of me. I wasn't playing the role of a nervous first-timer. I actually *was* a nervous first-timer.

Dr. Wilde sat across from me in an antique chair, and scribbled a few notes on his notepad. All the colors in the room—on the walls, in the paintings, even the bookbinders on his shelf—were all soft, muted and calming. On the wall was a framed diploma. He was a Doctor in Metaphysics. Okay, that didn't mean much to me. But at least it sounded impressive.

Finally, he stopped writing and stared at me.

"So how are you?"

That was all I needed to hear. I had spent the entire drive over trying to come up with what I would say. I needed to pretend I was there to talk about myself, which has never been a challenge for me. Again, my life as an actor was a marked advantage.

For the next forty minutes, I rambled on about my years as a child star, my life with Charlie, our recent fight. I had to censor myself along the way. I couldn't come out and say our fight was over my need to investigate the death of a man with whom I was once involved. And, oh, and by the way, he was one of your patients. So I was selective with the details.

Every time Dr. Wilde tried to interject a point, I talked right over him. I wasn't interested in what he had to say about me, I was focused on getting to Willard. With ten minutes left in the session, I finally worked up the nerve to steer the conversation in that direction.

"And to make matters worse, a dear friend of mine died unexpectedly a couple of weeks ago, and I've had a tough time dealing with it."

"How did your friend die?"

"He was murdered."

Dr. Wilde dropped his pen. Without missing a beat, he reached down, picked it up, and tried acting as nonchalant as possible. He jotted a few words on his notepad, and then looked up at me.

I never blinked, never took my eyes off him.

"Do you know who did it?"

"Not yet."

"What do the police say?"

"They think it was an accident."

"But you don't?"

I shook my head.

Dr. Wilde cleared his throat and leaned forward, resting his elbows on his knees. He was definitely intrigued. I decided it was time to put all my cards on the table, and gauge his reaction.

I told him the story of Eli the tattooed hustler, how he had lied to me, and how he had tried to drown me in the lap pool at his sugar daddy's estate. I spoke of how my friend's mother was convinced her son was unhappy and had given up on his life, and how her young user husband had warned me to stop poking my nose where it didn't belong. I also recounted how I had spotted the hustler and the mother's husband conducting a mysterious business transaction in a darkened movie theatre at the Beverly Center.

At this point, Dr. Wilde was sitting on the edge of his seat. He was undoubtedly a huge *Dynasty* fan in the eighties, because he was enthralled by my gripping, melodramatic storyline. If life was a television show, then the last few weeks of mine could have been a few heavily-promoted sweeps episodes.

I sat back, hugged the pillow tighter, and worked up a few tears.

I threw my hands over my face for effect and sobbed, "This is so embarrassing. I can't believe I'm crying. It's only my first session!"

"It's quite all right. That's what you're here for. Just let it all out."

"I don't know what to do, Doctor. They say he was drunk and he just tripped and fell into the pool and that's how he drowned. But I don't believe it. I know there was more to it."

I opened my fingers just enough to see Dr. Wilde's face. His mind was racing. The details suddenly seemed familiar. I had to strike now.

"Someone's hiding something. Someone doesn't want me to get to the truth. My own boyfriend thinks I'm nuts. But I need to know what really happened. Willard deserves that much."

"Willard?"

"Yes. My friend. Willard Ray Hornsby."

Dr. Wilde sat back in his chair. "How did you get my name?"

"Willard used to talk about how much you helped him work through his issues. Of course that was before he . . ." I let my voice trail off. The tears kept streaming down my cheeks. But I wasn't acting. Talking about Willard was heightening my emotions.

Dr. Wilde gave me a concerned look. "If you're here to discuss the problem Willard was having, I'm afraid I can't do that."

So there was one specific problem. That was a start. I just had to manipulate the discussion a little more to my advantage.

"Oh, don't worry. I already know all about that. Willard confided everything to me."

"I see," his eyes betraying a hint of suspicion.

He wasn't going to give me any more than that. My biggest beef with therapists was how they made you do all the talking.

I had to keep fishing. "I felt so bad he was going through that whole mess. Sometimes he was so consumed by it and I felt so help-less because there was nothing I could do to fix it."

"You can't blame yourself. It was Willard's responsibility to re-move himself from such a toxic situation."

I was getting close. I knew I was getting close. If he didn't shut me down in the next few minutes and claim conflict of interest, I was confident I could at least get a few of the sordid details. I took a risk, hoping for a pay off.

"I thought about talking to his mother at one point. I was hoping she might know what to do. I don't know why I didn't."

"Well, it probably wouldn't have done much good. Willard was es-tranged from her at that point. And given the fact that her husband was the problem, I'm not sure how sympathetic she would have been."

It was Spiro! Willard had a problem with Spiro. But what kind of problem? It was the hardest acting job of my life to maintain my composure, to pretend I already knew everything Dr. Wilde was telling me. My mind was flooding with questions I wanted to fire at him about Willard and Spiro and Tamara, but I had to play it cool or he'd kick me out on my ass.

"So you think there wasn't anything I could do?"

"No. You can't blame yourself for not solving Willard's troubles, particularly something as traumatic as what he was dealing with. Have you struggled with these feelings of helplessness before?"

Who cared about me? I wasn't there to talk about me. I wanted to know everything he knew about Willard's conflict with Spiro. "Yes. Many times. Most of my life I've felt helpless. From the mo-ment my mother pushed me into acting when I was four. I felt I had no choice. I was told what to say, how to act, who I should be."

We were moving away from Willard now, and honing in on me. Normally I would relish the attention, but not today, not when there was so much at stake.

"Willard felt the same way, you know," I said. "He felt helpless most of his life too, especially toward the end. Specifically over what was happening with Spiro."

Dr. Wilde opened his mouth to respond, but his eyes glanced at the clock and he closed his notepad.

"I'm afraid we're out of time."

He looked almost relieved as we both stood up. I could tell my session had rattled him. I had blindsided him with my relationship to Willard, and he struggled not to cross any ethical lines. But in the end, I got what I needed. Willard was grappling with a crisis, and Spiro was at the center of it.

With each step, I was getting closer.

I handed Dr. Wilde a check and shook his hand. Before I slipped out the door, he gently stopped me by the arm with his hand and said in his soft, soothing, feminine voice, "Would you like to make another appointment?"

"Oh. Sure. I'll call you tomorrow to set one up."

He knew I was lying. Therapists always knew.

He nodded, and said, "I strongly suspect you were bluffing today about knowing what Willard was going through, and I may have crossed some lines with what I told you."

And here I thought I had been so sly tricking him.

He patted me on the back as he steered me towards the exit. "But since Willard is no longer with us, I'm hoping it won't come back to haunt me."

"I won't say a word, believe me."

"And if what I told you makes life harder for that son-of-a-bitch stepfather of his, then I won't feel as bad for violating any confidentiality rules."

"Thank you, Dr. Wilde."

He ushered me out, and went to meet his next patient. And I was left to wonder if there was anyone in Willard's life who didn't despise Spiro with a furious passion.

Chapter Fourteen

The sick cartoon image of a man lying prone in a coffin as the words "Happy Birthday . . . I hope it's your last" danced in a line above him filled the computer screen in front of me. I had copied the animated greeting from Willard's desktop and was now at my psychic Isis's apartment.

Besides being a dead-on clairvoyant, Isis was also a computer whiz, an expert hacker who could artfully break into any site or program with little effort. I was hoping Isis might be the key to uncovering the identity of the person who sent Willard this morbid, chilling sentiment.

The deal I struck with Isis was beneficial to both of us. If she gave me a name, I would whisk her over the hill to Glendale for her weekly shopping excursion to Price Club since she detested driving her rickety old 1983 Toyota Corolla on the L.A. freeways. This Price Club fixation was lost on me. Her apartment was jammed with super sized paper towels, mammoth cans of Raid, and gargantuan bottles of 409 cleaning fluid. One might think Isis was shopping for a military base, but in fact, she lived alone. She just couldn't pass up a good deal. I turned my attention back to Isis, who was wearing thick-rimmed glasses and making fast progress.

She had already managed to break into the greeting card site's secure server, and was now close to downloading the customer directory. Amazing. I was barely able to check my e-mail without a complete system crash.

As I hovered over her shoulder, she scanned down the list of names and addresses. I was certain we would see Spiro's name pop up any second. People often challenge me about Isis's psychic abilities. If she's so good, why can't she just pull the name out of the air? Why go to all the trouble of illegally obtaining confidential information off a Website? Well, most psychics, though gifted, are not miracle workers. They can only relate what the spirit guides tell them. So in this case, I was damn lucky my psychic was an expert hacker who was not above breaking the law in exchange for a chauffeured trip to her favorite discount store.

"Gladys Phelan," Isis said, as she swiveled around in her office chair and flashed me a self-satisfied smile.

"Who?"

"That's who sent the greeting to your friend Willard."

"Never heard of her."

I leaned over Isis's shoulder, and stared at the name. Gladys Phelan was not the name expected. I was disappointed it wasn't Spiro.

Isis continued punching keys, hoping to turn up more information. She was all worked up, typing furiously. She loved a challenge. She suddenly stopped, the glow from the screen giving her bifocals a bluish hue.

"Her credit card information has been automatically stored. She lives in Los Feliz. Got the address right here if you have a pen." I grabbed a ballpoint and started writing. Whoever Gladys was, she probably thought a secure server meant no one would ever trace the card back to her. She was undoubtedly a relative newcomer to the cyber world.

*   *   *

Los Feliz, with its trendy restaurants, alternative bookstores and kitschy nightclubs that were a throwback to another era, was fast becoming an artsy section of Los Angeles. A lot of hipster musicians and rising young actors populated the area, driving out the old guard. There was a melting pot feel to the small city pocket, especially since many young artists mingled with the multi-cultural families that lived on the side streets behind the bustling, tragically hip Vermont Avenue. There were also a sizable number of elderly residents who staked claim to the neighborhood decades earlier and were too stubborn to move out and make room for the youth brigade.

After I dropped Isis off at Price Club in Glendale, just a few minutes east of Los Feliz, I double-checked the address I had jotted down from the computer screen, and turned left onto Russell, a small street sandwiched between the much larger, busier, and built up Vermont and Hillhurst Avenues. There were rows of one-story houses on Russell, most with chipping paint and rusty security bars over the windows.

I parked the car in front of an unassuming beige structure that had a giant blue tarp over the leaky roof, probably to protect it from the heavy rains, probably last winter. No one had bothered to take it down. Maybe they figured the splash of color gave the house more of a personality.

I walked up the small, muddy yard with overgrown dull grass and rang the bell. I waited a minute, and then rang it again. I could hear someone stirring inside, but it took another full minute for the door to creak open.

"Gladys Phelan?"

A diminutive woman in her early seventies, white hair tied up in a bun and granny glasses resting on the tip of her nose, raised her hunched back as high as she could to get a good look at me.

"Yes?"

"My name is Jarrod Jarvis. I was wondering if I could have a moment of your time."

I didn't expect her to be accommodating. After all, we lived in a city with all sorts of kooks and criminals, but Gladys apparently didn't care anymore. She had seen it all, and was able to judge someone's character with a cursory glance.

"Come on in. Judge Judy's just wrapping up."

I followed her through the unkempt house with its stained wallpaper and scuffed furniture. She led me into the living room where I heard the final pounding notes of *The Judge Judy Show* theme blaring out of her twenty-three inch Sony color television set. It was the only new item in the whole house and all the chairs and tables were angled to make it the centerpiece of the room. Gladys was, from my estimation, an avid TV watcher.

"Can I get you something to drink?" she said.

"No, thank you, Mrs. Phelan. I was hoping you could answer a few questions for me."

Gladys, with one eye on the TV set, scooped up her remote and switched channels. "*Maury* is a rerun. So it's between *Jerry Springer* and *Montel Williams*. Frankly, both boys tend to get on my nerves. God, I miss Phil Donahue, don't you?"

I decided to humor her. "Oh, yes. Phil was a pioneer."

"I can take or leave Oprah," she said. "One day she's fat, one day she's thin. Make up your mind, I say. I used to think there was something wrong with my television set. Do you mind if I eat my crackers?"

Before I could answer, Gladys plopped down on her couch, and began to pick over a small plate of Ritz crackers on a TV tray. She carefully chose one, dipped it into a small jar of Jiffy peanut butter, and then swallowed it whole. There was a small glob of peanut butter left on the corner of her mouth, but I decided to keep quiet.

"Mrs. Phelan, are you aware of a Website called Greetings for You dot com?"

"Web for you dot what?"

"It's a website. On the Internet. You do have a computer, don't you?"

"In the back room. It was my husband's. I never get near it. Don't have any use for it."

Her eyes wandered back over to the TV set. She was caught up in a small screen real life family drama on *The Jerry Springer Show*. I was amazed he was still on the air. I tried to bring her back.

"Do you happen to know a Willard Ray Hornsby?"

"Don't think so." Her eyes never left the TV.

"He was the recipient of an on-line greeting card. It came from your computer account about a week and a half ago."

She shook her head, her eyes still glued to Jerry. "Wasn't me."

"What about your husband? Could he have sent it?"

"Harry died last February. I don't think that thing's been turned on once since he's been gone."

"Well, someone used it. Your credit card was charged and the e-mail address matches your AOL account."

This finally got her attention. She looked at me, a bit confused. She kept shaking her head. "Wasn't me. I wouldn't know the first thing about how to send something over the computer."

"Does anyone else have access to your husband's computer?"

"Couldn't imagine who. I live alone."

I believed her. Maybe someone broke in while she was napping, accessed her AOL account, used her credit card, and sent Willard the greeting. But that made no sense. At this point, Gladys was down to her last cracker, and a commercial break from Jerry prompted her to pad down to the kitchen to refurbish her plate.

I pulled a card from my wallet and placed it down on the beat up coffee table. "If you think of anybody, could you give me a call?"

"Uh huh." Gladys's mind was on what show she was going to watch after *Jerry Springer*, not my little unimportant mystery. I left the house, got back in my car, and drove towards the Price Club to retrieve Isis.

After dropping Isis and a trunk full of purchases off at her apartment in West Hollywood, I got trapped in rush hour traffic that kept me at a crawl towards Beachwood Canyon for a full forty-five minutes. By the time I wound my way up into the hills, the sun had set and darkness enveloped the Hollywood sign.

I pulled into the garage, got out and stopped as I clicked the car locks down with my remote. There was a quick high-pitched beep. Something was different tonight. I didn't hear the familiar jangling of Snickers's collar. This was strange. Our devoted dog never once failed to race into the kitchen and wait by the door to greet Charlie or me whenever she heard the rumble of the garage door opening. It didn't bother me at first. I figured she had probably just scurried out to the backyard through the doggy door to take care of her business and hadn't heard me arrive home.

As I entered through the kitchen, I flipped on the wall switch next to the refrigerator. No lights came on. I attributed this to the rolling black out scares the whole state had been experiencing over the last few months, and assumed it was our turn. But a quick glance out the window disproved this theory. The neighbors' lights were working.

I called for Snickers, but she still didn't come. There was suddenly a gnawing feeling in the pit of my stomach.

When one senses impending danger, there's always some kind of sign, some sort of internal alarm that goes off. I chose to ignore it, and pressed on.

I opened a kitchen drawer and fumbled around in the dark for a flashlight. Once I found it, I turned it on, but nothing happened. I had forgotten to buy new batteries. Damn. Typical. I only remembered such things when I needed them. I stood there in pitch-blackness, trying to figure out what to do next. That's when I heard the scratching. It was faint at first, but persistent.

I followed the sound downstairs to the bedrooms, grabbing the handrail as I descended the steps. Since our house was inverted and propped up against a hill, it became darker the further you went down. And far more ominous.

I felt my way into the master bedroom where the scratching was growing louder and more desperate now. It was coming from inside the closet. I gripped the handle of the door, and pulled it, but some-one had locked it.

Inside, I heard a frantic whimpering. It was Snickers. Who would lock her in there? Charlie had been out all day and the housekeeper only cleaned on Mondays. It took only a few seconds before I finally began to comprehend what was happening. The gnawing in my stomach went wild, jumping into my throat as I sensed a presence directly behind me, and felt an intruder's hot steady breath on the back of my neck.

Chapter Fifteen

I stood there, frozen in place, panic rising. I pretended for a moment not to notice the figure behind me, trying to buy a few precious seconds before the intruder either shot me or stabbed me in the back. I kept trying to pull open the closet door, my mind racing. The minute I turned around to face him, my fate was up for grabs.

I let go of the door handle, sucked in a sharp intake of breath, and decided I couldn't stall any longer if I wanted a fighting chance to survive. I whipped around like a blindfolded kid playing Marco Polo.

No one was there.

My eyes adjusted to the darkness and scanned the room for signs of movement. But it was still. The only sound I heard was Snickers' scratching and whimpering from inside the closet.

Loud ringing from the phone interrupted the quiet. My heart skipped a beat. My nerves were shattered. Had I imagined the presence behind me, the breath on my neck? Had this ordeal done such a number on my nerves that I was now susceptible to violent home invasion fantasies?

The phone kept ringing. I walked over to the nightstand next to our bed and scooped it up.

"Hello?"

"It's me. I'm in Echo Park. Some guy's holed up in his apartment with a stockpile of weapons and his landlord as a hostage. Seems a receptionist at his office hasn't responded to his love letters, so he's decided to get her attention this way."

I was so relieved to hear Charlie's voice. "When are you coming home?"

"We've been here four hours already. SWAT team is on standby. Guy's getting antsy. I'm hoping something happens soon, but it may be a while."

"Just come home as soon as you can, okay?"

"Is everything all right? You sound kind of weird."

"I think someone's been here. I found Snickers locked in the closet and the lights aren't working."

Charlie's cell phone kept cutting out. I couldn't hear what he was saying and he couldn't hear me. "Snickers was . . . where?"

"Forget it. I'm going over to Laurette's. I don't feel safe . . ."

A hand clamped tightly over my mouth, cutting off my words, and I felt the pointed tip of a knife press firmly in my back. I dropped the phone and could only hear Charlie's faint voice cutting in and out. "Jarrod . . . are you . . . can you hear . . . Jarrod . . . ?"

And then, an insidious, hard voice that sent shivers down my whole body hissed in my ear, "Leave it alone."

He pressed the knife harder, breaking the skin, and I felt blood trickle down the back of my spine. He kept his hand in place, yanking my head back, almost snapping my neck as he spoke again, "You hear me? I said leave it alone."

Those were the same words Spiro warned me with after Willard's funeral. Was this Spiro? They were also the same words Eli scribbled on that note he left on my windshield? Could this be Eli?

My head was spinning, the pain in my back throbbing and relentless. The intruder's strong hand pressed firmly over my nose and mouth cut off my oxygen. I couldn't breathe. I had to act fast.

When I was fourteen, I guest starred on an episode of *Simon and Simon* where I played a math whiz who was coerced by his evil uncle into participating in a series of bank frauds. When the Simon brothers uncovered the plot, my uncle held a gun to my head in order to secure his escape, but I was able to wrest free using a self-defense maneuver the stunt coordinator taught me. I had forgotten all about it until now.

Pulling myself forward, I jabbed my elbow back, slamming it full force into the intruder's stomach. A whoosh of air escaped his mouth as he doubled over and let go. I felt a razor sharp pain in my lower lip. He was wearing some kind of ring and as I wrenched myself free of the assailant, it got caught and tore away flesh. I tasted blood.

Rushing as far as I could away from him, and, more importantly, the tip of his knife, I whirled around to get my first good look at him. He was wearing a black ski mask, a zipped up black vest with no shirt on underneath and blue jeans. His eyes, wild with rage, penetrated me like a wounded tiger in the jungle. He stopped to catch his breath, his knife thrust out to keep me at bay.

I didn't wait for him to recover. I raced upstairs, heading straight for the front door. Snickers barked wildly, but I knew she was safe. The intruder wanted me, not my dog. As I scrambled up to the top floor landing, I could see out the kitchen window. The married couple next door in matching purple and white sweat suits was out for an evening stroll in the hills, and just passing by my house. As I opened my mouth to yell for them, the intruder slammed into me. We crashed to the floor with a sickening thud.

I was on my back. He wrapped his arms around my legs like a steel bar. I kicked and struggled, desperate to wriggle free from his grasp, but he was strong and pumped up on adrenaline. I saw the handle of the knife sticking out of his back pocket and stretched my arm to reach it. My fingers were only an inch from it. I tried lifting my head, extending my body just enough to get my fingers around it. The attacker was able to crawl up my legs, push me down on my back and straddle my waist.

There was relief in his eyes. He was in control again. But when he reached for the knife in his back pocket, the relief gave way to concern. The knife wasn't there. It was clutched in my hand, and in a frantic act to save myself, I plunged it forward, prepared to drive it straight into his chest. I had never killed anyone before, but I was so full of fear and self-preservation, I was prepared to take a life tonight.

But it wasn't meant to be.

His left hand caught my arm just as it propelled forward, and with all his might, he slammed it down, smashing it against the floor. A pain ripped through my arm as my fingers instinctively splayed open, and the knife clattered across the kitchen floor.

I was still on my back, trapped between his powerful knees that held me there, and looked up at him one last time. He didn't speak. He didn't have to. His eyes said it all. They were narrowed and angry, full of bile and contempt. He raised his fist and I finally saw what had cut deep into my lip. It was a gold ring with a small green emerald in its center. I wasn't sure if it was a class ring, an engagement ring, or some fraternity ring. I just saw it jetting forward, decorating a fist that was about to slam into my face.

My only thought, as an actor, was "Oh God! Not the face!" I turned away but the blow caught me on the right cheek. The pain was excruciating. I glanced up to see him raising his fist to strike again.

Suddenly sirens blared up the street, rising in volume as they got closer and closer to the house. Charlie. He must have called a patrol unit to check out the house after we got cut off. The noise distracted the intruder long enough for me to slam my hands against his chest and push him off me. I slid out from underneath him, crawled to me knees and grabbed the flashlight I had left on the kitchen counter when I first got home.

The intruder was searching the floor for his knife when I brought the flashlight down, cracking it hard against the back of his head. He dropped to the floor with a thump. A patrol car screeched to a stop just outside the front door.

I stumbled through the dark, and managed to get the door open. There I found myself face to face with a pair of young, handsome officers in their mid-twenties, with buzz cuts and hardened jaws. L.A. cops always look like kick ass marines.

"He's in the kitchen," I said, spitting out blood.

One grabbed his gun from his belt, flipped on his flashlight, and stealthily made his way into the kitchen. The other pulled a handkerchief from his back pocket and handed it to me. I dabbed the blood that was streaming from my lip and mouth.

We heard the first officer call out from the kitchen. "There's no one here."

"He must have gone back downstairs," I said as I coughed and sputtered, trying to catch my breath.

We searched the whole house together. In the few moments it took for me to let the officers in, my assailant must have escaped to the garden off the bottom level of the house and retreated out the broken backyard fence where he probably came from in the first place. He also found his knife, so there was nothing left behind for the police to examine. Once again, I was left to explain some rather bizarre, questionable circumstances. A smashed window leading into the laundry room at least gave the officers some evidence to support a break-in.

I wasn't going to sit by and let the mysterious attacker's trail get cold.

I snatched up the phone and dialed Willard's mother Tamara. It took four rings, but she finally picked up. I could tell her scratchy, annoyed voice wanted to know who the hell was calling her at this late hour as she answered. "Yes. Who is it?"

"Tamara, it's Jarrod Jarvis."

There was a pause. "What is it, Jarrod? Is something wrong?"

"I want to know if Spiro is there with you."

"Yes."

"Is he there at this very moment?"

"Yes. We're having a quiet night at home. We're . . . um . . . watching TV." She didn't relish in telling me what they were really doing.

"I'd like you to put him on the line."

Tamara hesitated, not sure what I was up to, but she decided to indulge me. So she told me to hang on while she got Spiro. After a few moments, Spiro's gruff voice came on the line.

"What?"

"Been there all night, Spiro?"

"Yeah. What of it?"

"Someone just attacked me in my home, and I wanted to make sure it wasn't you."

"Sorry. Can't help you. But if it makes you feel any better, I sure as hell wish it *had* been me."

He slammed down the phone in my ear. What a lovely guy. I thought about the various possibilities. The intruder could have been someone Spiro hired. There was still Eli the tattooed hustler. Perhaps what I witnessed in the movie theatre at the Beverly Center was Spiro paying Eli to frighten me into giving up this crusade.

I found the key to the bedroom closet door and freed Snickers, who was more traumatized by the evening's events than I was. She followed me from room to room, sticking as close to my heels as possible without tripping me up while I checked one more time to make sure the intruder was truly gone from the premises.

A two-bit hustler shoving my head under water was cause for concern, but a knife-wielding madman invading my home was far more troubling. If Spiro was behind this, and the attack was designed to scare me off, then his plan was working. A part of me wanted to drop the whole matter right now, and just move on with my life.

The cops were kind enough to go outside, find the fuse box, and restore electricity. They offered to stay with me until Charlie arrived home, but I thanked them and sent them on their way. I didn't honestly believe the goon would come back. He had already made his point.

When I turned on the television and curled up on the couch with Snickers, waiting to hear the garage door squeal open signaling Charlie's arrival home, I happened to stumble across an old rerun of *Highway to Heaven* starring the late, beloved Michael Landon. It happened to be an episode where Michael and his bearded sidekick, Victor French, were helping a runaway deal with his drug-addicted mother and abusive stepfather in Madison, Wisconsin. A fifteen-year-old Willard Ray Hornsby played the boy. We both worked a lot in those days. Willard was so good in the episode, probably because it mirrored his real life.

I am and always have been a true-blooded Californian. And as a true-blooded Californian, it's required that I believe in any new age pursuits, psychic phenomena and universal signs. I was close to giving up this unending, frustrating search. It had been an exhausting quest, each turn in the road leading to another dead end. And more questions just kept piling up, making the puzzle that much harder to solve. But as I contemplated dropping the whole matter once again, the first face I saw was Willard Ray Hornsby himself. Playing a troubled boy in a long forgotten TV show. It was a sign. A sign I should continue. And I would. I would continue to push and prod and perhaps put myself in further danger. Willard's youthful face on my television set was sending me a message. And I wasn't about to let him down.

Chapter Sixteen

When the officers left, they must have radioed Charlie, because within ten minutes he was home, and holding me in his arms. He came close to losing me tonight and it had shaken him up pretty bad.

I, of course, was thrilled to see his angst-ridden face. It was proof that the big lug loved me. I no longer had to convince Charlie there was more to Willard's death than what the police and forensics people had already determined in their official reports. Too many bizarre occurrences had finally forced him to accept what I had so adamantly believed from the beginning. Someone had wanted Willard dead.

And now he or she wanted me dead too.

I didn't care that Spiro was tucked safely away inside his mansion in Bel Air with his sugar mommy Tamara. I had seen enough in the past week to know he was paying hustlers off, pulling strings from behind the scenes, warning me every step of the way to keep my nose out of it. Spiro was, in my mind, the devil. And if he didn't carry out the dirty deed of knocking off Willard himself and making it look like an accident, then he had certainly orchestrated it. And it was my mission to prove it.

Charlie combed the house for any clues left behind by the assailant, but I knew it was a fruitless search. The knife was the only key piece of evidence and the attacker fled with it as I let the cops in the house. But Charlie had to keep busy so his mind wouldn't wander to the scene he almost came home to find—his lover sprawled out on the kitchen floor in a pool of blood.

As the victim of the attack, I was doing much better emotionally than Charlie. I had already been pounced on once by a wild-eyed tattooed hustler in Laurel Canyon. I was getting used to violence and mayhem and it just strengthened my resolve, kept me focused and pissed me off enough to doggedly pursue more clues.

I fired up the laptop and cradled it in my lap as I clicked on the Internet Movie Database, the incredibly detailed Website full of entertainment industry factoids. All you have to do is punch in a name, and a complete list of film and television credits immediately downloads for your convenience.

I wasn't one hundred percent sure what I was looking for, but I knew Spiro was a struggling actor before he met Tamara, and won a few bit parts in a string of forgettable projects. I was hoping something might jump out at me. A name. Someone who might provide a little insight. It was a reach, but I had nothing else to go on at this point.

After typing "Spiro Spiridakis" into the little search box, I waited the few seconds for the computer to pull up a list of titles. Then, I painstakingly clicked on each and every barely released independent film and quickly cancelled TV show he had appeared in so I could pour over all the names in the cast and crews that Spiro worked with during his brief career.

For such a short stint in the acting profession, Spiro had certainly racked up a bunch of credits. Granted, most of them were glorified extra parts, but his swarthy good looks and Greek pedigree served him well, even after he gave up his dream of being an actor.

Having finished his third search of the house, Charlie sauntered into the bedroom where I was propped up against a pillow, clicking and searching, clicking and searching. He kissed me on the forehead.

"I turned on the house alarm before I came downstairs."

I looked up at him and gave him a reassuring grin. "I don't think he's coming back tonight."

"I know. I just thought it was a good idea."

It dawned on me that Charlie, as a cop, was used to always staying alert in situations fraught with danger. He was just worried about me.

"I'm okay, really. You didn't have to turn on the alarm."

When we moved into the house, we installed a high tech security system to monitor every window and door throughout the entire house. After I accidentally set it off six times and Snickers set it off eight times, triggering a migraine-inducing screaming horn heard for miles that called in three neighborhood patrol cars with armed guards to the scene, we decided as a family that it just wasn't worth it. It had been dormant for years. Until tonight. Charlie was trying to make me feel safe, and I loved him for it.

Charlie tossed off his clothes. There was a biting chill in the air, so he hurried into bed and slid under the covers. He snuggled up next to me, wrapping his arm around my waist, trying to pull me closer. As much as I wanted to just snap off the light and fall asleep in his arms, I couldn't help but notice a name in the cast list of a small independent movie in which Spiro appeared.

The film was a Quentin Tarantino rip-off in the mid-nineties that never got a theatrical release but was eventually sold to an Encore movie channel. Lots of blood, guts, guns, and self-consciously hip dialogue. According to the plot summary, Spiro played a small time hood (talk about type casting) who gets knocked off in the first five minutes of the story. Playing his buddy, who is tortured by a group of gangsters into revealing the whereabouts of a lost suitcase full of cash, was an actor by the name of Malcolm Randall.

I knew Malcolm. We had been in the same acting class a few

years ago. The one thing I remembered about Malcolm was his incurable need to gossip. If anybody could give me the skinny on Spiro, it would be him.

Charlie began to snore softly, his head resting on my chest, the glow from the laptop illuminating his face, tranquil at last. I closed the computer and gently moved his head over to the pillow as I picked up the phone and started making calls. Out of work actors have a strong information network, and not just when it comes to auditions and the best yoga classes. I knew I could track down Malcolm within minutes, and before I put down the phone and burrowed under the covers with Charlie for the night, I had the address of his new acting class, and the night this week that he would be there.

Leonard Short was a renowned acting teacher in Hollywood. His own career had short-circuited in the early eighties and ever since then he had chosen to share his knowledge of the craft with a few working actors and an army of wannabes. Leonard never got to play Hamlet or Romeo or even King Lear. If someone were to cast him as a Shakespearean character, the role most suited for him physically would be Puck, the mischievous midget fairy from *A Midsummer Night's Dream*. Leonard's shortcoming was his stature. He was, in a word, short. He overcompensated for this by yelling, mostly at his students. Ordering them to reach deeper into their souls to find the pain and anguish they could channel into whatever roles he assigned them in his popular Tuesday night scene analysis class.

Leonard projected a sensitive veneer to draw his students in. But mostly he relished in tearing them down once they finished a scene. It was a source of power he used to manipulate time and time again. He especially ripped into the young women, exposing their weaknesses and frailties all for the sake of "art." It was also a sure fire way to get his female students into bed. He'd beat them up so bad, their self-esteem would be shot. Then, the "sensitive" Leonard would offer them a ride home to discuss what he was trying to accomplish with his sadistic scare tactics. And just when they were feeling their most vulnerable and exposed, he would talk his way into their pants.

After six months of studying with Leonard, I caught on to what he was about and dropped the class. He was never cruel to me unless I was working on a show. Then it was impossible for him to contain his jealousy. He'd assign me the most challenging role he could find, usually Eugene O'Neill. Some testosterone-laden depressed alcoholic. That way he could tear into me when I couldn't pull it off convincingly. But when I was out of work and unable to get an audition, I'd be blessed with a light comedy, Noel Coward or Paul Rudnick, something that played to my strengths, and he'd guffaw as I plowed effortlessly through it. Acting classes in Los Angeles were often equivalents to psychological torture.

Leonard's class was held in a rundown warehouse on Formosa Avenue, just south of West Hollywood. The class was a mixed bag. Most of the students were in their twenties and early thirties, fresh in town, hoping this was a quick detour before becoming the next Sandra Bullock or Brad Pitt. A lot of them had haunted, scarred looks on their faces, so I assumed they had been in Leonard's class for at least a few months.

There was no sign of Malcolm as I took a seat in the back and watched the students set up the tiny stage for the first scene. It was Academy Awards night, and all the students had been paired up to perform classic scenes from Oscar winning movies. On the chalkboard just left of the stage was a list of tonight's featured movies including *Sophie's Choice*, *Misery*, and *Good Will Hunting*. You had to love Hollywood. Even most stage productions were based on movies. My guess is you'd have to go to New York in order to find an acting class that would bother with a Tony Awards night. Very few people in L.A. would ever dream of mounting a stage production of an actual stage play. What would be the point? How would that get them in front of a camera?

Leonard burst into the tiny theatre with all the fanfare of a royal procession. Students leapt from their seats to greet him, and he soaked up the fawning respect with a wide smile. I was hoping he wouldn't see me, but Leonard made a habit of scanning the room after his grand entrance. You never know when a shy young girl from Toledo might show up to audit. He was always on the prowl for a potential conquest. There was no escaping his gaze. His eyes settled on me.

"Well, it looks like we have a special guest star tonight. Jarrod Jarvis."

All heads swiveled to get a look. A few recognized me from my days on *Go to Your Room!* But most of them just wanted to size up the competition.

"Have you decided to grace our little class with your presence again, Jarrod? I know we'd all love to have you."

"Um, well, yes, I've been meaning to come back for a while, but I just haven't had the time . . ."

His face tightened and he visibly braced himself. "Oh. Have you been working?"

"Oh no. Not much."

The tension drained from his face. He was elated over my unemployment. "Well, why don't you sit in tonight, and then we'll have a chat after class. I have a Noel Coward scene I'd love for you to work on."

If I had even copped to a Trident gum commercial, he would have forced me into a blistering, impossibly dour scene from O'Neill's *The Hairy Ape.* To hell with Academy Awards night.

Up first was a classic scene from *Sophie's Choice* where Meryl Streep tells Peter MacNichol the agonizing decision the Nazis forced her to make over which child she was going to save and which child she was going to ship off to the ovens. A voluptuous young woman with a curvy body and long golden hair joined a wiry, intense kid with wire-rimmed glasses on the stage.

Leonard sat back in his chair and cupped his hands behind his head. "Meryl Streep won her first Oscar in 1981 for this masterpiece directed by Alan J. Pakula. It co-starred Kevin Kline and Peter MacNichol. Here's Anna and Steve doing a scene from *Sophie's Choice.*"

It took every ounce of self-control not to correct him. Meryl Streep won her first Oscar in the Supporting Actress category three years earlier for *Kramer vs. Kramer* and she won for *Sophie's Choice* in 1982 not 1981. I wanted so much to show Leonard up in front of his class. But I wasn't there to exact revenge on an acting teacher with a master/slave fetish. I was there to speak with Malcolm, who still hadn't shown up.

Anna and Steve launched into the scene with gusto and pulled out all the acting tricks they knew, from long reflective pauses (a favorite of mine I use to remember my next line) to jittery hand movements that keep the focus off your face, which is usually filled with abject fear.

Anna was quite good. She had perfected a flawless accent for her Polish/Catholic Post World War II immigrant and she delivered a moving, believable interpretation that would have made even Meryl proud. Steve, on the other hand, was hopelessly miscast. He jumped about like Tom Green on amphetamines, mangling the words with a thick, affected southern accent, and trying to step on Anna's lines in a blatant selfish attempt to wrest the scene away from her.

"Stop," Leonard said as he held up his hand. "Obviously one of you thought a lot about the scene before tonight and the other is just winging it. Steve, incredible focus, I felt you were there right from the start. Anna, I don't know what to say. I want to say you have potential to be a good actress, but you're not showing me anything."

Well, it was no mystery who Leonard would try to get in the sack tonight. I felt sick to my stomach as I watched him rail against this fragile creature with an abundance of talent. I wanted to jump to my feet and tell her not to listen to him, to follow her instincts and she'd probably do quite well in this town. I was very close to leaping to her rescue, but I knew it wouldn't do any good. She would automatically heed the word of her beloved teacher and acting guru. Anna would have to discover the truth about Leonard and her budding talent on her own. Especially since Malcolm Randall, nearly a half hour late, finally hurried into the theatre.

He was carrying a blanket and typewriter and was wearing striped pajamas. I guessed he was playing the James Caan role in tonight's scene from *Misery*. He glanced around the room for his scene partner. There was no one in the warehouse who remotely resembled Kathy Bates. So far she was a no show.

I glanced over to Anna and Steve. She stood in front of the class, her arms folded, feeling alone and humiliated. Steve stood a few feet away from her, trying to distance himself, his mind reeling from Leonard's praise, fighting back an urge to dance across the stage with joy. I tuned out Leonard's self-serving rant, and quietly stood up and tiptoed over to Malcolm.

Malcolm always looked good. Not a hair out of place. A year-round suntan. A sinewy perfectly formed body. That was the blessing and the curse for actors. They were always out of work, but it gave them plenty of time to take care of themselves.

I snuck up behind him and tapped him on the shoulder. When he turned around, his face registered surprise.

"Jarrod, what are you doing here?"

"Auditing."

"I thought you hated Leonard's class."

"I do. I came to see you."

"I really can't talk now. I'm up next and I can't find my scene partner. She always flakes. Always. I hate it when Leonard pairs us up."

"How about after class?"

118

"Can't. I have a date. With a director. Don't want to name names. But he won the Audience Award at Sundance last year."

Malcolm ran outside in search of his missing scene partner. Even in his nervous state, he never missed an opportunity to brag about the big fish he occasionally reeled in.

Anna and Steve were off and rolling again. I knew I only had a few minutes left before I lost Malcolm.

When Malcolm hurried back inside, dread in his face, I approached him again. "I just want to ask you about someone. Spiro Spiridakis."

Malcolm stared at me. The name seemed to stir up all kinds of emotion. But the one that was easiest to read was fear.

"I don't want to talk about him," he said.

"I think he may have had something to do with his stepson's death."

"Sorry. Not going there." For a legendary big mouth, Malcolm was certainly tight-lipped about Spiro.

Anna and Steve wrapped up their scene. Leonard scuffled down to the stage to scream in Anna's face about commitment and focus. The clock was ticking. Malcolm was up next, and I knew I'd never get him to talk to me after that. Not with his big date probably waiting for him up the street at the Formosa Café.

There was still no sign of Malcolm's scene partner. On the stage, Anna's eyes filled with tears, and sensitive Leonard took over, comforting her, shushing her apologetic whispers. Steve was so full of himself, so pleased with his whole sense of being, he practically floated off the stage.

Cradling a spent, distraught Anna in his arms, Leonard turned to his enraptured crowd of disciples. "Who's up next?"

"I am," said Malcolm. "But Christine isn't here."

Leonard's eyes narrowed. He despised students blowing off his class. He took it as a personal affront, as if they were blowing off *him*.

"Does anybody else know the part?" he said.

"I do!" I can't believe the words came out of my mouth. But I was determined to get Malcolm to talk, and this was the only way I could think of to do it.

Leonard chuckled, amused at the thought of me playing the same role as Kathy Bates.

"It's my favorite movie," I said. "I know it by heart."

"Take five minutes, everybody," Leonard said with an impish grin. "Then we're in for a real treat." Leonard pulled a pack of cigarettes out of his corduroy shirt, and raced outside to make sure Anna had a ride home . . . with him.

I turned to see Malcolm, staring at me with a pale, stricken face. He couldn't believe what had just happened.

I smiled. "What scene are we doing? I hope it's the one where I chop off your feet with an axe."

"Why are you doing this?" he said. "Is it because I got that Tylenol P.M. spot last year and you didn't?"

"Here's the deal, Malcolm. You tell me everything you know about Spiro, or else . . ."

"Or else what?"

"I feed you the wrong cue lines." It was an actor's worst nightmare. We depend on cue lines to keep the scene flowing and the thought of not getting them sent shivers down Malcolm's spine.

"Leonard knows you just got a guest spot on *Gilmore Girls*," I said. "He's itching to tear you apart. And since I'm not a pretty starlet with a big chest, chances are he'll be focusing on you tonight."

"Okay, okay. Spiro's a nasty, evil pig. Happy?"

"I'm going to need more than that."

Malcolm glanced around, and then lifted his pajama top, revealing a white scar five inches long down the side of his rib cage. "He got mad at me one night and decided to show me how much by grabbing an iron poker out of the fireplace and branding me. That was three years ago. The scar is there for life."

I swallowed hard. I had no idea just how violent Spiro could get.

It made me regret how much I had been rattling his cage over the last few weeks.

"Why was he mad?"

"I was making us a pot roast for dinner and I accidentally burned it. It really pissed him off."

Ding. Ding. Ding. Cue bells and whistles. If Malcolm was making Spiro a pot roast, then that could only mean . . .

"Yes, it's what you think, Jarrod. We were lovers. We lived together for almost a year."

I couldn't believe it. Spiro Spiridakis, Tamara's tough as nails gorgeous Greek boy toy, was a draft pick for our team.

The class ambled back inside. Time was up.

"Do you keep in touch with him anymore?" I said.

"Are you kidding? The day he hooked up with Tamara, I ceased to exist. He denied we were ever involved, said he was straight, and never looked back. How else was he ever going to get his hands on all that money?"

Leonard strutted back to his seat. His booming voice filled the air. "Next up, a scene from *Misery*, based on the Stephen King novel, directed by Rob Reiner. Kathy Bates won the 1991 Oscar for Best Supporting Actress."

It was Best Actress, not Best Supporting Actress. And it was 1990, you moron. But there was no time to expose Leonard Short's ignorance. My priority now was exposing the secret life of Spiro Spiridakis. Right after I debuted my impression of a psychotic axe-wielding Kathy Bates.

Chapter Seventeen

Susie Chan was more beautiful than I remembered. Almost thirty-five, she looked more to be in her early twenties. There was a youthful vitality in her face, a bounce in her voice. Her mood was always positive without being overly enthusiastic. I expected medical examiners to be more somber and reclusive, but not Susie. She was outgoing and fun and I absolutely hated her. This is another giant flaw in my personality. I can never get my mind around liking anyone Charlie ever dated, and in Susie's case, someone he married. If he had dated Mother Theresa or Ghandi, I would have found some way to get them on my shit list.

Luckily, Susie didn't think much of me either. After all, I was the man who stole her husband away from her. That was what happened in her mind anyway. The fact that she left him and he came out of the closet months before meeting me didn't matter. So if Susie and I had one thing in common, it was a mutual abhorrence for one another.

Despite these feelings, I insisted on joining Charlie and Susie for dinner at Off-Vine, an upscale eatery in the heart of a rather rundown section of Hollywood. The restaurant was housed in a small yellow wood framed house off the beaten path, off Vine

Street in fact. It was typical California cuisine with lots of fish, chicken and pasta dishes and was a favorite among theatergoers who ventured into the area to see *The Lion King* at the restored Pantages Theatre.

What bothered me most when Charlie told me he was dining with Susie at Off-Vine was its obvious romantic atmosphere. I didn't expect Susie to hypnotize Charlie into believing he was a heterosexual so he would leave me and go back to her, but I would have preferred a louder, more central location for them to break bread.

So, for the first time ever, I invited myself. Charlie was surprised, but didn't seem to mind me tagging along. Susie, on the other hand, was downright shocked at my sudden appearance, but her bubbly personality instantly covered up any reservations she had about me joining the party.

I ordered an expensive bottle of wine in an effort to get Susie drunk. On the surface, I knew her to be the utmost professional, not one to gossip about things she shouldn't. After a few glasses of wine, however, she got giggly and a lot chattier. My goal was to get an insider's perspective on Willard's autopsy in the hopes of uncovering an overlooked piece of evidence that might support a murder theory. So the more I could ply her with wine the better my chances were for some useful information.

Charlie knew exactly what I was doing, but he was still shaken from my near death experience. I was not above capitalizing on the slack he was cutting me. And I knew the reason he was so amenable to me joining him and Susie was because he still wasn't comfortable with the idea of me sitting home alone.

As we finished our salads and waited for our entrees, I ordered another bottle of wine. Charlie sighed, but didn't stop me. Susie polished off her second glass, and eagerly waited for her third. I had endured her stories of her parents' visit, her cat's pregnancy, and her flirtation with a cute, criminally young UCLA medical student who was interning for her. Finally, the opportunity presented itself. I leaned forward.

"I read about you in the papers all the time, Susie. You're becoming quite famous."

"It's only because I'm a coroner in L.A. If I were in Omaha, nobody would care. But here, I get to cut open lots of famous dead people."

"Someday someone's going to base a movie on your work."

"Maybe they'll get Lucy Liu to play me. People say we look alike."

I was in no position to disagree. "You're right. I didn't see it until right now. It's an amazing resemblance."

"I loved watching her in that *Ally McBeal* show. But clearly, I'm not that bitchy."

Again, I was in no position to disagree. "Clearly."

Charlie was amused as he watched me suck up to Susie. He finished his salad, and sat back to enjoy the show.

Richard, the slim, handsome Italian waiter I never failed to flirt with when I came here, arrived with a fresh bottle of wine. But tonight I didn't even glance his way. I couldn't risk losing any momentum with Susie.

"By the way," I said with about as much subtlety as Eminem at the Queen Mother's tea party, "Thanks again for that autopsy report."

She waited for Richard to pop the cork and fill her glass. He stopped half way, and she gave him an annoyed stare. "Keep going."

He filled it to the rim, one of his eyebrows raised as he did it. Richard could say a lot with one eyebrow. He then tucked the bottle into an ice bucket and moved off to one of his other tables.

Susie took a big gulp of wine and laughed. "Well, Charlie said you were obsessed with finding some proof your friend was murdered, so we both figured it was the only way to shut you up." Susie giggled and covered her mouth. "Oops. I didn't mean for it to come out like that."

"It was true. I was totally obsessed. But your report put my mind at ease."

"Good. Glad I could help." Her words were labored. It was getting harder for her to put them together. I reached over and poured her another glass. Charlie folded his arms, anxious to see where this was going.

"One thing did nag at me about the report."

"What was that?" She took another gulp.

"Just a small thing. There were traces of soap found in Willard's lungs. Charlie said he probably washed his face or took a bath and accidentally swallowed some, but I was curious. Could it be from something else?"

Susie set down her glass and thought about it. For a minute, I thought she might pass out and fall face first on the table, but then, she popped her head back up and giggled again. "He took a bath. Forensics found a ring of the same soap around the tub. Probably right before he fell into the pool."

I had no idea where I was going, but I began to think out loud. "Let's say, for the hell of it, it *was* a murder."

"But it wasn't."

"Indulge me," I said evenly as I filled her glass with more wine.

"Okay," she burped.

"Isn't it possible that someone could have drowned Willard in the tub?"

"It's possible, but unlikely."

"Why?"

"Because he was found in the pool!" Susie checked the wine bottle to make sure there was still enough in there for one more round.

"What if someone drowned him in the bathtub, and then dragged him downstairs, poured tequila down his throat, rearranged the patio furniture, and dumped him head first into the pool to make it look like an accident?"

"Why not just leave him in the tub?" Charlie asked.

"Because accidentally drowning in two feet of water seems highly unlikely," Susie slurred, a glazed look in her eye. She was slowly but surely coming over to my side. I had her thinking.

Charlie knew he was losing Susie so he pressed on. "But there were no signs of forced entry, and if Willard was in the tub, how could he answer the door?"

"It was someone he knew. Someone who would have a key," I said.

"Jarrod, this makes no sense," Charlie said. "Do you know how hard it is to drown someone in a tub and not leave a mark? There were no bruises anywhere on him."

Charlie had me. Richard arrived with our entrees and set them down. Charlie, with a self-satisfied smile, dug into his salmon. I started in on my blackened turkey breast, and Susie tried to eat her pecan-breaded chicken, but she was so drunk, her fork kept missing it.

"The Brides in the Bath Theory," Susie managed to spit out in between fruitless stabs at her plate.

Charlie and I looked at her, waiting for more, but she was too determined to get any tiny morsel of her meal into her mouth. Finally, she managed to stab a lone green bean and triumphantly popped it between her lips.

Contented, she rambled on. "Famous old murder case in England. This guy, George J. Smith, married three women. All of them died in the bathtub. Of course, the police were convinced George did it, but had a hell of a time making a case. There were absolutely no signs of a struggle and none of the victims had any bruises."

"So how'd he do it?" Both Charlie and I were enthralled.

"A forensics pathologist conducted an experiment. He enlisted the help of an expert swimmer and had her sit in a full bathtub. They had a policeman stand at the end of the tub nearest her feet and grab her heels, yanking them up. Her feet flew up and the rest of her body slid under the water. The water filled her lungs before she even had a chance to hold her breath. She nearly drowned. And there wasn't a mark on her."

"That's how the killer drowned Willard! He probably saw it on the Discovery Channel or something!"

Susie was getting excited. "He was already dead from drowning, so whoever did it decided to play with the circumstances to throw us off!"

In a surprise twist, Charlie's ex-wife and I were bonding. Poor Charlie just sat there, dumbfounded.

I was pumped up. Susie had provided a plausible theory that would explain how the killer could have pulled off the murder. Now the only question was, who did it?

When the check came an hour later, I slapped down my American Express to cover it. Susie had more than earned a free meal. She was too drunk to drive, so Charlie took her by the arm and led her to his car. I had Richard the hunky Italian waiter call me a cab.

My mind raced all the way home, and it kept racing even after I entered the front door. Snickers scampered to my feet, panting with unbridled excitement. Since she wasn't locked in the bedroom closet, I felt reasonably safe to roam about the house without fear of someone jumping me.

I flipped on the kitchen light, and found two messages waiting for me on the phone answering machine. One was from Laurette, wondering if I had thought any more about those personal appearance offers that were flooding her office. But all of them still wanted me to discuss my recent high profile arrest. The fighting spirit in Laurette's voice was fading fast. So was the tabloid show heat. Laurette knew in her heart that I would never agree, but felt obligated as my manager to relay the offers to me anyway. I made a mental note to call her back as the machine played the second message.

"Hi, Jarrod, it's Vito Wilde." He didn't have to tell me. I would have recognized the high-pitched feminine Laura Bush voice anywhere. "I need to meet with you as soon as possible. I know who murdered Willard Ray Hornsby."

Chapter Eighteen

If someone told me I would be line dancing with a hardy, sweet-faced cowboy at a gay country-western bar in the Valley in order to hear some dishy information, I would have laughed in his face. But there I was on a hot Sunday afternoon at the Rawhide in North Hollywood, standing off to the side by myself nursing a Bud light.

Vito Wilde had told me to meet him here at six, and it was already five past seven. I was getting antsy and nervous and was about to call his pager when a big, lumbering sweetheart in a red and blue patchwork shirt and ivory cowboy hat cautiously approached me and held out his hand.

"The name's Stuart. Want to have a go with me?"

I nearly choked on my beer. I was more at home in a bar pounding out the hits of Annie Lennox or even Gloria Gaynor, not Tricia Yearwood and the Dixie Chicks.

"I'm sorry, I don't line dance."

"Awwww, come on, why don't you just give it a whirl? It's not so hard once you're out there."

His charm was overwhelming, and I had to keep telling myself I was in a fulfilling, loving, monogamous relationship. But then again, what was the harm of one tiny little dance? It wasn't even dark out yet. I tentatively gave him my hand, and he led me out onto the floor where twelve same sex couples twirled and clapped and stomped their feet. I felt naked without the proper boots and Stetson, but I made the best of it, and Stuart wisely took the lead. He positioned me in front of him, slid his arm around my waist, took my left hand with his other and glided me out into the sea of line dancers. I wish I could say I adapted flawlessly, but Stuart's throbbing feet would probably suggest otherwise. I nailed him with my heel three times before we even got through the intro of the song. I was facing away from him but I sensed that he was wincing in pain. Gentleman that he was, he never said a word. And he didn't stop. He kept going. And I got him two more times. He slowed his pace, and tightened his grip on my hand, but still never complained, not once. God, I love cowboys.

I saw Vito Wilde enter through the front door and cross to the bar. He wore a patchwork shirt just like Stuart's, but Vito's was green and yellow. He ordered a beer on tap and looked around for me. Sweat poured down his agitated face, and his weighty frame heaved up and down with labored breathing. I turned around and smiled at Stuart.

"Mind if we take a break?"

The look on Stuart's face said it all. He was enormously relieved, but didn't want to hurt my feelings.

"I'll catch you on the next go around."

Stuart limped off the dance floor to a group of pals outside on the patio.

I hurried over to Vito, who had just spotted me. He grabbed my wrist and pulled me close to him. He had an intense, foul odor, the kind a lot of big men get when they've exerted too much energy.

"Someone's following me, I don't know who, but I could hazard a guess."

"Spiro?"

Vito nodded, then glanced at the door nervously, and fingered his beard. "He thinks I'm going to tell someone what I know."

"What, Vito? What do you know?"

He swallowed his beer in one gulp, and then slammed down his plastic cup in front of the bartender for another.

"I didn't want to tell you this before because of ethical considerations, but I'm afraid if something happens to me . . ."

"Please, Vito, tell me."

He glanced around the bar, half expecting Spiro to appear at any moment. He took a deep breath, still debating with himself on whether he should break his confidentiality agreement. I didn't want to push him anymore, but I wasn't going to let him leave without telling me.

"For Willard's sake, for the sake of the people who loved him and miss him, just say it!"

"Willard came to his session about a month ago. He was very upset. In fact, I'd never seen him so distressed."

"Spiro?"

"Yes. Willard's mother had invited Willard out to her weekend getaway ranch in the desert. I remember he didn't want to go, but it had been weeks since he last saw his mother. I had been encouraging him to come to terms with his relationship with her, and suggested that it might be a good idea if he went."

"So he did."

"Yes. I was hoping they would talk, maybe start working on a healthier approach to their relationship, but I never thought . . ."

This was hard for Vito. He still wasn't convinced he was doing the right thing. I, however, was.

"What happened, Vito?"

"Nothing the first night. They barbecued steaks on the grill, polished off a few bottles of wine and went to bed. Willard was actually feeling pretty good about making the trip. But then, the next day, Tamara drove down to Desert Hot Springs to get a massage at a spa, and she left Spiro alone at the house with Willard, and that's when . . ."

I knew what he was going to say, so I finished his sentence for him. ". . . Spiro made a pass at Willard."

"Yes. The bastard. Willard had gone for a swim. Spiro decided to join him. Basically attacked him in the pool. Willard pushed him away, and told him to never try anything like that again. His own stepson."

"What did Spiro do after Willard rebuffed his advances?"

"Nothing at first. When Tamara returned home, Spiro just pretended it never happened. But Willard was a basket case. He feigned a stomach flu, and got the hell out of there. Drove back to L.A. that night. When he came to see me the following Tuesday, he was a mess. He didn't know what he was going to do. He was literally shaking in my office."

"How did you advise him?"

"I told him he had to tell his mother. He couldn't just bury something like that. I was thinking of his mental well being."

"Did he tell her?"

"I don't know if he ever got the chance."

"So you believe Spiro killed Willard?"

Vito's voice dropped a few octaves, startling me with its sudden infusion of masculinity. "I *know* he did. After our session, I went outside for a smoke before my next appointment and I saw Spiro confront Willard in the parking lot. He had been following him. They argued. I couldn't make out all they were saying, but I heard Willard threaten to tell Tamara everything. Spiro had this wild look in his eyes, like he was going to explode. He just kept jabbing Willard in the chest with his finger, warning him not to do anything he'd regret . . ." Vito took a swig of his beer before continuing in a sad, soft voice. "That was two days before he died."

"Why didn't you go to the police with this?"

"They still think it was an accident. You're the only one who's convinced it was murder."

I finally had a motive.

"I'm sorry I didn't tell you before," Vito said. "But I've been struggling with all the implications."

"Your client is dead," I said. "You're not obligated to keep his secrets anymore." I was beginning to wonder if Vito's Doctor of Metaphysics degree came from one of those Universities by mail.

"Well, I just really felt you ought to know before . . ." His pager went off. He glanced down and checked the number. "Office emergency. Would you excuse me?"

"Sure."

Vito asked the bartender where the nearest pay phone was and lumbered off down a back hallway leading to the rest rooms. I ordered another Bud Light and tried to process all this new information. I had suspected Spiro all along, and now with Vito finally fessing up to the secret Willard discussed in his therapy sessions, a D.A. would be hard-pressed not to pursue a case against Tamara's no good husband.

Ten minutes passed, then twenty. A buddy of Stuart, the sweet-faced cowboy, smiled at me from across the room. He was about to saunter over and ask me to dance, but I could see Stuart stop him and whisper a warning in his ear about my clumsy feet, so the guy demurred from taking any unnecessary risks.

After a half hour of waiting for Vito to return, I chugged the last of my fourth Bud Light and went in back to find Vito. He wasn't there. My cell phone was in the car with a dead battery, so I picked up the pay phone, punched in my MCI card number, and dialed home.

Charlie scooped up the phone on the first ring. I told him I was on my way home after a quick pit stop in the bathroom. Charlie didn't ask what I was doing at Rawhide. He already knew and chose not to make an issue out of it.

After hanging up, I pushed the men's room door open and went inside. I unzipped at the urinal to relieve myself, and noticed in the bathroom mirror someone's feet underneath the stall. They were angled out in an uncomfortable, distracting position. I was trying to remember if the black, scuffed shoes were the same ones Vito was wearing.

"Vito? Is that you?"

Silence. The man was either being rude or he was pee shy and couldn't bring himself to carry on a conversation while in such a compromising position. I finished and zipped back up, and then heard a thump. It was like a head hitting the metal door of the stall.

"Vito?"

I crossed over to the door and pulled on the latch. It didn't budge. It was either jammed or locked from the inside.

I debated about what to do next. I could just leave the man in peace, or harass him some more. Naturally I chose the latter. I went into the next stall, leapt up on the toilet seat, and gripped the divider, pulling myself up far enough so I could peek over the edge.

A large man's body was slumped over, his head resting against the stall door. I immediately recognized Vito's green and yellow patchwork shirt.

"Vito, are you okay?"

I stood on the tips of my toes on the toilet seat so I could reach far enough down to touch his head. There was still no movement. I gently took a clump of his hair in my hand and slowly drew his head back. The first thing I saw was his eyes. They were wide open, pleading and horrified. His mouth was contorted into a silent scream, and dark blood drenched the front of his shirt.

Vito Wilde's throat had been slashed.

Chapter Nineteen

Rawhide always buzzed with activity during its Sunday afternoon line dancing beer bust, but nobody anticipated the hysteria and panic that would spin out of control on this particular weekend.

I tried cordoning off the bathroom to keep patrons from entering until the police arrived, but this was a beer bust. You pay five bucks and drink unlimited amounts of beer on tap. My guess was the place was packed with roughly two hundred people. We're talking two hundred bladders filled to capacity. There was no way I was going to keep Vito Wilde's murder in the men's room quiet.

The sleepy-eyed bartender with a very dated Flock of Seagulls haircut and a weathered brown leather vest that didn't even try to cover his enormous belly was the first to confront me. Several patrons were complaining that I wouldn't let anyone into one of the restrooms. A gay bar is one of the few places in the world where the men's room line is longer than the ladies' room line. With me pinned up against the door, guys started spilling into the empty ladies' room. But the hallway soon clogged up and the natives quickly got restless.

"Move out of the way, buddy. People have to piss," the bartender said as he barreled through the aggravated crowd.

"I can't," I said in as low a voice as possible. "Something happened in there and I don't want to cause a panic."

"What?"

He leaned in closer, as did the dozen other cowboys lined up to take a leak. I felt discretion was vital at this point, so I whispered in his ear. "A man's been murdered. And his body's in your bathroom."

"Holy shit! Murdered?"

An audible buzz spread faster than melted butter on a dinner roll. There was a powerful surge forward. All I saw in front of me were dozens of cowboy hats in various styles and colors crowding me in, all anxious for a glimpse at the corpse.

The bartender tried shoving me aside to get a better look. He was the type who slowed his vehicle down and bottled up traffic whenever he spotted a car wreck on the highway. He was bigger than me, and managed to reach over my head with his left hand and swing the door open. The guys in the front were able to get a quick look at the pale, stiff, bleeding body of Vito Wilde.

"Jesus!" one of the cowboys said as he covered his mouth and bolted out a side door.

I kept the crowd at bay as best I could, knowing it was important to keep the crime scene clean. Not only was I married to a cop, I had also played a murder victim/corpse in a teaser for *CSI: Crime Scene Investigation*. It took seven takes to get the scene where William Peterson examined me right, because I found him so sexy, I kept giggling every time he touched me.

The sirens that pierced the air brought some welcome relief. Flock of Seagulls man finally backed off and went to greet the cops, undoubtedly to claim credit for keeping things calm until they got there.

Since we were in the valley, I didn't recognize any of the officers who pushed their way through. Charlie's division was downtown

Los Angeles. One of the cops, a tiny young Hispanic woman with a kind face and a compact, curvy body escorted me outside away from the fracas.

"Bartender says you're the one who found the body."

I nodded.

"Did you know the victim?"

I nodded again.

"Want to tell me?"

"His name's Vito Wilde. He's a therapist. He was treating a friend of mine who died recently."

"This friend of yours, was he murdered too?"

"Police don't seem to think so. But I do. Vito had information that was going to help me prove it."

She gave me a quizzical look, not sure how to digest this. She paused, and then continued, "So you think Mr. Wilde knew who killed your friend, and that person is the one who murdered Mr. Wilde?"

"Yes."

"So don't keep me in suspense. Who do you think it is?"

"His name is Spiro Spiridakis. And I've got his number for you in my car." I didn't care that Spiro had an airtight alibi the night I was attacked in my home. He was going down.

I heard a voice behind me. "Why is it wherever you go, there's trouble?"

I turned to find Charlie standing behind me. He had thrown on some jeans and a t-shirt and rushed over the hill to make sure I was all right.

Charlie grabbed me in a hug and whispered in my ear, "Someday I hope you stop scaring me like this." Then he let go, and flashed his badge to the cop guarding the back door to the bar and disappeared inside. I was left with the small Hispanic lady cop, who was still trying to piece together my elaborate story.

It was starting to get cold outside, and most of the bar patrons had already been herded behind plastic yellow police tape hastily draped across the front and back of the bar. A crowd was gathering, and my lady cop friend ditched me to keep the area secure. I stood there alone, this horribly violent murder scene behind me.

It dawned on me that if curiosity seekers were already on the scene, then it was only a matter of time before . . .

Flash!

The flashbulb from a camera blinded me. Omigod! The press was here, and what a story they had this time. The former child star recently arrested for breaking and entering was now mixed up in a murder. All of the reporters on the scene had watched TV when they were kids. They all knew exactly who I was.

I made a mad dash for Charlie's car.

When Charlie came out of the bar about an hour later, the local news teams lunged for him, salivating for any tidbits of information they could feed to their post prime time audience. Charlie was out of his jurisdiction and didn't want to step on any toes, so he directed them to another officer who was more than happy to dish a lot of nothing to the quote-hungry reporters.

Charlie ducked away from the madness and slid into the driver's seat. I was slumped down, frazzled from the whole experience. I knew I would once again be featured across the front pages of the tabloids. This was why Ellery Queen never acted in breakfast cereal commercials as a child. It would have been a real hindrance to his stellar career as a detective.

"Anything?" I asked Charlie.

"Nope, not yet. Forensics is still scouring the area, but I don't expect them to find much. Whoever killed Vito did it quick and clean."

"You mean Spiro."

"It wasn't him, Jarrod."

"What are you talking about? We have a motive for both murders now," I said. "Spiro made a pass at Willard, and was terrified he was going to tell Mother. It would have done irreparable harm to Spiro's cash flow. And he knew Willard told his therapist everything, and that eventually Vito might speak out. He had to get rid of him too."

"I had a squad car stop by Tamara's house. Spiro answered the door. If he had been at Rawhide, there would have been no way for him to get back over the hill to Bel Air that fast."

"Then it was Eli. Spiro hired him to attack me in order to scare me off and then hired him again to get rid of Vito."

Charlie shook his head. "Sent a squad car over there too. He was in the middle of giving a 'massage' to a prominent studio executive."

"He was home? So then who . . . ?"

Charlie put his arm around me. "We'll get to the bottom of it. I promise. We'll figure it out."

With more and more questions mounting, I was beginning to believe my boyfriend was dead wrong, and Willard Ray Hornsby's death would fade away with time, just another bizarre mystery chronicled in a new edition of *Hollywood Babylon*.

Chapter Twenty

When Charlie and I arrived home and got ready for bed, reports of Vito Wilde's murder at the Rawhide bar were all over the late night news. It was a fast breaking story, and the frenzied media didn't overlook Vito's connection to Willard Ray Hornsby. They also didn't miss my connection to the whole mess, and wasted no time in putting up the photo of me taken outside the bar for the whole city to enjoy.

Charlie was in the bathroom brushing his teeth, so I was left alone in bed, clutching a sleepy Snickers as I stared at my surprised face on television. My first reaction was alarm at my haggard, worn appearance. I wanted the station to run a scroll underneath explaining to viewers that I had just discovered a dead body and then had to spend twenty minutes guarding it until the police arrived. But alas, they didn't offer that courtesy.

My second visceral reaction came when the field reporter at the scene suggested my possible involvement in the crime, since I seemed to be popping up everywhere a corpse was found. The news team speculated on how I might be connected to this recent spate of murders. The weatherman joked that I was around more dead bodies than the old lady on *Murder She Wrote*. You just have to love local news in L.A. I wanted to tell the jerk to stick to his storm fronts and save the commentary for someone with half a brain.

At that moment, the perky blonde news anchor introduced a new interview subject, who happened to be in the studio, respected Los Angeles coroner Susie Chan.

Susie was decked out in a powder blue power suit, fitted with smart earrings and had an impeccable camera-ready coif.

Once I found my voice, I cried out, "Charlie, get in here!"

He came stumbling out of the bathroom in his underwear, toothbrush in his mouth, and paste foam staining the sides of his mouth. He almost choked on the toothbrush at the sight of Susie. He was used to seeing her on television; it was just strange to see her commenting on this particular story. Even Snickers poked her head up, intrigued. There was a recognizable voice coming from the big box in the room.

The first question out of the bubblehead news anchor's mouth was about me. She wanted to know if Susie had any opinion as to why I always seemed to be at the scene of these crimes.

"First of all, let's make a distinction," she said in her very best professional, power hungry voice. "Willard Ray Hornsby's death was *not* a murder. If you read my autopsy report, which the L.A. Times printed last week, you'll see I ruled that death as an unfortunate accident. Vito Wilde's death is most certainly a homicide. There does seem to be a connection, however. Mr. Hornsby was a patient of Mr. Wilde's. As for Mr. Jarvis's propensity to show up on the scene every time someone expires, that's for the police to look into."

I was flabbergasted. After all our bonding at Off-Vine, Susie was selling me out on the eleven o'clock news.

I turned to Charlie. "Did you hear that? She's all but saying I'm the killer!"

Charlie didn't want to fan the flames, so he talked in his calm, even voice. "She didn't say that."

"She implied it! And did you notice how she's pretending we

don't know each other by calling me Mr. Jarvis? She's distancing herself. And what about her famous bathtub murder theory? She's not even talking about that!"

The news anchor glanced at the teleprompter for her next question. Hopefully with time and experience, she'd get better at pretending the questions came off the top of her head.

"So aside from Mr. Jarvis and their doctor/patient relationship, did these two men have anything else in common?"

"Yes. Both were openly gay men."

"What does that have to do with anything?" I was now shouting at the television. "You never got over your husband coming out of the closet, did you, Susie!" I crawled to the edge of the bed on my knees, still shouting. "I always knew you were homophobic!"

Charlie gently took me by the arm and pulled me back beside him. His best course of action at this point was to keep me calm. But I was wild with rage.

"I never trusted her! I knew she'd eventually show her true colors!"

Susie leaned forward, drawing the news anchor closer to her, as if she were about to share a secret just between the two of them. Of course, they were miked so the whole city could hear her intimate revelation. "And they were both HIV positive."

This bit of news stopped me dead. Susie continued on with her theories regarding the similarities between these two men, but I didn't hear another word. I was stunned. Willard had never shared that news with me. The first question that popped into my head was why this didn't show up in Susie's autopsy report. I grabbed Charlie's cell phone off the nightstand before he could stop me and pressed the speed dial button for Susie.

And then, right on television, there was a ringing. Susie stopped talking and froze, like a child caught sneaking candy. The news anchor stared at her numbly. She wasn't used to anything unexpected happening. That would require her to think on the spot, and most news anchors are not adequately trained in doing that. Susie reached down underneath the news desk and pulled her phone out of her purse. She held it up.

"I'm sorry. It might be an emergency." She flipped the phone up. "Susie Chan."

"Susie, it's me, Jarrod. Why the hell didn't you tell me that Willard was HIV positive?"

The news anchor touched her earpiece. The producer in the booth was probably screaming at her to regain control of the situation. But the anchor just sat there shaking. This was a first and she didn't know what to do.

Susie looked into the camera right at me. "I thought you knew."

The news anchor, ashen-faced, stuttered, "Thought I knew what?"

Susie pointed to the phone, but I don't think the news anchor understood yet that she wasn't talking to her.

Charlie had his hands over his face. He knew Susie would be livid over this. He was going to get it from both sides.

"Of course I didn't know! Why wasn't it in the autopsy report?"

Susie covered her mouth so the viewing audience wouldn't hear. But they heard every word. "That was just a preliminary report. Not all the blood tests were back. Look, if you don't mind, I can't talk about this right now."

"Fine. So what did you think of the restaurant the other night? Did you like your pecan-breaded chicken?"

Susie's face burned a crimson red. I loved tripping her up like this. It was a euphoric victory.

Someone in the booth was now feeding the still shell-shocked news anchor words to say because she finally turned to the camera, and chirped, "Sports and weather are up next. We'll be right back."

The station mercifully cut to a commercial.

"You're a bastard, Jarrod!" Susie was screaming now. She knew she was off the air.

"Yeah, well, what's with you acting like I'm a complete stranger on TV? You afraid I'm going to smear your pristine reputation if it gets out I'm shacking up with your ex-husband?"

Charlie was on top of things enough to grab the phone out of my hand at that point. He glared at me as he spoke frantically into the phone. "Hi, Susie, it's me." He settled back to endure her unexpurgated rant. He felt he had to after I torpedoed her live interview on the news.

I, on the other hand, was feeling pretty damn good. Susie was a grandstander and attention hog, and she deserved a little humility.

But I did sometimes feel sorry for Charlie, having to put up with me like this. However, I felt sorrier for Willard. I seemed to be the only one interested in putting all the pieces together. And this latest startling bit of information was one hell of a big piece. It was just a hunch, but deep down in my soul I knew this was the clue that would lead me to the mother lode of answers.

Chapter Twenty-One

During the heyday of *Go To Your Room!* I had a stalker. I was fourteen years old at the time, and completely unprepared for the obsessive advances of a persistent inmate at Angola State Prison who was convinced that we were soul mates meant to be together for all eternity.

He wrote an average of fifteen letters a week to me, each one becoming more aggressive and frustrated the longer I failed to respond. It came as no surprise that the inmate was mentally deficient, and had been in and out of institutions most of his life. I found out his first crime was at the age of eleven when he slaughtered his parents in their sleep for refusing to allow him to stay up and watch *The Sonny and Cher Comedy Hour.*

So when he escaped from his cell during a riot and disappeared just as we launched our second wildly successful season, there were a few tense weeks on the set while the escaped con was still at large. He was recaptured just two miles from my house after he got into a scuffle with a crossing guard who didn't know which street I lived on. The inmate was convinced there was a vast conspiracy at work and the crossing guard was an emissary from the evil forces bent on keeping us apart. The crossing guard managed to beat him off with her hand-held stop sign until a squad car arrived on the scene and arrested him.

That was my extreme story of someone who wouldn't take no for an answer during my days of fame, but it stayed with me, and ever since then I have been extra careful whenever I leave the house. I tend to be hyper aware of everybody around me, and I'm always prepared to react if I get any strange, uneasy feeling in the pit of my stomach. It's been years since I've gotten a fan letter, so the chances of acquiring another obsessive fan are remote. But I've never forgotten the trauma of those terrifying few weeks, so an alarm system has been permanently installed inside of me to detect anyone who might choose to invade my personal space. Most people, having not gone through such an ordeal, don't notice their surroundings or those who fill it. Tamara Schulberg-Spiridakis was one of those people.

I followed her all morning, and not once did she get an inkling that someone was on her tail. Granted, she did have a brush with fame after snaring her loaded geriatric media mogul, but since the marriage only lasted a couple of weeks, her fame was fleeting. She simply disappeared from the society pages and trade papers after settling her lawsuit against his estate.

So she wasn't trained like I was to watch for anyone who might be trailing her. She had her nails done at Skin Sense, a tiny beauty salon on Third Street near the Beverly Center, then had her hair rinsed and styled at Umberto, one of the trendier salons in Beverly Hills. I also went to Umberto for sheer camp value. I may not see Gwyneth Paltrow under a dryer, but I did spot Monica Lewinsky getting highlights once.

I lingered outside until Tamara was finished, then pretended to be just passing by. I knew if I showed up on her doorstep in Bel Air, Spiro would be on hand to shoo me away. I couldn't call and ask her to meet me because that would give her time to prepare. She would be ready for any questions I decided to lob her way. No, a surprise run in on a busy street in Beverly Hills was my best option, and the time to strike was now.

"Tamara!"

She looked up at me, startled. She had to be asking herself why I always seemed to be popping up in the most unexpected places.

"Jarrod, what are you doing here?"

"Meeting a friend for lunch at the Mandarin."

That was plausible. The Mandarin, a popular Chinese eatery, was within walking distance, and since I was standing outside the parking structure next to Umberto, it made sense.

"We seem to be running into each other all over the place," she said.

"Fate. We're meant to be together."

She let out a nervous laugh, not sure what I meant. She checked to make sure her new hairdo was still in place. It struck me as a nervous gesture.

"Well . . . take care, Jarrod." She tried pushing past me.

"Tamara, did you know Willard's therapist Vito Wilde was murdered?"

She nodded. "How could I not know? It's been all over the news and the phone's been ringing off the hook." Then she rose up erect, her eyes full of judgment and suspicion. "I've seen you on the news too. A lot of people are saying you had something to do with it."

"A lot of people? Or Spiro?"

"Well, it does seem ironic that you were so hell bent on proving Spiro is somehow involved with all the horrible things that have been happening, and now it looks like the evidence points to you."

"It's not me and you know it."

"All I know is, you discovered my son's body, you were caught breaking into his house, and now you were on the scene when his therapist was murdered."

"I'm just trying to dig up the truth."

"And I believed you. I was the one who sent you to Dr. Wilde. I feel responsible. If I hadn't given you his name, maybe he'd still be alive."

"Tamara, Vito was convinced that Willard was murdered. He had his own ideas about who he thought did it."

"Let me guess. He thinks it was Spiro too."

I didn't respond. I didn't have to. I just let it hang there.

"Spiro is a good man, despite what you might think," she said. "He loves me."

"Did you know he made a pass at your son before he died?"

She just stood there for a moment, staring at me, stunned that I would even consider making such an inflammatory accusation.

"It's true," I said. "Dr. Wilde was helping Willard work through how to deal with it."

"I'm really getting tired of your fairy tales, Jarrod."

"You said yourself that when Dr. Wilde called you after the funeral, he told you Willard was dealing with a specific problem in therapy. Well, when I spoke with Dr. Wilde, he told me it was Spiro. He made unwanted advances towards Willard in Palm Springs when you were off at some spa."

"That's a lie. A vicious, hurtful lie."

"It's the truth."

"If Spiro did such a thing, then why didn't Willard tell me?"

"Maybe he was afraid you'd react the way you're reacting now."

This stopped her in her tracks. She was fighting back tears now, but she wasn't going to break down. She didn't want to give me the satisfaction. "Like I've said all along, my son had a lot of emotional problems. And if something happened, and I'm not saying it did, who's to say it wasn't Willard who made the advances?"

"Do you honestly believe that Spiro is completely innocent in all this?"

"He's my husband."

"Willard was your son."

"I know where you're going with this," she said. "You've created this whole scenario where my husband went after my own son, got scared I might find out, and killed him so he couldn't talk. You're a fool if you believe that, Jarrod. Spiro may be many things, but he's not a killer. He's not capable of it."

"Vito Wilde was convinced he was capable of it."

"How would he know? Vito Wilde was treating my son, not Spiro. There was no way he could ever have drawn a conclusion like that."

"He was going by what your son told him."

"My son was an actor. And we all know how dramatic actors can be, don't we, Jarrod?"

"Did you know Willard was HIV positive?"

She flinched. "Yes, I knew."

We stood there in silence. Tamara dropped her head, took a deep breath, and stared at the sidewalk. "I know what you're thinking. You're thinking I flipped out when Willard told me, I deserted him, let him deal with it alone." She looked back up, and her eyes penetrated mine. "Nothing could be further from the truth."

"Why don't you tell me the truth then?"

"He was diagnosed years ago, around the time he was twenty-two, twenty-three years old. He never told me. We weren't speaking at the time. He hadn't worked in a few years, his SAG insurance had run out, so he had no health coverage. He just ignored the symptoms until he had full blown AIDS."

"I didn't know . . ."

"He was near death. I had no clue he was going through any of this. I would've helped him financially, paid for everything. He was desperate for medication, but he just couldn't afford it. Luckily he had this life insurance policy worth about thirty grand. He figured if he sold it, it might provide him with enough cash to buy some meds."

I knew all about this racket. AIDS victims who were strapped for cash would sell their policies to investors looking for a quick pay out. People would purchase the policy, knowing that AIDS was a fatal disease and the policyholder usually had only a few months to live. It was an easy way to make a fast buck. The investor knew the AIDS patient was going to die soon, so he'd get his money back with a tidy profit in hardly any time at all. It was a ghoulish, reprehensible investment, but dying young men, who were desperate for any kind of financial relief, saw it as a necessity. The only problem was, by the late nineties, advances in AIDS research had come up with the "cocktail," a combination of pills that held the virus at bay. Now people infected with AIDS were living longer, a lot longer, and these investors weren't too happy about it. It could potentially be decades before they would be able to cash in and get their money back.

Tamara folded her arms, hugging herself. "By selling the policy, Willard got a healthy chunk of change in his bank account, and was able to finally see a doctor and get on the meds. His condition improved dramatically. It was only months later, when his symptoms subsided and we reconciled, that he finally told me what he had been going through. At that point, I offered to help any way I could."

"Did you tell Spiro about Willard's HIV status?"

"No. That was between my son and me."

"Tamara, do you know which insurance company handled the sale of Willard's life insurance policy?"

"Grand Future Insurance. Both of us had life insurance policies there."

"Did Willard happen to mention who handled the sale?"

For the first time, a slight smile crossed Tamara's face. "Lance Zinni, a real character that one."

"Why do you say that?"

"He was rather star struck. He remembered watching Willard when he was just a kid. You would have thought he was dealing with Robert DeNiro. He was always tripping over his tongue he was so excited around Willard."

This was good news. If Lance Zinni was enamored of Willard, then chances were he might remember me too. After all, Willard was never on the cover of *TV Guide*. I made it twice. I could have been setting myself up for a colossal ego bruising, but my gut feeling told me Lance Zinni would welcome me with open arms. And if I played my cards right, he would tell me who bought Willard Ray Hornsby's life insurance policy.

Chapter Twenty-Two

"**B**aby, don't even go there!" I said, with all the enthusiasm of a beagle chasing a tennis ball. Lance Zinni threw his head back and howled, nearly falling out of his chair. We weren't in his office because he didn't have one. He was at a small cubicle sectioned off from the rest of the employees at Grand Future Insurance, and from what I could gather from my five minutes with Lance, his co-workers preferred it that way.

"Man, that cracked me up when I was a kid! Baby, don't even go there!" He held his ample gut that jiggled up and down as he bawled with laughter.

I chortled along with Lance, trying hard to ignore the creased, worn pictures of various supermodels that had been torn out of the *Sports Illustrated* Swimsuit Issue and taped up to the cork wall in Lance's cubicle. He treated his workspace like a high school locker, which was quite disturbing since I was guessing Lance was in his late thirties. And I was being generous.

As he prattled on, meticulously listing his favorite *Go To Your Room!* episodes in chronological order, I had a hideous image of him sitting at home late at night, in his underwear, flipping the remote between TV Land and those soft porn movies they show after midnight on Showtime.

When I had called Lance that morning and told him I was interested in buying a life insurance policy, he was polite but distracted. I could only imagine what he was doing. Probably downloading photos of Rebecca Romijn-Stamos on his desktop computer.

When I gave him my name, there was a long pause before Lance asked point blank, "You mean Jarrod 'Baby, don't even go there!' Jarvis?"

"The one and only."

After that, Lance and I were the best of friends. After briefing him on the current whereabouts of the rest of the cast, Lance eagerly asked me when I could come in to talk about a policy.

"I know you're a busy man, Lance, so I don't expect to get in today . . ."

"It just so happens I've had a cancellation. How about in a half hour, say ten o'clock?" I could hear him covering the mouthpiece of the phone and barking something to a secretary. I presumed he was ordering her to cancel his ten o'clock. Lance was so anxious to meet me he cleared all his appointments before lunch in case I ran into traffic.

When I got to the Grand Future Insurance Company offices in Sherman Oaks, it was everything I imagined. A small four-room office on the second level of a strip mall. I assumed Tamara bought these policies for herself and her son long before she had figured out a workable way to marry loads of money. The offices were drab, the walls were peeling, and the desks were in desperate need of refinishing. A lethargic, frumpy receptionist, who clutched her Coffee Bean and Tea Leaf cup in one hand and chewed her nails on the other, glanced up at me.

"You here to see Lance?"

"Yes. He's expecting me."

"Now there's one hell of an understatement."

It was official. I liked this receptionist. Just enough sarcasm to warrant the admiration of any quick-witted gay man.

She stopped chewing her nails and picked up the phone. She punched in a number, and a phone rang just a few feet away from her behind a partition. I heard a man's hurried, excited voice. "Yes?"

The receptionist popped a stick of gum in her mouth. "He's here."

A head shot up from behind the partition. It was Lance. And our friendship was born.

Lance decided to break the ice by regaling me with tales of the stars from his childhood he had encountered over the years. Most he met at annual autograph conventions held at the Beverly Garland Holiday Inn, just off the 101 Hollywood Freeway. Every year, an events organization dredged up long forgotten TV stars from the sixties and seventies and trotted them out on a Saturday for all their fans to see. They propped them up at cardboard tables in a large convention room, and for a fee, you could get a picture of yourself with them, or at least walk away with an autograph. It was the only place you could see a doctor from *Emergency* chatting it up with a female sweat hog from *Welcome Back, Kotter.* I had been asked several times over the years to participate, but wisely chose not to attend. I think one afternoon promoting myself as a has been would have sent me down Judy Garland Lane with a fistful of pills, never to return.

I indulged Lance for as long as I could. Finally, when he stopped to catch his breath after a scintillating story about how he once fetched a Diet Pepsi for Kitten from *Father Knows Best*, I decided it was time to get to the point.

"So what kind of life insurance policies do you offer, Lance?"

"Oh, well, we have a wide range," he fumbled through some papers on his desk, disappointed I had shifted gears so abruptly. "It depends on what you're looking for."

"I'd like to have the same one my friend Willard Ray Hornsby had."

He lit up. "You knew Willard?"

"Yes. We were old friends."

"I was so sorry to hear he died. Such a tragedy. He was another one I watched on TV when I was growing up."

"Let me put on my big surprise face."

My sarcasm was lost on Lance, but I heard the receptionist chuckling on the other side of the partition. I liked her more every minute.

"I'm not sure I remember exactly the terms of his policy," Lance said. "His mother bought it a while ago."

"You don't have a copy of it anymore?"

"Not in his file. He sold it. Going on a few years now, I think."

This was it. I was close. I had been remarkably lucky in my past attempts to con information out of people. I prayed my luck wouldn't run out.

"Do you remember who he sold the policy to?"

"Let me think now . . ." I held my breath as he thought about it. I was at the mercy of Lance Zinni's mind, and it scared me. "What was her name?"

"It was a woman?"

"It was a married couple, but I dealt with the wife mostly."

Had this mysterious woman ever guest-starred on *Baretta*, I'm sure the name would have just rolled right off Lance's tongue. But alas, she was a non-pro, so to Lance, she was somebody just not worth remembering.

"Nope. Sorry, drawing a blank."

Now there was a shock. I gave Lance a half-hearted smile. "Wouldn't there be a record of the sales transaction on your computer?"

"Yes."

Finally. Some progress.

"But we had a system crash about six months ago. Lost our whole hard drive and most of our old records. We've been busy rebuilding the database ever since."

"Guess this just isn't my day."

"Sorry." Lance seemed genuinely disappointed he couldn't help me.

I asked for some paperwork to fill out to make my visit appear legitimate. Lance pushed a sheaf of papers in front of me.

"Mrs. Phelan."

"What?" I said.

Lance shrugged. "I didn't say anything."

Then I heard the tiny voice again. "Mrs. Phelan." It was coming from the other side of the partition. I poked my head up over it to see the receptionist, looking back at me, with a grin on her face.

"I remember her. She and her husband used to have both home and auto policies with us. Her name is Gladys Phelan."

I recognized the name immediately. Gladys was the elderly woman in Los Feliz who denied knowing Willard, or how that ominous birthday card he had received shortly before his death was sent from her computer.

And for this key piece of information, I would've married that fabulously deadpan receptionist who had been eavesdropping.

Chapter Twenty-Three

I roared back over the hill on the 101 Freeway, leaving the Valley and returning to Hollywood. I took the Sunset Boulevard exit, which deposited me just on the outskirts of Los Feliz, and made my way back to the small beige one story house on Russell Street where Gladys Phelan resided.

I checked the time on the dashboard digital clock. Jerry Springer was just about to start. Mrs. Phelan wouldn't want to give me much of her attention if Jerry was on. But this time I was armed with information that she couldn't just brush off. The old lady had lied to me, and I was through treating her with kid gloves.

After parking right in front of the small house that still had the blue rain tarp on the roof, I marched up to the front door, and gave it three hard raps. There was the faint chatter of the television inside, so I knew she was home. After a minute, I rapped again, and again.

Finally, I heard some movement and the door opened. Gladys still had her hair tied in a bun, still wore her thick granny glasses, and remarkably, still had a tiny glob of peanut butter on the side of her mouth. She held her plate of Ritz crackers and looked up at me.

"Yes? Can I help you?"

"Mrs. Phelan, do you remember me, I'm Jarrod Jarvis?"

"Nope. Can't say that I do."

"I was here a few days ago. About the online greeting card that came from your computer."

"I don't want to buy anything you're selling."

She tried to close the door, but I managed to insert my foot inside to block it. There wasn't a trace of fear in her face, just contempt. I was keeping her from Jerry.

"Mrs. Phelan, we need to talk. You lied to me."

"I don't remember you at all. Just go away."

Her demeanor was much nastier than during my first visit. She had thought playing the daffy old lady would satisfy my suspicions that she was somehow not involved in this mess. But now that I was back with a fistful of accusations, she dropped the act and simply said, "Get the fuck out of here before I call the cops."

"Good. Let's do that, shall we? And then you can tell them all about how you sent a threatening greeting card to the man whose life insurance you and your husband bought. And how a few days after it was sent, he turned up dead."

She stopped trying to slam the door on my foot, and I saw her body heave a big sigh. She knew I was onto something, but she wasn't about to give me an inch.

"I don't know what the hell you're talking about."

"I think you do," I said. "You and your husband knew Willard Ray Hornsby was HIV positive. You knew he needed money. So you bought his life insurance policy as an investment through Grand Future Insurance. You figured he didn't have long to live. The disease was fatal. You'd have the cash back plus a tidy profit in no time."

She dropped her plate of Ritz crackers. The plate didn't break but the crackers scattered all over the floor. Hearing the plan out loud made it sound even more ghoulish.

Gladys refused to make eye contact with me as I continued. "But you never anticipated the advances in medicine. AIDS is now more of a chronic disease than a fatal one. And Willard's health improved immeasurably. He wasn't going anywhere, and you weren't going to get your money. So you killed him."

She finally met my gaze. Her eyes were on fire she was so filled with fury. "My husband handled all our business. I never knew what he did with our money."

"The good folks at Grand Future Insurance say you were the one they dealt with, not your husband. Care to try again?"

"Fine. We bought the policy. My husband's retirement pension wasn't covering our monthly expenses, so we decided to find a way to make some quick and easy investments. Our agent at Grand Future suggested buying Mr. Hornsby's policy. We didn't see anything wrong with it. He needed the money and we wanted to earn more on what little we had."

She reached down and picked up the crackers off the floor and put them back on her plate.

"It was awful," she said. "Mr. Hornsby got better, and we were broke. The agent assured us he wasn't going to live to see Christmas. But he did, and several more after that. We had no way to pay the taxes on the house or any of our bills. The stress got to be so much it finally killed Harry. Sad thing is, my situation improved once I got Harry's life insurance. I didn't need Mr. Hornsby's policy anymore."

"So you're saying you didn't send him the on-line greeting card?"

She shook her head. "Frankly, I forgot all about him."

"Mrs. Phelan, the fact is the card came from your computer. Sooner or later, you're going to have to explain that, and I'm afraid it might have to be to the police."

This shook her up a bit. She didn't want to go to jail. There would be no guarantee of a television set. She'd miss Jerry and Judge Judy and Montel and all her beloved friends. "I'm seventy-six years old. And I have a heart condition. How could I hurt anybody?"

"You could've had somebody do it for you."

"But I told you, I didn't need the money anymore. It doesn't make any sense."

"Then who *did* need the money?"

She was pleading with me now. Her aggressive attitude melted away as I continued to back her into a corner. I was afraid to push her too hard now that she had mentioned a heart condition, but I wasn't leaving without her giving me something.

"I don't know," she wailed. "Please, just leave me alone."

"If not you, then who else would benefit from that policy?"

She froze. Something dawned on her. "No. He's a good boy. He would never . . ."

"Who, Mrs. Phelan?"

"Nobody. He's not involved."

"Would you rather tell the cops? I have enough evidence already for them to haul you downtown for questioning. It could take hours. You'll never get back in time for the rest of your talk shows."

She heaved another sigh. The plate shook as her hand trembled. "Theodore. He's my only grandchild. His parents are gone. So when I go, he gets everything, including the policy. But I'm telling you, Teddy had nothing to do with whatever happened to Mr. Hornsby."

"When was the last time he was here for a visit?"

"It's been weeks. He's very busy, always working."

"How many weeks?"

"I'm not sure. He hardly ever comes around anymore. He was here once about five or six weeks ago, but I was at the grocery store. He left a note."

"Six weeks. Right around the time Willard got that greeting card."

"It's not him. I promise."

"Where can I find him?"

"I don't know where he lives."

"You don't have your only grandson's address?"

"No. He lives somewhere in Hollywood. I told you, I rarely see him anymore. He calls every once and a while to check up on me, but he's stopped coming around."

She was shutting down on me. She had shifted into protection mode. Her own suspicions of Theodore were rising, and she wasn't going to exacerbate his situation by telling me too much.

She was back to playing the frail old lady. "Please, I haven't taken my medicine. I'm feeling very weak. Could you just go?"

"All right, Mrs. Phelan, I'll leave now. But if Theodore does get in touch with you, I'd appreciate it if you called me." I knew she wouldn't. I just had to say it.

"I will," she lied and closed the door. I heard three bolts snap into place. I had startled her to the point where she would probably never answer the door for anybody again.

As I walked back to the Beamer, I knew I had it. My body pumped with adrenaline. After weeks of pounding the pavement, asking questions, alienating strangers and friends, there was finally an end in sight. Theodore wanted that money, and he wanted it bad enough to kill for it. All I needed now was for Charlie to pick him up, and squeeze a confession out of him. The only problem was, I had no idea where to find Mrs. Phelan's grandson. I wasn't even sure if Phelan was his last name. And there was no way in hell Gladys Phelan was going to tell me what it was.

I drove up Beachwood Canyon towards home, and was surprised as I turned the last corner to see Isis, my trusty Egyptian psychic, sitting on the stone steps leading up to my front door. She looked pensive, a floral print shawl wrapped tightly around her shoulders. She waved when she saw me, but there was no smile on her face. I swung the car to the curb, and jumped out to greet her.

"Isis, how did you get up here? You don't have a car."

"I took the bus."

"Must be important for you to endure public transportation."

"It is. Can we go inside?"

"Absolutely."

Snickers was jumping up and down inside, trying to get a good look out the window at who was with me. I opened the door and escorted Isis inside. Snickers, excited over my arrival and a new visitor, wasted no time sniffing us both up and down.

Isis made a beeline for the couch, and sunk into it. She folded her arms and stared straight ahead.

"Can I get you something to drink?" I said.

"No, I'm fine."

I could have used a stiff drink. Isis was making me very nervous. I picked up Snickers in my arms and sat down beside her. She stared off into space for a few more moments, and then shifted her body so she could look at me.

"I had to come," Isis said. "I had a dream last night. A very disturbing dream."

"What? What? Am I going to get hit by a bus?"

"No. Of course not."

I chuckled, a little relieved.

"But you *are* in extreme danger," she said.

The smile was gone from my face in an instant. I figured if Isis was making a house call and even took a bus to get here, it had to be bad.

"What kind of danger?" I said.

She took a deep breath, and held my hand. "Someone is going to attack you. Someone desperately wants you to hurry up and cross over . . ."

"Cross over? You mean . . . ?"

"Dead. Someone wants you gone from this world already. Buried. A memory. There's no putting it delicately."

"In my last reading you said someone I knew was going to be murdered. Is it me? After all, I know myself pretty well."

"No. That prediction has already come to pass."

Willard.

"This is different," she said as she rocked back and forth, eyes shut tight.

"Did you see who it was?"

"No."

"Well, can you tell me if it a man or a woman?"

"I don't see gender. Just spirits. And this is a spirit you don't want to mess with, believe me."

"Someone's already attacked me right here in my own home. Is it the same person?"

"I don't know."

"Do you know when this person plans on doing it? Or how?"

Isis solemnly shook her head. "There's a dark energy around you, Jarrod. You must proceed with caution."

I stopped breathing. Even Snickers stopped breathing. We just took this grave news in. I wasn't sure how to process it. I already knew there was someone out there who tried to kill me. But when you have a psychic sitting in your living room saying this person is going to keep trying until he gets it right, it's downright chilling.

"You have to tell me more, Isis," I said urgently. "What else do you see?"

Psychic visions are never black and white. Isis was trying hard to describe what she was seeing, but other than a vague warning, she couldn't muster many specifics.

"Is it Teddy?"

"No," she answered. "I'm sure it isn't someone named Teddy."

If Gladys Phelan's grandson didn't yet know I was close to exposing him, then it would explain why he wasn't concerned with bumping me off yet. But that was little consolation at this point. Isis was a good psychic, and she saw I had an enemy who wanted me dead today. There was only one other person whose name popped into my head.

"What about Spiro?"

Isis convulsed. Her whole body shook, and she gripped the arm of the couch to keep herself upright. Snickers leapt off my lap, and scampered across the room, taking cover underneath the piano bench.

I grasped Isis's hand and held it tight. "It's Spiro, isn't it?"

"It could be him. He has a very dark energy."

"But Spiro has an alibi the night I was attacked."

"I know. But he wishes you weren't around. And it is possible that he could take dramatic steps to insure that you won't be."

"But if it's not him, then who?"

"I'm not sure. But you're fighting for your life. I wish I knew the outcome . . . Just be careful, please, my friend, be very careful."

I wish I could say Isis's batting average wasn't very good. But with me, she was usually dead on, which absolutely scared the living hell out of me.

Chapter Twenty-Four

Iknew in order to find Gladys Phelan's grandson, I had to get a hold of a picture. And to do that would mean breaking into her house and stealing one. I had already been arrested once for breaking and entering in the last month. If I tried it again, not only would it mean another splash on the front page of the tabloids, but also the certain end of my relationship with Charlie. He had put up with a lot from me in the weeks following Willard's death and his tolerance was waning faster than Pat Robertson at a Gay Pride March.

Still, when Charlie arrived home amidst much fanfare from Snickers and me, I filled him in on my day's activities and the progress of my ongoing investigation, hoping he might volunteer to secure a search warrant and get a picture from the old lady himself. He didn't volunteer anything. After a hard day of tracking a gang of gun toting bank robbers, Charlie simply wanted to go to sleep.

I followed him down to the bedroom, and watched him toss off his shirt, wriggle out of his pants, and collapse on the bed in his underwear. He was on his stomach. I crawled on the bed, and gently lowered myself on top of him, nuzzling the back of his neck.

I whispered in his ear, "I love you."

He grunted a reply. I couldn't make out what it was, so I just assumed it was "I love you too."

I debated telling him about Isis's visit. I knew that would get him up on his feet and on the phone to his cohorts downtown, but I decided against it. He was exhausted, and it was time I stopped relying on his patience, his job, his ex-wife, and most importantly, his love for me to see this through. My life as a child star encouraged me to count on others to do everything for me. For the five years I was on a weekly prime time sitcom, adults ran around catering to my every whim—a soda, a sandwich, a script draft, a puzzle, a back rub, a new toy—whatever little Jarrod Jarvis wanted. Even when the fame had faded, I surrounded myself with people willing to indulge me. And Charlie, my beloved Charlie, despite his protests to the contrary, was there to make me happy as well. And he did a damn fine job of it. Like nobody else could.

No, I was not going to ask him for a search warrant, nor was I going to worry him by spilling the sordid details of Isis's prediction. This was my problem, not his. And whatever fallout came from it was mine and mine alone to handle. I wasn't going to just sit here waiting for Spiro or Theodore or whoever to try and take me out again. I was going to go on the offensive. Spiro seemed to have an alibi every time something bad happened. So if I wanted to prove he was involved in Willard's death, the attack on me, or even the JFK assassination, then I had to tail him, every moment of every day. That would be the only way I could prove he was a lying scoundrel.

I slowly lifted myself off Charlie and padded out of the room, leaving him to snore softly into the pillow.

I staked out Tamara and Spiro's Bel Air home for six hours before a neighborhood patrol car stopped to ask what I was doing there. I never understood these guys. They're not trained in crime fighting, they're allowed to carry a gun, and they honestly believe they're entitled to intimidate non-residents. I've always thought they were much more of a menace than the thieves they're supposed to protect the rich folks from, and this dirt bag was no different. He pulled up behind my car in his white patrol car, his headlights on high beam, presumably to confuse and disorient me enough for him to gain control of the situation. He swaggered up to my window, which I dutifully opened with the press of a button.

He was young, probably twenty-eight, with a cropped haircut and bulging muscles. He looked good in his dull gray patrol uniform and knew it. I would have bet he had the shirt custom cut to fit his sculpted frame.

"Mind telling me why you're parked here?" he said in a flat Southern California laid-back voice.

I had already grabbed my trusty Thomas Guide, and was flipping through the pages of local maps as I feigned annoyance. "Am I anywhere near the La Brea Tar Pits?"

"Nope. This is Bel Air. You're north west of the Tar Pits. 'Bout a twenty minute drive."

"Seems everything in L.A. is a twenty minute drive."

He didn't crack a smile. What a surprise. "It's five-thirty in the morning. What are you doing sight-seeing so early?"

He had a point. It never dawned on me that he would come out with an intelligent thought. I wasn't prepared for it.

"I want to beat the crowds." It was lame and we both knew it.

"Is this a rental?" he said as he inspected the Beamer.

"No. I'm visiting a friend. Out from Alabama." I added a twinge of a Southern accent at this point to add credence to my cover. He didn't seem to notice that I had no accent before I said I was from Alabama.

"What's your friend's name?"

"Charlie. Detective Charlie Peters. Works downtown. We're old college buddies."

I may not have been willing to ask Charlie for any more help, but I certainly wasn't above using his name if the situation warranted it.

"Got his number right here if you want to call," I offered.

He stared a long time, sizing me up. I looked harmless enough. And he knew he could take me in a fight, which gave him peace of mind.

"No. That's okay. I believe you." He had no idea who I was. He probably never watched *Go To Your Room!* Too busy pumping iron. I was relieved and hated him for it at the same time.

"What you want to do is go back down to Sunset, make a left, take Sunset east, all the way to West Hollywood . . ."

He couldn't have picked a worse time to be helpful. It was at that moment the gate separating the world from Tamara's Bel Air mansion swung open, and a snappy red Jaguar sped out. I caught a glimpse of a yawning Spiro behind the wheel as he zipped past me and the droning neighborhood patrol watchman.

"Then you'll want to make a right on Fairfax, which is just past the Virgin Megastore, take that down to Wilshire . . ."

"Thanks," I chirped as I jammed the car into gear and roared away. He wasn't finished but there was no time for pleasantries. Spiro was already half-way down the hill towards Sunset Boulevard.

I jerked the wheel to loop around the bends of Bel Air in a desperate effort to catch up with the Jaguar. The tires on the Beamer squealed as if I were in the opening credits sequence of *Starsky and Hutch*.

Luckily it was early enough that there were very few cars on the road. Once I hit the traffic light at Sunset, I sighed with relief as I saw the Jaguar turn left towards Beverly Hills.

I jerked the wheel again and kept it steady as the Beamer screeched around the grass divider in the middle of the boulevard and tore off after the Jaguar. I tailed it for a few more miles past the Beverly Hills Hotel and finally into West Hollywood.

You always know you're leaving Beverly Hills when the immaculate floral foliage abruptly vanishes in favor of an urban enclave of nightclubs and oversized billboards trumpeting the latest Hollywood movie releases. It was going on six a.m. I pulled over to the curb as Spiro turned the Jaguar into a Starbuck's and got out.

He was wearing a tight green tank top and shorts. He disappeared inside and emerged a few minutes later with a container of piping hot coffee.

He hopped back into the Jaguar, and drove further east, pulling into the large Virgin Megastore complex, which housed not only the massive two level record shop, but also a Wolfgang Puck restaurant, clothing store, day spa, and the always busy Crunch Fitness Center. I knew from Spiro's attire that he was bound for the gym.

I parked one level down from him to avoid being spotted, and then took the elevator to the top level of the complex and the entrance to Crunch.

I wasn't a member of the gym, so I gave Althea, the stunning African-American female receptionist with her perky smile and even perkier breasts, a song and dance about how much all my friends just adored Crunch, and it was high time I considered switching from Gold's. Gold's was their chief competitor, so I knew she would be more than happy to accommodate me.

After signing over a guest pass, she gave me a quick rundown of the facilities. She was so chatty and thorough, I started to fear Spiro would finish and head back to Bel Air before I even had a chance to find him. I heard about the Yoga classes, the hip-hop classes, the personal trainer programs, the state-of-the-art machines, and the steam room. She was a walking brochure. I could never tell if people in Los Angeles really loved their jobs or were just programmed to always be enthusiastic and helpful.

When she finally reached the conclusion of her memorized presentation, she offered to hook me up with one of their on staff trainers. I politely declined, explaining how I was a pro at using all the machines and would just check out the place on my own. Althea flashed me one more winning smile, and then retreated back behind the counter to greet more newcomers.

I scanned the work out room and saw no sign of Spiro. Then, right behind me, I heard a familiar voice. "Jarrod?"

At first I thought Spiro had found me and I had completely blown my surveillance. But the voice had a more feminine tone, and I turned to find Terry Duran, Willard's personal trainer.

"Oh, hi," I said, still searching for Spiro. "I thought you worked at Custom Fitness."

"I do. I have clients at gyms all over town."

As nice as Terry Duran was, I had no time to waste engaging in small talk with her. I didn't want to lose Spiro.

"Have you figured out what happened yet?" she said.

"You mean regarding Willard's death?"

"Yes. Last time I saw you, you were looking for someone who sent him a nasty birthday card."

"Haven't found out who yet. But I'm close. Real close."

I barely glanced at her as I looked around. I didn't want her to think I was one of those horny gay boys who spent all his time at the gym checking out the butts and abs of other male patrons. But that's exactly the impression I gave.

Finally, I saw Spiro on one of the treadmills, engrossed in the *L.A. Times*. Sweat poured down his face, and he had to keep toweling himself off as he caught up on the morning's headlines.

Terry knew I was distracted, so she decided to leave me alone. "Well, good luck, Jarrod. I hope you find the answers you've been looking for."

"Me too." I watched Spiro step down off the treadmill, and saunter into the men's locker room. I suddenly felt bad for ignoring Terry. She was about to disappear in the crowd, when I finally turned to her.

"Still dealing with all those money hassles?" I asked, remembering how important it was to her that Willard pay for his personal training sessions.

"Nope," she smiled. "Picked up a few new clients. Things are much better now."

"Good. Glad to hear it. You take care, Terry."

"Let me know how it all works out," she said as she crossed over to the front desk to greet a client.

I whipped back around and hurried over to the men's locker room.

I felt a burst of hot, steaming air as I entered. There were about ten men in there. A few in white towels shaving in front of the large glass mirror above the row of sinks. A couple more in the shower. Still more stood in front of various open lockers, adjusting ties, rolling on deodorant or slapping their faces with aftershave. I heard one of the showers stop, and the door swing open. I ducked behind an open locker door to watch as Spiro dried himself off, wrapped the wet towel around his waist, and ran his fingers through his hair.

I slipped out of my clothes, grabbed a fresh towel, and padded over to the grooming station filled with shaving kits, combs and other amenities. I squirted some Gillette shaving lotion in my hand and covered my face with it when I saw Spiro round the corner and stop at the sink next to me.

"Good morning," he said, not recognizing my face underneath all the white foamy lotion.

"Morning," I grunted as low and indistinguishable as I could.

Spiro was so into himself he didn't even notice it was me. But if I went through with shaving, pretty soon there would be no foam left to cover my face. And if I just stood there with a Santa Claus beard, I would surely rouse suspicion. So I quickly shaved the foam away, wiped my face with a towel and kept it fastened there as I slipped into the steam room, which was located next to the row of sinks.

I was the only one in there, and the steam was so hot and thick I was barely able to breathe. I stared out the glass door at Spiro, who was immersed in his grooming. If I could stand the heat, I would stay here until he went back to his locker, and then I would wait until he dressed and follow him to his next destination.

I saw a man, wearing just a towel, approaching the steam room. My heart skipped a beat as I saw the shape of an eagle emblazoned on his arm. It was Eli, the tattooed hustler.

I stepped back, deep into the steam room and found a corner behind the tub of coals. It was excruciatingly hot, but I could hide there without anyone noticing me. Unless of course the steam evaporated, then I would be exposed.

I slid back as far as I could as the door to the steam room opened, and Eli entered. He sat just a few feet away from me, but had no idea I was there. He waited a few moments. Then, the door opened again, and Spiro walked inside. They looked around, but the steam was so thick, they couldn't tell who else was in there with them.

"Anybody here?" Spiro asked.

I kept quiet and clasped my knees tightly with my arms to stay hidden. I couldn't believe how much time these two spent together. Were they just secret lovers, sneaking around behind Tamara's back? Or was there something more sinister going on?

Spiro then picked up a bucket of water and poured it over the coals. His dark, hairy legs were only a few inches from my face. The oppressive steam scorched my bare skin, but I stayed silent.

Spiro took a seat on the blue tiled riser next to Eli. They never looked at each other as they spoke.

"I'm finally going to do it. This weekend."

"Do what?" Eli asked.

"Free myself from the old ball and chain."

"You mean . . . ?" Eli's voice quivered.

"She's been bugging me all month to take her to that spa in Palm Springs. Says she needs to get away. Bitch doesn't do anything all day. What the hell does she need to get away *from?*"

"I know you talked about doing it," said Eli. "But I never thought you'd go through with it."

"I'm so tired of her whining, pulled back, ugly face. I want out."

"Don't you think you ought to wait a while, you know, until all the hoopla about her son dies down?"

Spiro cupped his hands behind his head, and leaned back against the tiled wall. "I've had so many fantasies lately. Smothering her with a pillow while she sleeps. Spiking her martini with cyanide. It would be so easy, and then I'd finally be a free man . . ."

Eli's voice was shaky. "You're just going to leave her, right? You're not seriously thinking about . . ."

"I know two things, kid. I want to be done with women. And I want to be rich. Leaving her means no money. So you do the math."

I couldn't believe what I was hearing. I had stumbled upon a murder plot, and it had nothing to do with Willard Ray Hornsby. Spiro was going to kill his adoring wife Tamara.

At least that's what I thought. He didn't exactly come out and say it, but he heavily implied it. It wasn't enough to warrant a call to the police, but as I crouched behind the tub of scorching coals, my body burning from the intense heat, I knew I had to do something to stop Spiro before he got away with it.

Chapter Twenty-Five

As I raced to the bank of elevators that would carry me down to my car in the parking garage, my pager erupted in an incessant buzz. It was Laurette, calling with some new offer of tabloid exploitation. I was sure of it. But my thoughts were on Tamara Schulberg at the moment and her impending date with death. I fished for my keys that were buried amongst some loose change and gum in my pants pocket as I scuffled up to the Beamer. I heard the familiar beep of the car alarm disengaging as I hurriedly pressed the black button on my key chain, whipped open the door, and jumped inside. I revved up the engine, backed out too fast, and clipped a steel pole. I heard a headlight smash to bits, but didn't stop to check the damage. I just cursed to myself as I raced up the ramp towards the exit.

I had to warn Tamara. I wasn't sure if she would believe me. After all, our relationship was rocky enough. She had no reason to trust me. But I at least had to try. Tamara may have been a terrible mother to my old friend Willard, but she certainly didn't deserve to die.

I forgot to get my parking ticket validated at Crunch, so I lost precious time scrounging for enough change to get the parking attendant to open the gate. Neither of us had drunk our morning coffee yet, so there were no smiles exchanged between us. I hurled what quarters I could find at him in a fit of panic, and after stalling a few seconds just to piss me off, he raised the gate, and I sped out of the complex.

It was still early, so Sunset Boulevard wasn't clogged with morning rush hour traffic yet. I sailed through a few yellow lights, and one red without incident as I headed back towards Bel Air.

On the radio, Danny Bonaduce (another former child star from the popular seventies sitcom *The Partridge Family*, which chronicled the adventures of a widow and her five kids who formed a pop singing act) was discussing his wild pre-teen sexual adventures during the heyday of his fame. I guess I should have been glad a club member made good and had his own drive-time radio talk show, but this morning he just annoyed me.

I found myself talking to his disembodied voice. "You're an asshole, Danny."

He kept right on going, getting more graphic with his sordid sex tales.

"Bet you're lying," I said. "You were so ugly as a kid they could've stuck your face in dough and made monster cookies."

I thought that was a pretty good one. Too bad no one else was in the car to help me appreciate it.

Right now it seemed to me that all of us child stars were just sad, pathetic screw-ups, tragedies waiting to happen. It wasn't like I wanted to throw a big pity party or anything. I was just in one of my moods again, where I jump on the bandwagon and proclaim, "Being a child star ruined my life!" Not that kids with normal lives don't have a tough time of it. But it seemed the odds of a child star going down the wrong road in life are far greater.

Kitten from *Father Knows Best* turned tricks for drug money.

Buffy from *Family Affair* overdosed.

Ditto for Kimberly from *Different Strokes.*

And Willard Ray Hornsby was found face down in his lap pool surrounded by a couple of empty tequila bottles.

I swerved the car into the right lane and sped past a city bus.

It wasn't Danny Bonaduce's fault, and I didn't have to take it out on him. The guy was just trying to make a living on the radio. But he was there in the car with me, and I had to lash out at somebody.

"You're a washout as a human being, Danny. You beat up a poor transvestite, for Christ's sakes!"

Yes, even Danny, the Howard Stern of the West Coast, had been in trouble with the law. And now, after breaking into Willard's house with Laurette and getting caught, I was finally able to join the esteemed ranks of busted former child stars with a rap sheet.

As I sped back through Beverly Hills, this unexpected rant was interrupted by my cell phone chirping like a sparrow gone mad. I snatched it up, and bellowed, "What? Hello! What?"

I must have startled whoever was on the other end with my bark because there was a moment of dead air.

"Yes! Hello! Who is this?"

"Jarrod?"

It was Laurette. I rarely heard timidity in her voice. But she wasn't used to hearing me so gruff, not to mention speaking in such a deep, manly voice.

I softened just a bit. "Hi, Laurette. I'm a little stressed. What's up?"

The fire returned to her tone. "I've been paging you for the last hour. Where the hell have you been?"

"Stalking Spiro. You're not going to believe what I've stumbled onto!"

"I got a call this morning, Jarrod. They want you to come in for a meeting. This is big!"

"For the last time, no talk shows! I'm trying to put this arrest behind me now!"

"This is a pilot, Jarrod. An NBC comedy. They say it's a shoo-in for the fall schedule, and they're talking Thursday nights right after *Will and Grace!*"

"An audition?"

"No. A meeting. You don't have to audition. Both the producers *and* the network think you're perfect for the role. Can you believe it? That never happens!"

"What's the part?"

"Who cares? It's NBC! Thursday night! After *Will and Grace!*"

"When do they want to meet?"

"This morning."

"I can't."

"Are you crazy? The last pilot meeting we had was for the Food Network. Drop what you're doing and get your ass over to Burbank!"

"Laurette, Spiro's going to murder Tamara!"

"What?"

She thought she didn't hear me right. So I told her again.

"I overheard Spiro talking with Eli the tattooed hustler in a steam room. It sounded like he was going to bump off Tamara in Palm Springs this weekend! I'm on my way to her house now to warn her!"

There was a pregnant pause. Laurette wanted to be sympathetic, and under normal circumstances I'm sure she would have been, but after all, she was a Hollywood talent manager.

"Is there any way you could foil the murder plot after the network meeting?"

"No!"

"I know, I know. I just had to ask."

"He's got his sights set on the Schulberg fortune, and he knows with Tamara gone, it'll all be his."

"And you think he knocked off Willard to get him out of the way?"

"Absolutely. He didn't want him sniffing around his mother's bank accounts if something happened to her."

"He's evil!"

"Hello! I've been saying that all along!"

"Well, truth be told, Jarrod, the man may be a murderer, but he has helped jumpstart your sagging career."

"My career is not the hot issue, Laurette!"

I desperately wanted to turn the car around and scoot over the hill to NBC. This was one of those opportunities that came around once every twenty years, if at all. I worked for so many years to re-build my shattered career, and finally the universal forces came to-gether to make it all a reality. If I had any fears of winding up as a wax figure in the Museum of Child Stars Gone Bad, then showing up for that pilot meeting would certainly erase them permanently. It was now or never.

As much as every little voice inside of me screamed at me to make that meeting, my gut was urging me on. I kept the car steady, west bound for Bel Air. This was a matter of life and death, and if anything happened to Tamara while I was schmoozing with the network brass at NBC, I would never forgive myself.

"Send my apologies to NBC," I said.

"Jarrod, please, be careful! If Spiro is racking up murders, I don't want him rubbing you out next!"

"I'm at least five minutes ahead of him. I left him back at the gym."

I veered the car through the majestic iron gates that lead up into the hills of Bel Air and raced towards Tamara's sprawling estate.

"You're absolutely sure you heard Spiro right? He was definitely talking about murdering her?" Laurette asked.

"Yes."

"Call Charlie. Wait for him to bring some back up before you do anything."

"I'm not *that* sure."

"Jarrod, don't do anything crazy. Just call . . ."

"Got to go. Call you later."

I hung up. I knew Laurette was right, but there was no time. I had to talk to Tamara before it was too late.

I squealed the car to a stop just outside the weathered gate that enclosed the house from the main road. I rolled down the window, reached out and pressed the white button on the call box. After a few moments, I heard a distinct Latino voice speak through the static. "Schulberg residence."

"I need to speak with Tamara. Is she there?"

"She not here. This the housekeeper."

"It's an emergency. Where can I find her?"

"She not here."

"I know! Where can I find her?"

"This the housekeeper."

I wanted to scream, or threaten deportation if the woman didn't cooperate. But anger never gets you anywhere. Kindness is always the best approach.

"What's your name?" I said, purring like a sleepy kitten.

"Rosalita."

"Hi, Rosalita. This is Jarrod, a good friend of Mrs. Schulberg's. I have a very important message for her."

"She not here."

"I know, Rosalita. You've told me that. Three times. But I need to speak with her."

"She gone. Won't be back until Sunday."

"Did she go to Palm Springs?"

"I'm not supposed to say."

"Do you know where in Palm Springs?"

"I'm not supposed to say."

"This is a matter of life and death, Rosalita. I have to talk to her!"

"Sorry."

There was a click and the static on the box cut off abruptly. Rosalita had hung up on me. Spiro was meeting her in Palm Springs. But where? I knew they were going to a spa, but which one? There were dozens of spas in Palm Springs and the surrounding area. I had no clue how to find them. But if I didn't try, then Tamara would certainly wind up dead and I'd never be able to live with myself.

The Spanish maid wasn't going to talk even if I showed up flanked by an army of INS agents.

I had one other option. I knew someone who would be able to tell me exactly where Spiro was meeting her. It would be risky, but I had no choice. Willard Ray Hornsby's mother and I had never gotten along in all the years we had known each other. The fact was I disliked her enormously for the choices she made and for the shoddy way she treated her only child.

But today, I knew I had to save her.

Chapter Twenty-Six

When I returned to the house in Laurel Canyon where Eli the tattooed hustler lived, I wasn't sure what to expect. The memories of him trying to drown me just days earlier were both vivid and disturbing, and it was possible he might perform an encore once he saw me again.

As I made my way towards the guest house in the back, I was relieved to see the three gardeners who had rescued me from the drink the last time, dutifully trimming the hedges and sweeping up stray leaves. The younger one with the dazzling white teeth flashed a blinding smile and waved enthusiastically.

"Watch your step, sir. I would hate to see you fall in the pool again!"

The other two older men all smiled politely and went about their business.

I nodded to the younger man. "Don't worry. Nothing's going to happen to me today." In fact, I was sure of it. With the gardeners milling about the backyard, Eli would be hard pressed to try something in plain view.

"Looking for somebody?" a voice asked from behind.

I turned to see Eli, wearing only a tight red Speedo and Armani sunglasses, lying on a chaise lounge and nursing an Amstel Light beer.

"Yes," I replied. "You."

"Well, lucky you. Here I am."

There was something off. I couldn't quite put my finger on it. But Eli was acting strange, like he had no recollection of our previous encounters. He stared at me with vacant eyes.

"I need some information. And you're going to tell me," I said. "You're going to be nice and behave this time, or I'll have my boyfriend the cop boot your ass in jail again."

Eli sized me up before responding, like he was deciding the best way to handle me. "I'm just soaking up the sun, enjoying my beer. I don't want to cause any trouble."

"I saw you at Crunch with Spiro. I heard everything. I don't know what your role is in all of this yet, but I do know if anything happens to Tamara Schulberg, you're going to be charged with accessory to murder."

"Now that would be a big pain, wouldn't it?"

It pissed me off that he was so calm, but I kept my cool. "I think you better tell me where in Palm Springs they went."

"Haven't a clue."

"I was in the steam room. I heard you talking. You know the place he was taking her. Tell me, or I call the cops."

That's when I noticed his nose. It was perfect. I remembered before it was bent, like it had been broken. Had he gotten surgery to fix it in the interim? It was very distracting.

Eli took a swig from the bottle and smiled. "Wish I could help you, but I can't."

I made my second observation. Eli the tattooed hustler had no tattoo. There wasn't a trace of that distinctive eagle on his arm. I finally woke up.

"What's your name?"

"Elliot."

"Eli's twin."

"Uh huh."

"Down visiting. From San Francisco, I bet."

"Uh huh."

He was quite pleased with himself. I was sure they tricked unsuspecting people all the time for kicks. I was just another rube to toy with.

A voice called out from behind me.

"You here for another swimming lesson?"

I turned to see Eli, in a matching red Speedo, emerging from the main house with a beer in his hand. The eagle glistened on his right arm. Thank God. Otherwise, I might have been dealing with triplets.

"Just having a nice chat with your brother here."

Elliot turned himself over on his stomach and let the harsh rays of the sun wash over his back. "He's looking for your pal Spiro. Says he knows all about his big plan."

"You don't know nothing," Eli said as he popped the top off his beer.

"Oh, that's where you're dead wrong, Eli. I know you no longer have an alibi for the night Willard Ray Hornsby was murdered."

He looked at me. I detected faint creases of worry on his forehead. Finally, he wasn't so cocky and cool. My surprise visit today had messed up his story pretty good.

"You said you were dancing in a bar in San Francisco the night Willard was murdered," I said. "You told me there were a bunch of old farts there who would corroborate your story. So tell me something, Eli, you think any of them will remember your eagle tattoo?"

I thought he might lunge at me right then and there and try to finish the job he started during my first visit, but the gardeners were still on the property trimming and sweeping so his hands were tied. I felt incredibly confident at this point because I knew I had him.

"You figured the cops would question all the men who were in the Castro bar that night, show them your picture, and they'd recognize you as the sexy dancer who got a whole lot of dollar bills stuffed in his g-string. But it wasn't you. It was your identical twin brother."

"I didn't kill *anybody*, you understand?"

"Then why'd you lie?"

"I told you . . . it's easier for the cops to pin a murder on someone like me, a pay and play kind of guy. I was protecting myself."

"Was it Spiro?"

"No. He never had any plan to kill Willard."

"Just his wife."

He didn't respond.

"Talk to me, Eli. Tell me where they went."

Eli glared at me defiantly but I noticed his hand shaking. He wasn't as tough as he pretended to be.

"If you don't talk, then a woman's going to wind up dead and it'll be on your conscience," I said.

"Tell him, Eli." Elliot stood up and put an arm on his brother's shoulder.

"Look, Spiro says a lot of things. It doesn't mean he's going to actually . . ."

Elliot grasped his brother's arm and shook it. "Do you really want to take that chance?"

It was obvious Elliot was the one who got the brains when they were being passed out. But at least, for the first time, I saw a trace of humanity in Eli.

He stared at the ground, and finally said in a low, defeated voice, "Two Bunch Palms."

I knew the place. It was a former compound hidden in the desert by a cluster of majestic palm trees once owned by gangster Al Capone. In recent years it had been transformed into a world-class spa. I dragged Charlie there two years ago to celebrate our first anniversary. I spoiled myself with salt glow herbal wraps and exfoliating mud baths, while a bored Charlie mostly just read a Tom Clancy novel.

I darted back to my car without saying another word. It was a two-hour drive to the desert and both Tamara and Spiro had a good head start. Eli was young, scared and stupid. But I believed him. Okay, he did try to drown me, but I was beginning to wonder if he would have ultimately had the guts to finish the job if the gardeners hadn't surprised him. He was just a street kid who got charmed by yet another slick older man, much like the older man who owned the guesthouse where he lived. Eli was Spiro's pawn. He was drafting this kid into all kinds of sordid affairs, including a possible murder plot. He was in way over his head, and had crippling low self-esteem. Poor kid figured just because he was a hustler, the cops would use him as a scapegoat. Which would explain the elaborate lie involving his twin brother.

I jumped behind the wheel, and tore off down the hill. The plan was to hop onto the Hollywood Freeway, which connects to the San Bernardino Freeway, and ultimately spills out into the desert. I prayed traffic would be on my side, and that I would make it to the spa on time.

I debated calling ahead to the Palm Springs police and warning them about the impending murder attempt. But would they believe a disgraced actor who had been plastered all over the tabloids lately? No one was willing to take me seriously, especially the police. And since I wasn't even one hundred percent sure what I heard in the steam room was an actual murder plot, I opted for calling the spa instead. I knew if I didn't immediately get Tamara on the phone, she would never call me back. Why spoil her romantic weekend getaway by talking to *me?* But I at least had to try.

The desk clerk told me Tamara and Spiro hadn't checked in yet. I left my name and cell phone number and said it was an emergency before I hung up.

One thing nagged at me as I careened from lane to lane in an effort to make it outside the city limits, where the unrelenting sea of cars would eventually ease up. If Eli was telling the truth, and my gut told me that he was, then Spiro didn't murder Willard. Eli maintained he never planned on it. So maybe it *was* an accident. Or maybe Spiro got rough with Willard and accidentally killed him and didn't bother to tell Eli. Or maybe this mysterious Theodore Phelan was behind the killing. I still had no idea where to find him. I didn't even know what he looked like. But I had a gnawing feeling that he was already in the equation. I just had to figure out how.

Chapter Twenty-Seven

Dashing Robert Wagner and gorgeous Stefanie Powers played the globe-trotting, impossibly happy married couple Jonathan and Jennifer Hart, who lived off their millions and solved murders for sport in the hit eighties crime series *Hart to Hart*. Yes, it was a knock off of those classic *Thin Man* movies of the thirties, but hell, those were in boring black and white and not as accessible as the Technicolor Harts, who had an adorable dog Freeway, a raspy-voiced, devoted manservant Max, and a custom-made Lear jet at their disposal. I worshipped the Harts, and even wrote letters as a child begging them to adopt me.

Even after I was cast in my own television series, I spent my free hours lobbying the producers to secure Wagner and Powers for a guest shot just so I could finally be reunited with my "other parents." But the stars were well beyond making appearances on highly rated yet critically reviled Friday night family comedies.

They had definitely made an indelible impression on me, and even now, as I raced along the 10 Freeway, east towards Palm Springs, this entire surreal quest to stop a murder at a spa once owned by Al Capone, harkened back to one of those high society murder escapades I watched on *Hart to Hart* as a kid.

In fact, it was a bit scary as I realized just how much I had modeled my life after them—a fancy house in the hills, a happy marriage, an adorable dog with a cutesy name. All that was missing was a manservant, but there was still time. I just hoped that when I got to the spa to confront Spiro, I would be able to muster the same class and style the Harts displayed as they outwitted the bad guys.

I grabbed the cell phone and punched the speed dial button. An annoying beep kept alerting me to the fact that the battery was low, so I knew I didn't have much time to talk. And just to make things even more difficult, I had left the cigarette lighter adapter at home. No chance of juicing it up while I drove.

I hate cell phones and the people who use them, especially in moving vehicles. They're a menace, and already statistics have shown a spike in the number of automobile accidents because of them. But here I was, on a busy California freeway, making a call.

A wailing semi horn jolted me to attention. I had drifted into another lane while searching for Charlie's speed dial button, practically colliding with an eighteen-wheeler. I cursed out loud as I jerked the wheel back to my rightful lane.

I saw the trucker flash me the finger, so I gave him a sheepish shrug to let him know I was aware that it was my fault. There wasn't much else I could do. I was the perfect example of why there should be a law against operating a cell phone without a hands free set. The line crackled and cut out as it rang.

"Come on, Charlie, come on, pick up . . ."

It rang a few more times before I heard a click and then the distant, barely audible voice of my boyfriend.

"Charlie Peters."

"Hi, it's me."

"I can barely hear you . . . Where are you calling from?"

"The car. Listen, my battery's low and I don't have much time. I'm on my way to Palm Springs . . ."

"Where?"

"Palm Springs!"

"What for?"

I tried to fill him in on everything, but the phone kept cutting out and he was only getting bits and pieces.

"You're going to do what?" he asked.

"Stop a murder!"

I knew if he got the whole story, he'd insist I turn the car around and head straight home. He wouldn't hear of me putting myself in peril again. Charlie would just call ahead to the local authorities and send them out to the spa to check out my wild, improbable story. But even though I had overheard Spiro's insidious plot in the steam room, there was still the chance that I was off base. That he was only fantasizing out loud and had no real intention of offing his wife. And once again I would be proven wrong, be publicly humiliated, and lose what little credibility I had left. No, this time I needed to handle things by myself.

I checked the digital clock on the dashboard. Ten forty-five. Tamara and Spiro were probably just pulling onto the private grounds. He wouldn't try anything so soon after their arrival, and their first spa appointment wouldn't be scheduled until at least noon to give them time to check into their bungalow. I had some time.

"Jarrod, are you there?" Charlie's voice bellowed in my ear during a brief moment of clear reception.

"Yes, I'm here. I'll call you after I get to Two Bunch."

"Listen to me, Jarrod, I didn't hear a lot of what you said, but I got enough. I don't want you to . . ."

And then, mercifully, the phone cut out for good. The battery was on life support.

I knew exactly what he was going to say. But how could he possibly be angry with me if I legitimately didn't hear him tell me not to get myself into the middle of anything?

I wasn't sure what I would do once I got to the spa, but the point was to make my presence known so Spiro wouldn't be tempted to try anything. And if I could just corner Tamara somehow and tell her what I heard, she might finally see Spiro for the murderous, money-grubbing cad he was. And even if she didn't believe me, the seed would be planted in her mind, and perhaps a grain of suspicion might grow to the point where she couldn't trust him, and would finally have to leave him. That was the most I could hope for at this point.

But then, in typical California commuting fashion, traffic came to a grinding halt. I was about a mile away from the interchange where four separate freeways converge, just west of the industrial city of Riverside. The bottleneck was more severe than usual, and after tuning into a local radio station for a commuter report, I discovered there was a three-car pile-up ahead.

This was not good. By the time I cleared this mess, I would still be another hour away from Two Bunch. Both Tamara and Spiro, in separate cars, already had a good start, and the longer it took me, the more time Spiro would have to set the wheels in motion for Tamara's ultimate demise.

The accident slowed down the flow of traffic, but it was the gawkers, the curiosity seekers who hit the brakes and craned their necks for any sight of blood and carnage that brought the cars to a full stop. California drivers by nature are a soft bunch. A light rain on the west coast arouses about as much panic as a tropical storm in the south, a blizzard in the east, or a tornado in the north. Cars can be backed up for miles if there's a lone tube sock in the road. I didn't need this delay today, and as I passed the sight of the smashed-up cars, I glanced out to make sure it wasn't Tamara or Spiro.

A Mexican family of four sat sullenly on the roadside, their only means of transportation, a beat up Toyota truck, damaged beyond repair. A few feet away, a tight-faced bottle blonde with teased hair and a cell phone clamped to her ear shouted directions to AAA next to her dented Infiniti.

It would have been easier if it had been Tamara or Spiro. But I tapped my foot impatiently, muttered obscenities at the cars ahead of me, and waited for the traffic to clear. I had no reason to complain. At least I was in a luxury car with a six CD changer and perfect temperature control.

Finally, after an exhausting wait, the lanes opened up and I was on my way again. I knew from my previous visit that Two Bunch Palms had tight security, and no one would be allowed past the gate without a room reservation. So I lost more precious time, pulling off the freeway, finding a pay phone since my car phone battery was nearly kaput, and placing a call to the spa's reservation line. Luckily, there was one room close to the hot pools still available, and I booked it with my American Express. This way, I was a legitimate guest and Spiro would not be able to protest.

By the time I jumped back in the car and was speeding past the barren hills and sporadic cactus trees towards Desert Hot Springs, the outside temperature had soared to over a hundred degrees.

Just as I relaxed a bit, confident I would make it in time, the flashing red lights of a police car filled the back window, urging me to pull over. My heart was in my throat as the older, graying, seen-it-all highway patrolman got out of his car behind me and shuffled up to the driver's window. *What now*, I thought?

"Got a broken tail light."

Great. My bad driving in the Crunch Gym parking lot might cost Tamara Schulberg her life. After a painstakingly slow process of issuing me a warning, the patrolman ripped the official looking piece of paper off his pad and handed it to me. For a brief moment, I wanted to grab his arm and spill everything, how I was on my way to stop a murder, and how he should follow me in case Spiro got out of control. But a cooler head prevailed, and I simply thanked him for the warning. Then I pulled the car back on the road for the last ten minutes of the drive. He followed me for five more miles, so I had to stay close to the speed limit, but after he took an exit towards downtown Palm Springs, I hit the accelerator to make up for lost time.

It was after one in the afternoon by the time I rolled up to the gate that led into this swank private oasis in the middle of the desert.

The smiling, handsome guard (the entire staff of the spa was friendly and nobody was deficient in the looks department) checked off my name, and the gate opened, welcoming me inside.

The grounds were immaculately kept, and the buildings, which included a dining room, spa, and individual bungalows, were built of stone and wood that seemed to melt into the vast, lush foliage of palm trees and natural hot springs.

After checking in, I didn't even bother stopping by my room first. I headed straight past the lush greenery and a small, almost hidden pool where a few guests were lounging about reading Hollywood movie scripts and a couple of self-help books. It was absolutely quiet, as there are only two rules at Two Bunch—don't make a lot of noise and let yourself be pampered.

I swung open the door that led to the underground spa and hurried down the steps to the reception desk. A bright-faced young woman with an impeccable complexion smiled at me and asked if I had an appointment.

"No," I said as casually as I could, "I'm just seeing what time my friends are done with theirs."

"Oh, well, let's have a look. What are their names?"

"Tamara and Spiro."

She perused the slips of paper that were neatly lined up across the desk. Each one contained the name of a guest and what treatment they were currently enjoying, along with a line for them to sign when it was completed and another line highlighted with a yellow marker, where they could write in a tip for their therapist. She picked up one of the pieces of paper and studied it for a moment.

"Here they are. Tamara and Spiro are having a couple's mud bath right now. They'll be done at 2:30."

"Thank you."

I raced back up the stairs and hurried to the south side of the property where the mud baths were located, which I knew from my previous visit.

There was no one to greet me as I entered the open-air reception area, which struck me as odd. Two Bunch prided itself on making everything as easy as possible for their guests. If I had been here for an appointment, I wouldn't have known what to do.

I waited for a few seconds before a slight commotion in the back drew me through a curtain made of thin strands of bamboo. I saw several employees, all marked by their Two Bunch t-shirts with soft, muted colors and white nametags. They were clustered outside one of the mud bath rooms. There was a panicked buzz in the air as I made my way towards them. With each step, my heart sank a little more. I was too late. The traffic jam had delayed me too long. Tamara Schulberg was already dead.

"What's wrong?" I asked one of the employees. Her hair was pulled back into a ponytail giving me a full view of her pale, shocked face. Her hands were trembling.

"Sir, please step outside." Her voice was quivering. Needless to say, it did nothing to stop me.

"I have some friends here," I said as I blew past her. "I want to make sure they're okay."

She was too upset to stop me. And as I pushed my way through the throng of Two Bunch attendants, I was able to get a peek inside the mud bath room.

Sitting in a large wicker chair was Tamara Schulberg, shaking and near hysterics. She was caked in dried muck, and looked like an African tribal woman straight off the cover of *National Geographic*. She clutched a fistful of Kleenex and kept dabbing her eyes.

I breathed a sigh of relief. At least she was alive. I watched her for a few moments as she chattered incoherently to the staff that formed a half circle around her. She was manic, her arms flailing as she spoke.

Where was Spiro, I wondered? Searching the room for any sign of him, my eyes fell to the blue tiled bath that was filled to the brim with a gooey, dark, and filthy mixture of white clay, peat moss and hot mineral water.

I never go in for mud baths. The health benefits everybody raves about are lost on me. I tried it once and spent the next few weeks scrubbing it out of cracks I never knew I had. But it's a luxury for a lot of rich folks, so who am I to deny them the pleasure?

I stared at the dull brown sludge, trying to figure out what was going on, why Tamara was so distraught, and what she was so desperately trying to explain to the tense staff. And then I saw it—a man's arm perched just above the surface. It was sinewy and strong and completely still just resting there on the bed of moist dirt.

Two strapping Two Bunch attendants reached down, one grabbing the arm and lifting while the other reached down to get a grip on the torso. They hauled a man's hulking mud stained body out. That's when I recognized the naked corpse of Spiro Spiridakis, his tortured eyes wide open and staring lifelessly at me.

Chapter Twenty-Eight

A bulked-up officer squeezed into a tan cop's uniform stepped over to me and with a stern voice said, "Please, sir, this is a crime scene. You're going to have to leave."

"But I know Mrs. Schulberg . . ."

He wasn't going to ask twice. He clamped his hands on both my shoulders, and shoved me forcefully back out the door. I could hear Tamara's sobbing voice as she spoke with the other officers gathered around her.

"But it was self-defense. I had no choice . . ."

One of the officers, a woman, with dyed blonde hair and a shapely, curvy body, unhooked a pair of handcuffs from her belt and locked them on Tamara's wrist. She reminded me of Angie Dickinson, who played sexy forty-something Pepper Anderson on TV's *Police Woman* in the seventies. Another officer began reading Tamara her rights.

"You're not listening to me," Tamara cried. "Please, he tried to kill me."

"Tamara!" I yelled just as the door to the cabana was closing on me.

She looked at me, her face a mask of confusion.

"Jarrod?"

I smiled at her sympathetically. I could tell she was trying to figure out what the hell I was doing there. I noticed another officer slip on a pair of plastic gloves and pick up a gun that had been dropped by the side of the mud bath. He sealed it up in a bag.

"What . . . what are you doing here, Jarrod?"

"I was at the gym this morning . . . I overheard Spiro talking to a friend . . . they thought they were alone . . ."

Suddenly her face was full of hope. And for the first time, Willard's mother was relieved that I had once again horned my way into her life.

"He was planning on killing you," I continued. "I came here to try and stop him."

Tamara looked at the officers, who didn't know what to make of my sudden appearance, as if we were all characters in the third act of a Hercule Poirot mystery.

"Oh, Jarrod, thank God," Tamara said as she nearly collapsed, held up by the strong arms of the officers on both sides of her. "They're trying to arrest me for what happened."

"What *did* happen?" I asked.

"We came here for a romantic weekend. Everything's been so tense since Willard's death. We just needed to get away, even if only for a couple of days. We were scheduled for a mud bath treatment, but once the therapist left us alone, Spiro went crazy. He tried shoving me under. I started choking on the mud. He was suffocating me. I just couldn't believe . . . he was capable of doing such a thing."

I noticed the skeptical looks on the police officers' faces. I had to admit, it sounded far-fetched to me too. How could Spiro be so stupid as to do the deed during a mud bath treatment, with a gaggle of nosy spa employees right outside the door? The whole thing sounded completely preposterous. But here I was, backing up Tamara's story. I knew what I heard. Spiro had every intention of offing his wife sometime during their weekend getaway.

"So how did you manage to get away?" I said.

"I don't know," she said. "He held me under by the throat. His hands were so tight, I couldn't breathe, the mud was filling my lungs. But I remembered he always carried a gun, and his tote bag was at the edge of the tub . . . I was able to reach it, I felt for the gun and . . . and . . . I just started firing."

While Tamara recounted her story, a pair of paramedics arrived on the scene and lifted Spiro's lifeless body up onto a gurney. I looked down at him as they wheeled him away. He was covered in blood and mud, his eyes still open in surprise. I felt nothing. Spiro Spiridakis got what he deserved. I only wondered if Tamara was telling the absolute truth.

The officer who pushed me out of the room earlier was now interested in hauling me back inside. A few spa employees poked their heads in to see what was happening as the officer slammed the door on them.

He stood in front of me. "So you're saying he planned to kill her?"

"Yes," I nodded. "Sometime this weekend. That's what I overheard."

"So you believe her story?"

I nodded again.

The officers looked at me, perplexed. Before my entrance, they had figured out the entire scenario. Tamara and Spiro got into an argument. Tamara knew Spiro carried a .38 pistol. And when the fight spiraled out of control, Tamara reached for the gun, and in a blaze of anger, blew six holes in him. But now my sudden arrival threw a wrench in their whole theory, and they weren't too pleased about it.

There was a long silence before Angie Dickinson spoke. "I think we should all go downtown and talk this out some more."

Two Bunch Palms was located in Desert Hot Springs, about fifteen minutes east of Palm Springs. But when the staff of the spa called the local police department to report a shooting on the premises, the "big guns" from Palm Springs were called in, still small potatoes if you live in a teeming metropolis like Los Angeles. But this, after all, was the desert, and not much excitement happened out here. So everybody who carried a badge within a twenty-mile radius was hell bent on showing up.

The officers escorted me to the four squad cars parked in front of the spa's dining room. The flashing red lights managed to stir up a crowd of guests to watch all the commotion. They were decked out in their terrycloth bathrobes with the Two Bunch Palms insignia and their leather sandals, the proper attire for any guest of the spa, day or night.

I was sweating profusely as I was led towards the cars, the scorching sun a relentless reminder of our desert surroundings. We stood waiting for Tamara, who had been allowed to shower off the mud in one of the private cabanas and put on some clothes. When she finally arrived, she looked a bit more relaxed. I think my presence was giving her peace of mind. Who would have thought I of all people could be a comforting presence to her?

We were placed side by side in the back of one of the squad cars and Angie Dickinson got behind the wheel and off we went.

I immediately turned to Tamara. "I'm not sure these cops believe me, but I'll do whatever I can to help you, Tamara."

She threw her arms around my neck and hugged me tightly. She began to cry again. "I've never been so scared, Jarrod . . . I loved him . . . I thought he loved me . . ."

With Tamara at her most vulnerable, I knew this was my best opportunity to try and get her to open up a bit. Her guard was down, her mind was reeling, and we were still a good ten minutes from downtown Palm Springs.

"Tamara, do you know a Theodore Phelan?"

"Who?"

"I think he might have had something to do with Willard."

"No, I don't know anyone by that name."

"What about Spiro?"

"No, I don't think so. But then again, I guess I didn't know anything about Spiro after all, or who he might have known." The tears welled up again, and she was crying again. "Oh God, how could I have been so stupid?"

I rocked her in my arms gently, trying my best to be supportive.

Tamara clawed at my shirt as she sobbed. "I should've seen this coming." Then she laughed wryly, and spit out, "*She* should've seen this coming."

"She? Who's she?"

"Oh, it's nothing. Never mind."

"Tamara, anything you tell me could help. Even the smallest thing."

"It's silly. I went to this psychic reading yesterday. She warned me about Spiro. She kept talking about his dark energy. But she never said he would try and kill me. Guess she's not so good."

I couldn't be this lucky. I kept my voice steady. I didn't want to tip her off that I was about to burst.

"I didn't know you were into that kind of thing."

"I'm not. Willard was always trying to get me to go. He kept giving me this woman's card. And finally, last week, I was feeling so lost and helpless, and I found the card Willard gave me, so I finally called."

I didn't need the psychic's name. I knew it was the same one Willard suggested to me all those years ago when *I* felt so lost and helpless. Tamara Schulberg had received a psychic reading from my beloved Isis. And if anyone could fill in the blanks at this point, it would be her.

But first I had to endure a night of hard questions from the Palm Springs police department, and even Charlie's reach didn't extend to the desert. There would be no phone calls from my boyfriend to fix things. I was completely on my own. And so was Tamara. I was just curious to know if after hours of relentless questioning, her implausible story would still hold up.

Chapter Twenty-Nine

Since I wasn't officially under arrest, I was able to make more than one phone call. My first three were spent tracking down Charlie, who was busting a gang-operated car theft ring downtown. Sometimes it amazed me just how butch he was. If he hadn't just last week surprised me with tickets to the *Sound of Music* sing-a-long at the Hollywood Bowl, I would seriously question his allegiance to the gay community.

Charlie was stunned at the revelations I had stumbled upon in the desert, and dropped everything to race out to my rescue. But even with a flashing red siren slapped onto the roof of his Ford Explorer, it would still be after midnight before he could get there.

Next I called Isis. There was no answer. I waited twenty minutes and called again. Still no answer. I was desperate to talk to her, but common sense told me she was haunting the aisles at Price Club. And if that were the case, she would be gone for hours.

I watched Angie Dickinson escort Tamara out of the interrogation room. Tamara's eyes were red. Her face was pale. I think if she caught a glimpse of herself in the mirror, the shock of her appearance would have killed her. Tamara prided herself on looking stunning, even at her advanced age. She hadn't doled out thousands on new cheekbones and fat injections in her lips to look this haggard after a harrowing attempt on her life by her loving husband.

She saw me sitting in the hall, and came over to join me.

Angie Dickinson scowled at me and said, "We'll be ready for you in five minutes." And then she marched off towards the officers' break room.

Tamara plopped down in the hardback chair next to mine, and fumbled though the contents of her purse. "I know I have a hand mirror here somewhere." I had to distract her from finding that mirror, or all hell would have broken loose.

"How did it go in there?" I said.

She stopped searching for a moment, and stared straight ahead. "They don't believe it was self-defense. They think I'm lying about Spiro trying to drown me in the mud."

"But what about me? I overheard him planning it. They'll have to listen to me. I'm a credible witness. Sort of."

"But you hated Spiro. You've been running around accusing him of killing Willard for weeks. They believe you'll say anything to smear his name."

"There's someone else. The man Spiro confided in. He may not be the most upstanding citizen, but he did tell me you two were coming here. He cared enough to help me. Maybe he'll back me up."

"I hope so, Jarrod. I can't go to jail. I'll never survive in there."

"I don't understand why they won't believe us."

"They're hung up on some stupid little detail."

"What?"

"They want me to explain why there was a bullet in his back if he was facing me when he tried to drown me."

Good question, I thought. The police had a point. For all intents and purposes, Tamara's story didn't make a bit of sense if there was a bullet in his back. And it would explain their frustration with me for showing up to further stack the deck against the focus of their investigation. That Spiro never tried to do her in during a mud bath treatment. That what really happened was simple: Tamara murdered her husband in cold blood.

"So what did you tell them?" I said, as non-confrontational as possible.

She shrugged. "Not much."

She was strangely calm and serene. I found her whole demeanor a little spooky for someone who had just been through such a traumatic ordeal.

She continued in a soft, matter-of-fact voice. "I said he spun around after I shot him the first three times, fell into the mud bath, and I shot him again in my panic."

"And what about the other two bullets? If he was face down in the mud and there was only one bullet in his back, how did the other two find him?"

"I don't know. Maybe I shot him five times before he spun around. My mind's a little fuzzy. It all happened so fast. God, Jarrod, you're worse than the police."

She didn't have a concrete explanation of what really happened. And with me on the scene to back up her story, she didn't feel the burning need to clarify much of anything anymore. Let them prove otherwise.

Tamara Schulberg had just been blessed with a good deal of luck. If I hadn't sped to Palm Springs to save her from the vicious hands of her diabolical husband, her situation would be far more precarious, the probing questions from the Palm Springs police department far more troubling. There was no doubt in my mind that Spiro was planning on killing Tamara. I heard him tell Eli myself.

But what if Tamara had been planning to kill Spiro at the same time he was plotting to do away with her? What if she just happened to beat him to the punch? And this romantic getaway at the luxurious Two Bunch Palms just happened to be her crime scene of choice, too? The problem was, she hadn't thought her plan through carefully. She had hastily concocted the story of Spiro trying to drown her, the gun in the tote bag, the whole self-defense scenario.

It struck me that she might have been acting out of passion, which would explain the lack of forethought in planning his demise, and the giant holes in her story that my presence was helping to patch up.

We sat there in silence as I contemplated the reasons that might have led to Tamara confronting Spiro and ultimately riddling his body with bullets. It all boiled down to one name: Willard. Perhaps all my digging unearthed something that might have illuminated a light bulb above Tamara's head. Perhaps she finally faced the possibility that her husband, whether he did it himself or had someone else do it, was somehow connected to her only child's untimely end.

"Did Spiro kill Willard?" I said.

"No, Jarrod. He did not. I know you want some kind of closure, but believe me, he had nothing to do with it."

"Then why did you kill him?"

She glanced up at me in surprise. A look passed between us. We both knew the truth. Still, for her own well being, Tamara was sticking to her story.

"What are you talking about? I told you, it was self-defense."

I shook my head. "No. The police are right. Spiro may have been planning to murder you, but you had plans of your own. I want to know why."

"I thought you were on my side," she said, her eyes welling up with tears.

"I'm not on anybody's side. Except Willard's."

"What is this sick obsession you have with my son? Why won't you let it go?"

"Because I loved him!"

She stared at me in disbelief. Her eyes betrayed a wariness. She wasn't sure she wanted to hear the details of what I had to say, but I wasn't going to hold anything back anymore.

"That kiss at the rodeo, the one the tabloids splashed on the front pages all those years ago. That wasn't just a captured moment of two confused closet cases exploring some strange, suppressed feelings. That was a picture of two boys in love. He meant everything to me."

"Stop it. No more. He's gone. What's done is done."

I wasn't going to allow her to sweep any of this under the carpet anymore.

"We were only sixteen at the time," I said. "We were both scared about the repercussions, how our families would react. How the whole country would react."

"Why don't you just write a play about it? *Romeo and Julian*. It'll be a big hit with the gays. Just don't share it with me."

Tamara was squirming. Deep down she knew what Willard meant to me, and it made her extremely uncomfortable. I had downplayed my past feelings for Willard because I was afraid of hurting Charlie, the new man in my life, the most important man now. But I couldn't protect Charlie anymore. It had to all come out.

"You knew all along," I said. "Willard told you he loved me. That he was going to keep seeing me. Screw what Hollywood might think. He told you that, didn't he?"

"He was a boy. He couldn't have possibly known what was good for him at that age."

"That's why you forbade him to see me anymore, that's why you did everything in your power to destroy what we had."

"I had to. We were in debt. The settlement from my first divorce couldn't cover expenses. I needed him to keep working."

"So if the world knew Willard was a faggot, your gravy train would've derailed."

She shifted in her seat and refused to make eye contact with me. "Something like that, yes. But I never forced Willard into the business. He chose that for himself."

"He did it to please you. He figured if he were a big star, maybe you'd finally accept him. Why do you think he worked so hard to make it? He just wanted you to love him."

"I *did* love him."

"Did you ever tell him that? That's all he ever wanted to hear."

"I'm sure I did. Many times."

Tamara's eyes flickered, her mind searching for just one instance where she could remember when those words passed her lips. And from what I could see, she was drawing a blank.

"I loved him too, Tamara. I loved him with every fiber of my being. I would've given up my career for him."

The irony was, I was giving up my career for him now. He just wasn't alive to appreciate it.

"Stop it," Tamara said. "I don't want to hear anymore."

"Even after all these years, even now that he's dead, you still can't accept the fact that he was gay."

"He wasn't gay. He was confused. He would've straightened out eventually. But you went and put all kinds of sordid ideas into his head."

"He was who he was. Whether you like it or not. I had nothing to do with it."

"He didn't have many friends when he was a boy. He liked you and trusted you because you were both child actors, and you were both going through the same things. I thought you would be good for him. And then he got . . ."

She blamed me for corrupting her son. Turning him gay. She even blamed me for his contracting HIV. Her backward thinking was misguided and wrong, but I felt sorry for her. I felt sorry for myself too. I had never completely got over Willard. And reliving the past with his mother, dredging up these deep-rooted memories, was difficult and painful for both of us.

And now I understood why Charlie had been so reticent about me diving head first into this pool of secrets and lies. He was afraid of losing me to the past.

I put my hand out for her to take, but she moved away from me and folded her arms. She spoke evenly, her voice void of emotion. "Listen and listen good, Jarrod. I admit Willard and I drifted apart over the years, but after I married Spiro, I tried reconnecting with him. He didn't want anything to do with me, so I had to let him go.

And ever since he died, I've spent every waking moment regretting it, not having some kind of relationship with him while I had the chance. I loved my son. I would never hurt him intentionally. And Spiro didn't kill him. I know that for a fact because he was with me the night Willard died. And whether you choose to believe that or not, it's the truth. So go find this Theodore Phelan or whoever it is you think might be involved, because chances are the real answers are there, not with me."

"You still haven't told me why you killed Spiro."

She took a deep breath, made sure no one was around, and then turned her head slightly towards me without looking at me.

"Fortunately," she said, "I don't have to."

Chapter Thirty

By the time Charlie charged into the Palms Springs Police Department (after hitching a ride with a fellow detective who owned a weekend cabin near Joshua Tree), the officers were finished questioning me. Angie Dickinson spent two hours pumping me for information, and I told her everything I knew. Almost everything. I feigned ignorance when she asked if I knew who it was Spiro confided his plans to in the steam room at Crunch gym. I'm not sure why I was protecting Eli. But he did have enough of a conscience to tell me where Spiro was planning to knock off Tamara, and I did feel strongly that he could be of further help in the future.

My immediate plan was to return to L.A. and talk to him one more time. I still believed he was holding something back from me and I was determined to find out what. And I didn't want the Palm Springs police locking him up in a desert jail cell for collusion before I had the chance.

Charlie was a formidable presence in the precinct, hovering over the small town officers, barking questions about their procedure, and waving his badge around. The ploy worked. They wanted his ass out of there. And they knew he wasn't going to leave without me, so Angie Dickinson finally told me that I was free to go.

After retrieving the Beamer at Two Bunch, Charlie and I stopped at a convenience store on the edge of town to load up on soda and chips for the long drive home. He knew junk food would calm me down and bring me back to a better place.

Still, I was wired enough to try calling Isis three more times on Charlie's cell phone. There was still no answer. I recounted what Tamara had said about her psychic reading, and I was single-minded in my resolve to find out exactly what Isis saw. I wasn't going to let this wait until the sun came up.

By the time we could make out the lights of downtown Los Angeles in the distance, it was going on three o'clock in the morning.

"Don't go home. Head for Isis's apartment."

Charlie raised an eyebrow. "At this hour?"

"She'll be up." I had no idea if that was true, but it sounded confident enough to Charlie, who shot past our exit and took the 10 freeway west towards West Hollywood.

When I rang Isis's apartment, I was still jacked up on caffeine from the sodas and a sugar high from a Mounds bar Charlie had been kind enough to share with me. Charlie stood behind me, a little self-conscious to be calling on someone so late.

A raspy, annoyed voice came over the speaker next to the locked front door that led into the lobby. "Who is it?"

"It's me, Isis. Jarrod. I really need to talk to you."

Charlie leaned over my shoulder and spoke into the speaker. "If it's too late, we can come back tomorrow."

"It's not too late," Isis said. "I'm just reading a few tarot cards and watching TV."

I tossed a self-satisfied smile to Charlie as a buzzer rang, and we pushed the door open.

Isis was in a pink robe and big oversized fur slippers when we entered her apartment. Her hair was a tangled mess. She may not have been sleeping but she certainly wasn't expecting company. On the television was a Psychic Friends Network infomercial. Isis was obviously checking out the competition.

"Can I get you boys something to drink? I went to Price Club today so I'm all stocked up on the super size bottles."

Charlie declined. I was so high I figured another shot of caffeine wouldn't make any difference, so I asked for a Wild Cherry Pepsi. Isis had giant bottles of every kind of soda on the market stacked in her pantry. It didn't matter that she lived alone and could not possibly drink all of it before the expiration date. A good deal was a good deal.

After we sat down, Isis smiled.

"Is this about Tamara Schulberg?"

Charlie sat up. "How did you know—?"

I knocked Charlie's knee with mine to shut him up. I had a plan and I didn't want him spoiling it before I had a chance to put it into effect.

"No. I completely understand that your work as a psychic is confidential and it would be inappropriate for you to share information from another client's reading." I patted her thigh with my hand for punctuation.

"Uh huh." She eyed me suspiciously. This didn't sound like me at all, so she remained on her guard, rightly fearing I might be up to no good.

"You take your work very seriously and I would rather cut out my tongue than risk our friendship by asking you to compromise your obviously strong convictions," I said.

She was suppressing a smile now. This was too much, even for me.

Charlie leaned back on the couch, interlocked his fingers behind his head, and got comfortable. He figured we'd be here for a while.

"You know how you always have psychic visions in your dreams? Well, I had one last night. I had this dream," I said.

Isis's curious nature got the best of her. "A dream? What kind of dream?"

I had hooked her. Isis was obsessed with dream interpretation, and I knew she couldn't resist a challenge. It was also the only thing I could think of at the time.

"Screw the cherry soda," I said. "You got any vodka in the pantry? My throat's a little parched, and this is a pretty elaborate dream."

She was up on her feet in an instant, and heading towards the kitchen. Not only was Isis an amazing dream interpreter, but she was also a consummate hostess. And I was hoping that in the time it took for her to mix me a potent cocktail, I would be able to come up with some dream, any dream that would help bridge the conversation to Tamara Schulberg and her psychic reading a few days before.

Isis didn't have any orange juice or club soda, so we mixed the vodka with one of her super size bottles of Seven Up. Charlie declined. He had to be up early for a raid on another garage that supposedly housed some more car thieves. He was also tired from driving out to Palm Springs and back to fetch me.

I watched Isis fill our glasses liberally, and knew my time was running out. I had to think fast. Once we were settled down with our cocktails, the spotlight would be back on me, and Isis was expecting a doozy of a dream. The pressure was on for me to deliver.

Charlie knew exactly what I was doing, and checked his watch. He was resigned to my schemes, especially at this late hour, but was also interested in what malarkey would come spilling out of my mouth. I was kind of curious too.

As she stirred the drinks with her fingertips, she yawned. "Sorry, I'm a little tired. I had four Reiki clients in a row tonight. That's why I didn't pick up the phone when you called earlier."

Reiki is a spiritual form of healing accomplished through the power of touch. The therapist directs energy through her hands into the body's seven Chakras. Isis was recently annointed as a Reiki master, and was enormously proud of her accomplishments as a healer. She was also easy to flatter. That's when it came to me. I had my dream.

"You are such an amazing psychic, Isis. You already know what I dreamed, don't you?"

She looked at me with a glassy-eyed stare. She wanted to say yes, that her wise mind had already seen and studied what I was about to say, but unfortunately it hadn't. She didn't have a clue, but she knew I considered her my all-knowing guru, so she just stayed quiet.

"It's like we have this powerful mental connection," I said, laying it on thick. "It's freaky that you just mentioned Reiki because that's exactly what my dream was about."

"Oh. Yes. Okay. What exactly happened in this dream?"

"I was giving a Reiki treatment to this older woman. I couldn't quite see who it was. But she was more of an acquaintance than a friend. I was trying to rid her body of all this dark energy inside of her. You know, restore the peaceful glow of her aura. But I couldn't. It just wouldn't go away. What do you think the dark energy represents?"

"I'm not sure," Isis said, her voice tentative. She was still questioning my motives and didn't want to be tricked into talking out of school.

"I kept trying and trying, but the energy was too strong, so full of evil. And that's when this strange apparition appeared above us. It was a man, about my age, who kind of looked like me, and I had this great affection for him. He was just floating above me, crying this warning that I couldn't make out."

I was so caught up in my make-believe dream that I never stopped to think that I might talk myself into a corner. But there I was with Isis and Charlie on the edge of their seats, waiting to hear what came next, and I was stumped. This probably explains why I never excelled at improvisational acting.

So I stopped the story, grabbed the bottle of vodka, and refilled my glass, adding just a splash of Seven Up. I gulped down the cocktail and practically licked off the last remnants of liquor from the half melted ice cubes, hoping and praying that the dramatic pause would give me a few precious seconds to make up the rest of my dream.

Isis was tired of waiting. "What was this spirit trying to say?"

"It said that this dark energy took a human form and was hiding his true self from this woman. This energy, this wicked soul was trying to enslave her, but she didn't see it. It was almost as if he was playing the role of loving husband, but behind the scenes he was another person, this shadowy creature who was preying on her . . . or someone close to her."

Now I knew Spiro had made several passes at his own stepson, and I was betting that it must have come up in Tamara's reading in some form. Fortunately Isis had no idea that I was aware of this juicy tidbit, and I could see from the look on her face that it was killing her not to explain what I was seeing.

I looked at Isis, my eyes full of innocence. "Do you have any idea what it means?"

Isis was itching to divulge everything. Every fiber of her being wanted to talk, but her ethics kept getting in the way. She shook her head.

"Well, don't feel too bad," I said. "Not everybody's good at dream interpretation."

Isis's head snapped to attention. I had called her talents into question. It was too much for her to bear.

"The apparition represents Willard! He was warning his mother about her husband Spiro!"

"Go on."

She paused, debating with herself, and then shifted her gaze towards me. "Now, you can't tell anyone I told you this . . ."

I was next to her on the couch in an instant. "I wouldn't dream of it."

"Promise?"

"Of course."

"When Tamara came to me, she was very upset. Her marriage to

Spiro was crumbling. She felt he was just using her, and let me tell you something: The asshole *was* using her. But that's not the awful part . . ."

"What?" I asked, bursting with anticipation.

Isis became distracted by a loose thread on her bright pink robe. She began to pick at it. It got longer and longer as she pulled, threatening to unravel the garment entirely.

"Isis, talk to me. What were you going to say?"

She let go of the piece of thread and looked up. "You know, most people just want to be friends with me so I'll tell them they're going to win the lottery. They don't really care about me, just my gift. But you, you always loved me for me."

It was true. I did love Isis, and I was sure we would still be friends even if she weren't a dead-on psychic. But tonight, I was obsessed with her gift, and it made me feel like a first class heel because I was forcing her to compromise her principles. She knew it, which was why she was keeping me in such suspense.

"We have a very special relationship and I would never exploit it," I said as I leaned over and kissed her on the cheek. "Now get to the awful part!"

"Spiro did a horrible thing."

"He tried to get Willard into bed," Charlie said.

Isis sat back, disappointed. Charlie had been sitting on the couch, quiet as a mouse, and now at this critical point in our conversation, he decided to pipe in and spoil Isis's big moment. He had sucked the drama out of her revelation. I couldn't believe it. She spun around to Charlie.

"How did you know that?" she asked.

"Jarrod told me."

She whipped back around to me. "You already knew?"

I shot Charlie an angry look for ruining my manipulations, but the jig was up. I nodded somberly.

"Willard's therapist told me."

Isis snorted, indignant. "How could he violate his client's trust? Doesn't he have any professional ethics?" The irony of this statement, in light of her own gossipy nature, was lost on her.

"The therapist doesn't have to worry about ethics anymore. He's dead," Charlie said.

"Oh," Isis said, the anger draining out of her face.

I thought for a moment that we were done. My plan had been to use my dream to at least get Isis talking about Tamara's reading; first about Spiro's despicable behavior involving his stepson, and then perhaps something more that might help tie it all together. But Charlie's interruption threw all that into jeopardy.

"Charlie, maybe you ought to wait downstairs," I said trying to put a lilt in my voice to cover the fury. I failed miserably.

"Now don't be mad at Charlie," Isis said. "I've been reading you for ten years, Jarrod. I saw right through you the minute you came in the door."

I nodded, chastised, and then rose to leave.

"Not so fast. I know how much you cared about Willard. I adored him too. Next to you, he was one of my favorite clients. So I think his spirit will be okay with me sharing a few things with you."

I was back down on the couch. She had something good. I could feel it. And I could tell she was already in the mood to gossip, and Charlie's interruption was not going to deter her from getting some kind of rise out me.

"I saw it all. And, of course, at first Tamara insisted I was wrong. That it had to be the other way around. She tried conning herself into believing it was Willard who tried putting the moves on Spiro. But deep down she knew the truth, and I helped her to face the reality of what really happened."

"So when she left here, she was finally convinced Spiro was the one who betrayed her?" I said.

"Yes," Isis said.

I sat back and looked at Charlie and Isis. I must have chugged my last cocktail too fast. I was now seeing four of them.

"She was devastated," Isis said. "I mean, the poor woman came to me hoping I would advise her on how to fix her marriage and what do I do? I deliver the deathblow. She just kept sobbing and sobbing. I tried to comfort her. But I felt I was right in convincing her." Isis stared into space, remembering. "It was a very difficult reading."

"How did you leave it?" I asked.

"She was in such a state. She wanted me to try and raise her son's spirit so she could beg his forgiveness, but I don't do that sort of thing. I told her to get tickets to the *Crossing Over* show with that hottie John Edwards. I just said her marriage had been over for a long time, and this was the information she needed to end it immediately and move on. I warned her that when she confronted her husband he would try to dismiss me as a fake and say her son was lying. But she had to listen to what was in her heart, and in her heart she knew he had done it. She had to accept it. I told her she was strong enough to get past it. It was time for her to begin a new phase in her life, to put Spiro's dark energy behind her, and focus on the positive."

"What did she say?"

"She said she had every intention of focusing on the positive. She was going right home to kill the dirty, lying bastard." Isis stopped and thought for a moment. "I thought she was just being dramatic."

I wobbled a bit, using Charlie's knee to steady myself as I stared at Isis in shock. And my favorite psychic and Price Club spokeswoman sat back with a proud grin. She had gotten just the reaction out of me that she wanted.

Chapter Thirty-One

"I want to thank you, Jarrod," Tamara Schulberg said. "I never dreamed you would turn out to be my knight in shining armor."

I shrugged. "I just told the police what I heard."

She smiled. "I don't mean for backing up my story. I mean for dashing out to Palm Springs to save me. After how I've been acting, I'm surprised you didn't just sit back and let the bastard get away with it."

"I guess I'm not built that way."

Charlie and I had barely fallen into bed after returning home from Isis's apartment when the phone rang. It was Tamara, just back from the desert and desperate for me to rush over. I had known her son for most of my life, and this was the first invitation I had ever received to actually enter the formidable iron gates of her Bel Air home.

I let Charlie drift back to sleep, and then I jumped in the shower, threw some clothes on, and hopped in the car. There was very little traffic so early in the morning, and I made the trip to her house in less than half an hour.

I rang the buzzer, and Tamara's housekeeper opened the gates.

As I passed on through into the blooming foliage that lined the gravel driveway, I noticed the house was an exact replica of Tara, Scarlett O'Hara's Civil War plantation in *Gone With the Wind*. Tamara may have been a fixture of the Hollywood scene for decades now, but she was still a southern girl at heart, and this home was a testament to her heritage.

I parked the car and before I had a chance to ring the bell, the door opened and Tamara's housekeeper, a large stout woman with a stern face, ushered me in and led me through the hallway, past the kitchen, and into the backyard, where Tamara sat at a round glass table next to a kidney-shaped pool with a small waterfall.

She picked over a silver bowl of fresh strawberries and blueberries and clutched a champagne glass filled with what I assumed was a mimosa. When the housekeeper handed me my own champagne glass, one sip confirmed it. Tamara was always up for a buzz-inducing drink, even at six in the morning. Never too early to dull the pain.

I never expected Tamara to invite me over to her house to thank me. I thought, if anything, she would warn me to stop hounding her or else I would wind up with a gut full of lead like her nasty husband Spiro. But given everything this woman had been through in the last few weeks—losing her son, facing yet another bad choice in men (the worst yet), and escaping a near arrest for murder—she was a bit more reflective and subdued.

Tamara stared at the pool, her eyes hidden behind an expensive pair of Gucci sunglasses.

"You were right, Jarrod. I did blame you for Willard being gay. I needed some reason to explain it. And because you two were so close, I decided it had to be your fault. He probably would have been very happy with you. He'd probably still be alive."

Her face remained still, but I could tell she was crying. She adjusted her giant sunglasses to make sure I didn't see the tears streaming down her cheeks.

"We were kids," I said softly.

"What bothers me the most . . ." Her voice got caught in her throat. She was trying to maintain her composure, but talking about Willard was difficult for her.

She cleared her throat and continued. "What bothers me the most is that he wanted to please me so much that he gave up you, his first true love. He let you go because he was so desperate for me to accept him and love him. And yet, I kept distancing myself from him. My only son . . . I pushed him away . . . just because he wasn't what I wanted him to be."

"I think he knew you loved him."

"You're just being nice. He never knew. Sure, I used to tell him all the time when he was a big star. But then, after you two were in the tabloids, and the work stopped coming, I resented him. I thought his life was over at sixteen years old. And I never told him how I really felt ever again."

She threw her hands to her face and began sobbing. I sat there watching her in so much pain, and I felt helpless.

She grabbed a cloth napkin off the glass table and dabbed at her face.

"And then I go and marry Spiro . . . who . . . who does the un-thinkable . . . to my own son . . ."

Her voice trailed off. We sat there in silence for a while, and then she gathered the strength to continue, to get everything off her chest.

"I had heard rumors about Spiro after we got married. Christ, we even paid off a hustler or two to keep quiet about his past, but I never in a million years ever thought he would go after Willard. When I left the psychic, I ran home and just threw up. For hours. I stayed in the bathroom, hunched over the toilet, unable to lift my head. Every bone in my body ached." She swallowed the rest of her Mimosa. "And then I got mad. Frightfully mad. I wanted him to pay."

"And that's when you decided to kill him? I know you did, Tamara. It's only a matter of time before the police prove it."

She didn't even flinch. She just kept staring at the pool. I had no idea what was going on behind those large Gucci sunglasses, but I could tell she knew I was right.

"I didn't know what I was going to do," she said. "I was so confused. Did Willard kill himself because Spiro drove him to it? Did he get drunk to forget that his own stepfather had tried to put the moves on him? Or . . . did Spiro hire someone to . . . ?"

She let the idea hang in the air. Tamara picked up a strawberry and took a bite. "It wasn't premeditated. I didn't go to Palm Springs to murder him. I was going to confront him, have it out, demand a divorce. But when I broached the subject, he was so arrogant, so unapologetic. He didn't even care that I knew he made advances towards Willard. In his mind, he had already decided to kill me. I knew he carried a gun. I grabbed it and started firing. Bang! Bang! Bang! It felt so good. The shock in his face was worth the life sentence I would probably get for doing it. Honestly, Jarrod, deep down I felt killing Spiro was the first positive contribution besides Willard that I ever made to this world."

I noticed the housekeeper hovering by the open sliding glass doors that led into the kitchen. She was getting quite an earful. But she was loyal to her mistress, and would never rat on her. I, on the other hand, was the wild card. What made Tamara think I wouldn't rush right home and recount all the gory details to my policeman boyfriend? At the moment she didn't seem to care.

"I was consumed with so much anger, so much passion," she said. "I never bothered to stop and think of the logistics or how I would explain it. But then you just showed up out of nowhere with a story that put me in the clear. It might as well have been gift-wrapped with a big red bow on it."

"Tamara, why are you telling me all this?"

"Because . . . for so long I've been such a scared little rabbit, so afraid I might make Spiro angry . . . Well, now Spiro's gone . . ."

Thanks to her, I thought, but I wasn't about to say it.

"And now I want to set things right . . . with my son, with everyone. And if Willard is up there watching me, maybe just this once, he'll have reason to be proud. I don't even care if I go to jail."

"You won't go to jail."

She snorted. "It was a long drive back from Palm Springs this morning. I had plenty of time to think about telling you all of this, and what the consequences would be. Believe me, I went around and around and I kept coming back to a picture of me in a drab gray smock with an embroidered number on the front."

"We can always keep this between us," I said.

She looked at me. I couldn't tell if she was relieved or angry that I wasn't going to share this information with the police. In Tamara's mind, I believed there was a part of her who wanted to be punished for her past sins, and that giving up her freedom was a small price to pay for abandoning her only son. But I had other ideas.

"I'm never going to breathe a word about this to anyone, Tamara. Because I know in my heart that Spiro had every intention of killing you. He was a callous and ruthless human being and no one's ever going to miss him. What if you hadn't shot him in the mud bath? Then he would have found the opportunity to do the same to you. And now you'd be dead, and he'd be here to carry on. To hurt more people."

I stood up and put my hand on her shoulder. She gently rested her face on my forearm. "And the only other outcome I can think of," I said, "would be if you had managed to defend yourself from his attack, and if that had happened, then Spiro would still be dead and we'd both still be here now. So in my opinion, everything worked out the way it was supposed to."

She wasn't entirely convinced I was right. And to be honest, neither was I. But the logic made us both feel better, and I was betting this would be the last time either of us ever discussed it.

Tamara kissed my arm, and then stood up. She took her sunglasses off and smiled at me. For the first time I noticed she had the same haunting green eyes as Willard.

"You've got a good soul, Jarrod. I wish I had been smart enough to see that when you were sixteen. It might have saved us both a lot of heartache."

I gave her a peck on the cheek and turned to leave.

"Jarrod?"

I swiveled back around on my heel.

"There's one more thing. I didn't tell you this earlier when you were asking questions about the night Willard died because I was afraid it might somehow implicate Spiro, and I honestly didn't think it meant anything."

"What?"

"Earlier that day I heard Spiro on the phone. He was talking in hushed tones and being very secretive. I started to suspect he might be having an affair with another woman, maybe one of my friends he was always flirting with, so I picked up the other line to listen. He was talking to a young man. It sounded like Spiro was pressuring him to do something for him, and the young man sounded agitated, but before I could make out what they were talking about, Spiro hung up."

"Did you get the man's name?"

"No. But later I asked Spiro about it. He said it was a massage therapist. He knew Willard liked to get bodywork done to relieve his chronic tension, and this was a guy Willard hired on occasion. Spiro told me he was going to treat Willard to a massage for his birthday, and was just setting up the appointment."

I knew the young man she was talking about was Eli. And Eli had never mentioned that he had been at Willard's house the night he died. It was worth another trip to find out why he omitted such a crucial piece of information.

Tamara sighed. "I let myself believe whatever Spiro told me. I could barely accept the reality of my son being gay. To even speculate about my husband was too much to bear. I don't know what this man's relationship was to Spiro, but they sounded close. Close enough that this man was willing to drop everything and do whatever Spiro wanted."

"I promise you, we will get to the bottom of this. And you'll know what really happened to your son," I said. "I'll make sure of it."

She put her sunglasses back on and returned to her private world of grief as I bolted back through the house towards my car. I was heading straight for Laurel Canyon and one final confrontation with Eli the tattooed hustler and his identical twin brother Elliot.

Chapter Thirty-Two

As I roared up toward the top of Mulholland Drive, a famous twisting and treacherous stretch of road on top of a mountain that straddles the city of Los Angeles and the San Fernando Valley, I jammed my cell phone into its cradle for a quick charge-up. It had been dead since Palm Springs and was in desperate need of an energy boost. I finally remembered to bring along my cigarette lighter adapter from home. An actor without a cell phone was about as useful as a web designer without a computer.

I was overwhelmed with theories. Had Eli been conning me from the start? His valiant show of vulnerability during my last visit had completely won me over. I believed his sincere plea of innocence. I even bought into his fear of Spiro. Was it all an act? Did he help me out by telling me where Spiro planned on doing away with his wife just to throw the scent off him? And what about his walking reflection, Elliot? He was the one who persuaded his brother to talk. Was it out of concern for Tamara's fate, or part of a cool pact with his brother to cover up a murderous misdeed they had pulled off together?

As I jerked the wheel and flew up Laurel Canyon Boulevard on the city side of the hill, I knew I would have to wing it once I found the brothers. But I had been a pit bull all along, grabbing onto tiny pieces of evidence and not letting them go, and I wasn't about to soften up now when I was so close.

I didn't even make it to the house on Lookout Mountain. As I rounded a steep corner, I saw two lean hard bodies up ahead, both in matching blue shorts and white tank tops, jogging down the canyon road side by side.

I zipped past them before I had a chance to get a good look at them. Staring back at them through the rearview mirror, I concluded it had to be the twins. Who else had such gloriously matching tight asses? I must have stared a few seconds too long because when my eyes glanced back at the road in front of me, a speeding black SUV was directly in front of me. All I could see was a junior development executive with a smart suit and frizzy red hair, cell phone clamped to her ear, screaming at our impending collision.

I spun the wheel with all my might and slammed on the brakes. The Beamer squealed off the road, hurling dirt and brush into the air before barreling into a ditch and screaming to an abrupt stop. It was a miracle I didn't hit a tree, but nevertheless, the airbag sprung out of the steering wheel, pinning me in my seat. The SUV disappeared, racing to one of the studios around the bend where the D-girl inevitably had a breakfast meeting with Ben Affleck or another rising generation Y star of his magnitude.

I sat in my car, trapped for a few moments before a shadow fell over me. I looked up to see Eli and Elliot, both dripping with sweat that glistened in the morning sun, staring down at me with big smiles on their faces.

Eli spoke first, and I could only tell it was Eli from his eagle tattoo. "If you wanted to get our attention, you could have just waved."

"Are you all right?" Elliot asked as he and his brother opened the car door and tried to extricate me from the suffocating air bag.

"No, no I'm not all right," I said huffily.

Each twin grabbed one of my hands and yanked hard. I fell out of the car into their waiting arms. If I weren't so suspicious of them at this point, I would've enjoyed the moment more.

"Are you hurt?" Eli checked me over for wounds.

"No. I'm pissed. I'm pissed at you, Eli. For lying to me."

The brothers exchanged a quizzical look. Eli was cute on his own. But standing next to his brother, they were a pair of aces to die for. I attempted to put any carnal thoughts out of my mind by trying to remember that at one point Eli had gone to great efforts to drown me in a lap pool.

"You were at Willard's the night he died."

"No, I wasn't." His voice cracked. He was a terrible liar, which made me believe he had been telling me the truth before.

"Tamara Schulberg heard you on the phone with Spiro. He was hiring you for a job. Was it to kill Willard?"

"No!"

"Did you get him drunk and drown him in the pool?"

"No, I didn't do anything!"

"Come on, Eli, you expect me to believe that?"

"He didn't hurt anyone. Eli would never do anything like that," Elliot interjected as he put a comforting arm around his brother.

"In case you're both suffering from a memory lapse, Eli had no trouble dunking me when I asked too many questions about Willard!"

"He was scared," Elliot said, "He was only trying to warn you off."

"Why? What did you have to hide, Eli?"

Eli gazed at the gravel. Dust was settling from my hair-raising near accident, and morning traffic was picking up as we stood at the side of the road. "I did go over there that night, but I didn't kill him."

"I'm listening."

"Willard and I knew each other for a couple of months. He saw my ad in *Frontiers*, and started calling my voice mail. I'd go over to his house once, maybe twice a week. He really dug me, and to be honest, I really liked him. Even though he paid me for my time, I always looked forward to seeing him. We didn't always have sex. Sometimes we'd just hang out and talk. God, I used to think it was such a shame we hooked up the way we did, because if we had met at a cocktail party or in a bookstore, it might have been a completely different kind of relationship. Something real, you know?"

"Sounds like it was real," I said.

Eli nodded perfunctorily. He didn't necessarily believe me. Like most hustlers, no matter how good-looking they are, they rarely overflow with a lot of self-worth.

"He confided to me that he was having trouble with his stepfather," Eli said.

"I know all about that. How Spiro made a pass at Willard, and got rejected."

"He wouldn't take no for an answer. He kept following him. Everywhere Willard went. To auditions. To his therapist. There was no getting rid of him. He was terrified Willard was going to blow the whistle on him."

"What got you involved?" I asked.

"One night when I was leaving Willard's, I saw Spiro lurking in the shadows. He watched me leave. I was worried about what he was going to do to Willard, so I came back to check up on them. I heard them shouting. Willard was threatening to go to his mother if Spiro didn't leave him alone and Spiro was trying to push his way inside. Finally, Spiro gave up and left. About a week later, I got a call from Spiro. He wanted to hire me."

"To do what?"

"Scare the shit out of Willard."

Eli sighed, a shameful look on his face.

Elliot piped up, "Eli needed cash badly. We both owed a lot of money, and neither of us knew what we were going to do. We were under a lot of pressure, and the tips I was making up in San Francisco weren't going to cover our debts."

"So he offered to pay you to go rough up Willard a little bit, threaten to bash his head in with a baseball bat or something if he breathed a word to his mother," I said.

Eli nodded. "Something like that. Yeah."

Elliot, responding to an innate need to protect his twin, interjected, "It's true Eli went over there, but he wasn't going to hurt Willard. He was just going to try and reason with him."

"What happened?" I said.

"I called Willard, told him I knew it was his birthday, and offered to come over and give him a free massage. He said some friends were throwing him a party that night, but if I could get to his place by four-thirty, we'd have time for a session. When I got there, he was feeling pretty good. I guess he had just landed some kind of part on TV or something, so we celebrated."

"You gave him a massage?"

"Among other things."

"Then what happened?"

"I was going to hold him down while we were fooling around, slap his face a couple of times, and tell him who had really sent me there and why. But I couldn't. He was so happy. Between getting the part and you throwing him a party, he was walking on air. I couldn't ruin all that. It was then that I realized how much I cared for Willard. I could never do anything to hurt him."

"So you left him there alive?"

"Yes. I left and called Elliot in San Francisco. I didn't know what I was going to do. Spiro had already paid me a thousand bucks. I was a mess."

"I told him to keep the money and skip town," Elliot said. "Willard was heading off to your party. Calling his mother was the last thing on his mind. We knew we had some time before Spiro found out Eli didn't go through with it."

"I headed for San Francisco the next morning," Eli said. "I had been on the 5-freeway north about ten minutes when I heard on the radio that Willard had died. I knew then that Spiro would never find out that I didn't do what he paid me to do."

"Weren't you afraid Spiro would think it was you? That you went too far and accidentally killed Willard instead of just scaring him?" I asked.

"Maybe for half a second," Eli said, "But then I thought, if he tells anyone, he's only implicating himself."

"And you swear what you're telling me is true?"

"Yes," Eli said emphatically. "On my life."

I must have given him a look that said I wasn't one hundred percent convinced, because he followed up with, "On my brother's life."

I finally believed him.

"What time did you leave Willard that night, Eli?" I said.

"Five-thirty, six at the latest. Why?"

"I spoke with Willard on the phone around seven-fifteen and he was just leaving for my house. So whoever killed him had to have arrived sometime after we hung up."

Flashes of Willard's body face down in the pool kept distracting me. I saw the empty tequila bottles next to the chaise lounge. "There was a lot of alcohol found in his system. Did you two have a drink to celebrate his birthday?"

Eli shook his head.

"Not even a glass of wine? There were two glasses and a half empty bottle on his coffee table."

"Willard never drank before he worked out. He must have had it after."

"Excuse me?"

"He called his trainer while I was there. I remember him joking that he had to burn off ten pounds in forty-five minutes if he was going to spend the whole night stuffing himself with ice cream and cake."

There was no way Willard could have driven to Custom Fitness on Melrose Avenue, worked out with his trainer, showered, got dressed, and driven to Beachwood Canyon in such a short amount of time. I spoke with him by phone at seven-fifteen, which meant if he had worked out, it was an in-home session. That put one more person at his home the night he died: his personal trainer Terry Duran.

Chapter Thirty-Three

By the time I arrived at Custom Fitness on Melrose, the hot summer sun was descending in the west. A cool breeze swept through the city, and there was a strange tension in the air, as if the universe was trying to tell me something, but I unwisely chose to ignore the signs, again.

I raced up the steps to the second floor of the building and found the gym empty except for a perky brunette with a pixie cut, wearing a bright blue form-fitting spandex one-piece.

She flashed me a wide smile. "Can I help you?"

"I'm looking for Terry. She around?"

"Nope. Finished up with her last client about an hour ago."

"Oh, we were supposed to work out."

She frowned and checked the schedule. Obviously it was unlike Terry to forget about an appointment. Miss Perky perused the page, and flipped over to the next one.

"What's your name?" she asked, now frantic to get to the bottom of this scheduling snafu.

"Jarrod. Jarrod Jarvis."

"I don't see it. Are you sure it was for today?"

"I called to confirm this morning."

"Let me try her cell phone." She grabbed the receiver next to her and dialed. She smiled uncomfortably as she waited for Terry to pick up.

"Maybe she's just running late," I said.

"No. I'm sure she was done for the day. She said something about going over to her grandmother's house in Los Feliz."

Could her grandmother be Gladys Phelan? I was sure there were plenty of grandmothers in the Los Feliz area, but those bells and whistles were going off in my head again, which had to mean something. It was strange, however, that Mrs. Phelan talked non-stop about her grandson Theodore but never mentioned a granddaughter.

"Hi, Terry," Miss Perky said brightly, confident the matter would now be dealt with and solved. "I have a client of yours here with me. He says he was supposed to work out with you now . . ." She glanced up at me. "What was your name again?"

"Jarrod Jarvis."

"Right. Jarrod Jarvis." She listened for a moment, and then shifted nervously as Terry talked on the other end of the line.

"Terry says you're not a client, and you have no appointment," she said, a sheepish look on her face.

I grabbed the phone and said with a cheery grin, "Hi, Terry. Are you sure we don't have a session scheduled?"

"What's this about?" Terry said coolly. "I don't know anything about any appointment. What are you trying to pull?"

"I know you have six-thirty p.m. on Fridays free now that Willard is no longer with us. Am I right? Wasn't six-thirty on Friday reserved for Willard? I'm pretty sure it was. I know for a fact you were at his house on that day, at that time, the night he died."

There was a long interminable pause, and then I heard a loud click. I flashed Miss Perky a winning smile and handed the phone back to her. "Her cell phone cut out. Must be going through the canyon," I innocently offered.

"I suppose so," she said, not entirely convinced.

I had hit pay dirt. Terry's reaction had confirmed everything in my mind. And it was time to bring down the final curtain on this long-running show of deceit and murder.

I was on my way out the door when Miss Perky spoke up. "You'll have to forgive Terry. She's been a bit of a mess lately. Not only did she lose one of her clients, her therapist died too."

I stopped cold. "Her therapist?"

"Yes. Nice man. He was murdered. At a dance club in the valley of all places," she said, a disdainful look on her face as if she had just smelt a two-week-old piece of fish.

I spun around. "Was his name Vito Wilde?"

Miss Perky perked up. "Yes. I think it was."

I was out the door.

I knew it would be impossible for me to break into Vito Wilde's office and pore over his patient files. The office was locked and sealed off for the on-going police investigation. And the thought of calling Charlie wasn't a desirable option either. I knew he was home, taking a much-needed break from crime busting and bailing me out of jail, so I decided not to test the limits of our relationship. Besides, my cell phone was only partially recharged so I probably wouldn't have gotten past "Hello."

My only remaining alternative was to follow my hunch, and speed over to Los Feliz for one final chat with schizophrenic granny Gladys Phelan. I had no idea which personality to expect when I got there. Doddering, daffy talk show fan granny or cold, rude badass gutter mouth granny? Or maybe I'd find someone entirely new.

When I arrived at the familiar tiny house with the peeling paint, blue tarp, and unkempt yard, there was still that persistent sense of dread in the air.

I figured if things got rough and Granny jumped me, I could probably take her in a fight. Or maybe I was being too cocky.

I rapped on the door. No answer. I pressed my ear against the door to see if I could hear her television set. It was quiet inside. If the TV wasn't on, then she was definitely not home. I jiggled the door handle. It was locked. I snuck around back, stepping over weeds and dirt before finding a broken window that led into the basement. I reached my arm through, flipped the latch, and opened the loose, flimsy window frame with ease. I was becoming a pro at breaking and entering. But I knew if I got caught again, I'd be right back on the front pages of the tabloids. The headlines would scream, "FORMER CHILD STAR A SERIAL TRESPASSER! BREAKS IN BUT DOESN'T STEAL ANYTHING! WHAT SICK GAME WILL HE PLAY NEXT?"

The house was very still and sweltering hot. Beads of sweat formed on my brow as I made my way through the cluttered rooms, looking for anything that might connect Terry to Gladys and Teddy.

In the back bedroom, I found the computer. It was turned on. I placed my hand on top of the monitor and found it was warm. Somebody had been using it only minutes earlier.

Was Gladys home and just hiding in a closet waiting to spring out at me? She had sworn to me that she never touched the computer. Only her grandson Theodore ever had cause to use it. I swung around. Was Teddy hiding in the closet? Was he about to pounce on me? It was deathly quiet. I stood there, frozen for a moment, straining to hear any sounds that might alert me to someone else in the house, but there were none.

I started walking out of the room when I spotted a framed photo on the dresser. It was a snapshot of a young man, very handsome, probably in his early twenties. What struck me about him was how effeminate his features were. So smooth and delicate in the face, but his arms were thick and his legs muscular. I marveled at how much he looked like Terry Duran. Were they twins, like Eli and Elliot?

And then I noticed the ring on his finger in the picture. It was a gold ring with a small green emerald in its center. It could have been a graduation ring or a fraternity ring. But I knew it was the same ring the intruder wore who attacked me in my house that night with a knife.

The attacker had been Theodore Phelan, and Theodore Phelan was probably attempting to protect Terry, his sister or cousin or whoever.

Terry was the one who had been seeing Vito Wilde. And the night Vito Wilde met me at the bar in Silverlake he mentioned that someone was following him. He assumed it was Spiro, who was afraid that Willard was blabbing to his therapist all about his stepfather's unsavory advances. But what if it wasn't Spiro? What if it was another patient who was connected to Willard? What if this patient was afraid that Vito was going to tell me something else? Something that would put him or her in serious hot water? What was Terry hiding? What could be so dire that it caused her to murder two people and dispatch her brother Theodore to drive a knife through my chest to keep her secret?

And the fact that Gladys never mentioned Terry was still nagging at me. What was that all about?

I heard the door open, and someone shuffle inside. It was Gladys. She made her way to the kitchen, and I heard her start to unpack some grocery bags. I carefully slipped open a window, then slowly and quietly climbed out as the sweat from my forehead stung my eyes. I turned back to close the window so she wouldn't know I had been there when I felt movement behind me.

A blunt object struck the back of my head. A jolt of pain shot through my entire body. I had trouble keeping my balance, stumbled, and then everything went black.

Chapter Thirty-Four

My head was pounding when I opened my eyes and found myself engulfed in darkness. I tried to stretch my legs, but I was encased in what seemed like a coffin. Yet I was moving. I heard the hum of an engine, so it didn't take me long to figure out I was in the trunk of a car.

The panic slowly seeped through my body, spreading and growing like a cancer. I had been claustrophobic since I was twelve and we filmed the one hour third season opener of *Go To Your Room!* on location in Honolulu, Hawaii. In the episode, which was a direct rip-off of a famous *Brady Bunch* three-parter, I stumbled upon an ancient Polynesian artifact that some two-bit thugs wanted, and the show climaxed with me getting trapped in a cave. We were a family sitcom that had no business doing crime capers, but our new head writer was so distracted by a nasty palimony suit, he banged out whatever came into his head.

My parents didn't care about the implausibility of the script. They were just thrilled the whole family got a free trip to Hawaii.

When we filmed the scenes of me stuck in the cave, the director was so impressed with my performance he said, "I think I smell an Emmy."

But I wasn't acting. The short breaths were real. The cries for help were real. The intense feelings of isolation and alarm were all real. And ever since that day, the mere suggestion of being in an enclosed space stirred up panic attacks and meltdowns worthy of the late great Judy Garland.

I kicked the trunk lid over and over with my foot. It was as if I was trying to channel all the terror sweeping through my body into some kind of superhuman strength. I honestly thought I would be able to kick hard enough for it to pop open.

After several tries, common sense prevailed, and I chose to save my energy. What was I going to do? Theodore Phelan could be driving me out to the desert with plans to shoot me through the heart, and leave my body for the vultures as an all-you-can eat Sunday brunch. I had no idea how long I had been unconscious. Maybe hours. We might already be in Arizona or Nevada or even as far north as Oregon for all I knew.

As I rolled over on my back and tried to visualize myself in a wide-open meadow with lots of open space to move around and breathe, I felt a sharp, cutting pain in my left butt cheek. My cell phone! I had stuffed it in my back pocket earlier when I left the car to sneak inside Gladys' house. I could call Charlie. But I had only been able to charge it for a few minutes. I had no idea if the phone had enough juice to make even one call. I flipped it open, and held my breath. The orange lights illuminated and I sighed with enormous relief. My euphoria was quickly dashed, however, when the digital words, "LOW BATTERY" started flashing. I quickly punched the speed dial to home button, and waited. It rang once. Twice. The phone began to BEEP, warning me I didn't have much time before it would die.

After the third ring, I heard Charlie's voice. "Hello?"

"Charlie, it's me!"

"Where are you?"

The car rolled to a stop, and I heard the driver's side door open. Theodore was walking back towards the trunk. He inserted a key and unlocked it. I knew if he saw the phone, he would snatch it away from me, so I quickly jammed it back into my pocket making sure it was upside down so Charlie's voice would be muted but he would still be able to hear most of what was happening. I made a silent prayer that the phone wouldn't die before he could figure out where we were.

The trunk lid rose up, but it wasn't Teddy Phelan there to greet me. It was Terry Duran, her harsh, angry face illuminated in the moonlight.

"Get out," she said.

I sat up and tried to make out where we were. I noticed a long chain link fence that followed the side of the road before disappearing into the darkness. There were lots of trees blowing in the night breeze. At first I thought we had to be far outside the city limits, but then I saw a posted sign that read "Welcome to Lake Hollywood," along with a list of rules for the hiking trail around the scenic reservoir.

Lake Hollywood is a picturesque body of water nestled in the Hollywood hills high above the city. During the day, residents of the area hike around it, passing over a dam bridge. It's a breathtaking view. And nature lovers resigned to city life flock to it as an escape from clogged traffic and smoggy air. But at night it's desolate and quiet, with no streetlights and only the coyotes, squirrels, and lizards to inhabit the trails. If you don't know the area, you might think you were lost in the wilds of Montana, or somewhere far removed from a metropolitan city. But I knew Lake Hollywood like I knew my own backyard. Terry Duran didn't know I lived just over the hill, and that Charlie could swoop in and save the day in a matter of minutes. That is, if the cell phone had enough juice left for him to find out where I was.

"I said GET OUT!" Terry whipped a gun out of the back of her shorts and waved it menacingly at me. I immediately complied with her orders. I could hear Charlie's faint voice emanating from my pants pocket, but luckily the soft wind, the sound of crickets, and other night noises prevented Terry from catching on to what I was trying to do.

"So why did you bring me all the way out here to Lake Hollywood, Terry?" Charlie stopped talking. Either he was listening to what we were saying or the phone had just died. I was afraid I wouldn't live long enough to find out which one was true.

She cocked the gun and flashed a crooked smile. "Why do you think? You should have left it alone."

Leave it alone. Leave it alone. Those were the same words Theodore Phelan had whispered in my ear the night he attacked me in my home.

"You should've listened to me. Goddammit, why didn't you listen to me? Why didn't you stop poking around when I told you to?" She spit the words out with a fury that made my heart skip a beat. She was unbalanced and not thinking clearly, and that couldn't be good for me.

But she had never warned me to leave it alone. It had been Theodore. Or had it? That's when I noticed that she was wearing the same gold ring with an emerald center as the one Theodore Phelan wore in the picture I found at his grandmother's house. The same ring my attacker wore.

It finally hit me, all of it, and I gasped with shock, more from my stupidity than the actual revelation. Theodore and Terry didn't just look alike because they were siblings or cousins. They looked alike because they were the same person.

"You're Theodore," I said quietly.

"No," she barked. "I'm Terry!"

"You used to be Theodore, didn't you?"

She wavered, not sure whether she should admit anything to me. But then her face relaxed. Why not cop to it? It wasn't like I was ever going to leave these woods to tell anybody.

Terry nodded. "Yes, I was. Now turn around."

I did as she ordered. And I winced. Waiting for the pop of a gun. Waiting to feel the force of a bullet blast through me.

"Let's go for a walk," she said.

The fence leading into the path around the lake was secured with a bolted lock. But the chain tying the two separate fences that came together to make a barrier was loose enough to form a small opening. She pushed it back and motioned for me to slip through. You had to be Houdini to make it unscathed, but she wanted me to go, so I went. The wires on the fence cut into my flesh as I squeezed through. I bit my tongue as each movement ripped another gash in my skin.

Once I was through, I debated running. After all, she had to follow, and it would take some effort. Maybe I could make it. But I quickly dismissed that idea as she kept the gun trained on me and didn't even flinch as the sharp iron chains did a number on her legs. Once she was on the other side, her eyes narrowed.

"Move," she said.

I turned around and started walking.

"What's the plan? Are we going to do a few laps around the lake?" I said.

If by some miracle the phone was still working, I knew Charlie would now be able to pinpoint my exact location. But there were a lot of "ifs" in that theory, so I wasn't counting on my Superman to show up any time soon.

"So I take it your grandmother Gladys hasn't seen the new you?"

"Nope," she said flatly. "Hasn't seen me since I was Theodore. Must be close to a year now. She goes to the grocery store the same time every day. I wait until she leaves, and then I go over to her house and use her computer."

"So it was you who sent Willard that threatening birthday card?"

She didn't answer my question. She didn't have to answer it. I had it all figured out.

"You wanted him to die. He had to die. If he didn't, you'd never get your hands on Willard's big fat life insurance policy that your grandparents bought all those years ago. Your grandmother didn't need the money. Not the way she lived. And she had her husband's life insurance to live off. But you needed it. You needed it desperately. And I'm betting it has to do with the big change from Teddy to Terry. You look real. You got the hormone injections, the breasts look perky, everything's rolling along, but you're out of money. I'm guessing you still need a jockstrap when you play Squash."

"It's the last procedure, but I ran out of cash."

"You're not a real woman yet. You're just a chick with a dick. And it was driving you crazy."

"Yes," she said, trying to put a lid on her emotions but failing. "If my grandmother knew why I really needed the money, she'd never agree. So I kept my distance from her, and wrote her letters as Theodore so she wouldn't suspect. She already promised me a good chunk of the money from that life insurance policy. I was so close to getting my hands on it. I knew that Willard was going to die soon from AIDS, and I'd finally be able to afford the rest of my sex change. But he didn't die. He kept hanging on. And then he started taking that cocktail of pills the doctors came up with and his symptoms all but disappeared. They said he was going to live a long, long time, and I thought it was hopeless. I was never going to be able to live as who I really am."

"So you killed him to speed up the process."

I glanced back at Terry. She was looking off at the stars, contemplating. I knew, however, if I made any sudden movements, the gun would go off and I would be left lying on the path in a pool of blood. The scenario unfolded in my mind and I started thinking aloud.

"When you found out who he was, you started following him, working out at the same gym, befriending him, and then eventually you became his trainer. He had no clue that you used to be a man. On the night Willard was supposed to come to my house for a birthday party, you showed up for your scheduled session. You worked out for an hour, toasted his birthday with a glass of wine, and then when Willard went upstairs to take a bath, you pretended to leave. But you didn't. You snuck back, and you surprised him in the tub, yanked his legs up, and he slipped under the water and drowned. That's why there were traces of soap found in his lungs. You had been planning to do it like this for weeks because you knew Willard always took a bath after your sessions. Then, knowing Willard was a big drinker, you poured tequila down his throat to get his blood alcohol level up, dragged him to the pool in his back-yard and tossed him in it face first so the police would assume it was a drunken accident. If it worked, they would close the case quickly, and you could expect that tidy check from the insurance company in no time."

"Kudos to you, Magnum pee wee," she said, not wanting to hear anymore. But I was on a roll. I had been trying to unravel this scam for weeks, and nobody, not even a cold-blooded transsexual killer was going to prevent me from living out my well-deserved Columbo moment.

"You just sat back and waited for the mail to arrive with your check. That is, until I started showing up asking questions. And then, to make matters worse, your therapist, who Willard recom-mended to you, started talking to me. You had already told him too much, not that it was you who murdered Willard, but enough that eventually he might have started to suspect you. You were already following me around terrified I might figure it out, and then you saw me at Vito's office. When you saw us meet at the Rawhide Bar, you started to panic. You were afraid Vito would expose you, so you surprised him in the men's room and slashed his throat."

"I waited so long. Worked so hard. He was going to ruin every-thing talking to you."

"Funny thing is," I said as I stared Terry squarely in the eye. "He didn't suspect a thing. In fact, he thought Spiro was the killer, not you. You never even came up."

There was a flicker of regret on Terry's face. I could tell it both-ered her. She never wanted to kill Vito Wilde, but she was insane with worry and paranoia, and had managed to convince herself that the two of us were conspiring against her. Of course, the sad irony was Vito Wilde probably would've been able to help her. And as for her grandmother Gladys, she had been so protective of him I was certain she would have loved whoever he was, Teddy or Terry.

But none of that mattered now. What mattered was that I was standing at the edge of the lake amongst a cluster of trees. It was late at night. There was nobody around for miles. I had worked so hard to get here and solve this puzzle, and now I was about to die for it. Terry Duran was ready to pull the trigger and snuff out my life just as she had done to Willard Ray Hornsby and Vito Wilde.

Chapter Thirty-Five

As unbelievable as it may sound, given the fact Terry Duran was about to unload a cartridge of bullets into my chest, I felt sorry for her. After two and a half decades of hiding her real self, she was so close to finally being able to live and breathe as the woman she always knew she was. It must have been maddening to be a woman trapped inside a man's body. If just a few snips here and a couple of implants there could finally give her the freedom to live happily ever after, then I could have applauded her for her determination and effort.

But Terry was an altogether different case. She let her desire for a complete sex change grow into a dangerous obsession. And each frustrating setback she suffered began to slowly, methodically eat away at her sanity until she was willing to commit murder in order to turn her dream into a reality. And after one premeditated killing, another one didn't seem so extraordinary.

Vito Wilde failed to see the psychosis brewing inside Terry. Maybe he would have if he hadn't gotten his bogus degree through the mail. In any event, that fatal mistake cost him his life. And with two dead bodies left in her path, a third, namely me, didn't seem like that big of a deal.

I had run out of stalling tactics. Terry was working up the courage to finally pull the trigger and end it right there. Thoughts of Willard flashed through my mind. He wasn't just a gay kid like myself who I kissed at the rodeo when I was sixteen. Despite the years of separation, he was one of the defining people in my life. I thought I let go of my romantic feelings for him, but I simply buried them. And despite my happy relationship with Charlie, Willard's abrupt and unexpected death awakened a passion in me I never knew still lingered. And that, coupled with the fear of winding up just like him and a long line of other former child stars, was what drove me so hard to unlock the mystery of his demise. I always loved Willard Ray Hornsby. I loved him deeply despite how we drifted apart over the years. And because I was unable to let him go, I was now locked in a final showdown with his killer.

"I'm sorry, Jarrod," Terry said softly. "I'm sorry."

She raised the gun. Her eyes squinted as she started to pull the trigger. But then a pair of headlights cut through the darkness, momentarily distracting her. I didn't wait around to see who it was. I dove into the bushes out of the line of fire.

Terry snapped back, and losing all control, fired the pistol three times. One of the bullets pierced the edge of a tree trunk I was hiding behind. It passed so close to my cheek I felt a hot burning sensation as it whizzed past me.

And then I was up on my feet running. I threw my arms up in front of my face to protect it from the branches that I recklessly plunged through in an effort to put distance between me and Terry's gun.

Did the headlights mean the cell phone had stayed on long enough for Charlie to hear where we were? I was afraid to call out to him for fear of Terry finding me before he did. Terry was in a manic state now, left only with the single-minded mission of spraying me yet again with an unrelenting hail of bullets.

I stopped behind a tree and tried to control my asthmatic heaving. I could hear twigs snapping and an intense, disturbed voice

241

muttering obscenities only a few feet away. Terry knew I was close and it was frustrating her that she couldn't find me. It was like a child's game of hide and seek. I quietly lowered myself to the ground and rolled into some bushes.

I held my breath and waited. After a few moments, I saw a pair of shoes rustle through the leaves on the ground. They moved up and stopped about five inches from my face. Terry was so close I could see the scuff marks on her shoes. I was lying with my hand underneath my face, and I started to feel a tingling sensation. Damn it, my hand was falling asleep! Four years of yoga and I couldn't control my stupid hand from falling asleep? I shut my eyes and kept holding my breath, terrified that the smallest sound, the slightest movement would give me away. I tried meditating to forget about the tingling, which was growing in intensity.

"Jarrod!" It was Charlie. He was close, but not close enough. Terry froze, and considered what to do next. She quietly moved away from Charlie's voice and trudged off through the woods.

I slowly exhaled and stayed face down on my belly for another two minutes. I hoped Terry would keep walking away from my hiding place, and it would be Charlie who found me.

When I thought Terry was far enough away, I shook my hand violently to wake it up and get rid of that annoying, numbing, tingling feeling. That's when I heard the hissing start. I thought it was a sprinkler system turning on and I braced myself to get soaked. But after a few seconds, I was still dry and almost certain it wasn't sprinklers. What could it be? Please, God, don't tell me it's . . .

The arched back of a rattler sprung up from the leaves in front of me, coiled for attack. I must have settled into his bed when I hid in the bushes, and he was definitely ticked off that I awoke him from a deep sleep.

I couldn't make a sudden move or the snake would strike. They can jump about three feet. I was trapped, face to face with its sharp fangs dripping with venom. If ever I wanted to scream like a nellie queen, this was the time. I hated snakes. Charlie hated snakes. And whenever we hiked in the hills with Snickers, we always stayed keenly aware of any that might be lurking in the bushes. The Hollywood hills were infested with them, though I rarely saw any. Until tonight, that is. It's scales were course and its colors dull and muted. But when you can stir up so much fear, you don't have to be a looker.

I heard footsteps pounding through the brush. They stopped in a clearing just a few feet away from me. Was it Charlie or had Terry come back? I was afraid it was Charlie, and he was going to get a shot of venom in his leg if he took another step. If I cried out a warning, the snake would strike at me, probably sinking his fangs right in the middle of my forehead. Seconds passed like hours as I waited for the snake to act. He was up and ready, so he was going to attack somebody. The question now was who.

I knew I couldn't let the snake get Charlie, so the only option left was to lure it towards me. I rustled a bush with my fingers to get the snake's attention, but it was too late. I saw a shoe land directly in front of its face. I opened my mouth to yell a warning, but before any words escaped, I saw the snake's mouth close over the leg.

A blood-curdling scream pierced the air. It wasn't Charlie. It was Terry. She had circled around, hoping to surprise me. But now the surprise was on her. She reached down and ripped the snake off her, and hurled it into the woods. In a state of delirium and fear, she crashed through the trees and disappeared into the night.

I rolled out of the bushes and slammed into someone's legs. It was Charlie. He reached for his gun, but I grabbed his belt buckle and lifted myself up off the ground so he could see my dirt-and-sweat-smeared face in the moonlight.

"Charlie, it's me!"

His face, so full of worry and tension, finally melted into enormous relief, and he grabbed me into a hug, squeezing with all his might. Then I realized the snake could be winding its way back home, so I grabbed his hand and we hoofed it out of the woods and back onto the graveled walking path.

"I was so worried," Charlie said as he showed me the cell phone clenched in his hand. "I never thought I'd get here in time."

"You almost didn't."

"I love you, babe," he said as he clutched my shoulders with his big hands and kissed me on the lips.

"I love you," I said and meant it.

I reached into my back pocket and pulled out my cell phone and looked at it. "I know you're controversial and cause a lot of traffic accidents, but I love you too." And I kissed it. The "LOW BATTERY" warning was still flashing, so I shut it off to give it a much needed and well-deserved rest.

"Where's Terry?"

I shrugged. Charlie had his other hand wrapped around his police-issued revolver, and spun around. Terry could spring out at any moment, full of poisonous snake venom but still armed and dangerous. But she didn't. The lake was quiet again except for the sounds of a few police sirens in the distance. Charlie called for back up when he was racing to the lake.

Terry was nowhere to be found. And she wouldn't be found for another week, when a crew of parks and recreation workers accidentally speared her lifeless body while dredging Lake Hollywood. Investigators concluded that once the hopelessness of her situation finally registered, with the venom coursing through her veins further fueling her anxiety and panic, and with Charlie and the cops closing in, she finally gave up the struggle to cover her tracks. She relinquished her dream to complete the transformation to Terry Duran, and jumped headfirst off the bridge.

Once famous for its prominent role in the disaster film *Earthquake*, the bridge would be known from this day forward as the landmark where the transsexual killer Teddy/Terry took a swan dive, thus climaxing her murderous rampage. That's what the tabloids would scream, and yes, I would be permanently attached to the whole sordid story. I got more press coverage from this piece of Hollywood Babylon lore than I did from my whole notorious career. It was awful. But I knew the details weren't so sensational, so ready made for public consumption. Terry Duran wasn't a marauding maniac, neatly wrapped up for the nightly news. She was far more complex. Yes, she was desperate and disturbed. Yes, her obsessions led to the tragic deaths of two vibrant men in their prime. But she was human and sad and not an excuse for the right wing to go on television and denounce "her kind" and call her "the result of sexual perversion."

It angered me that her story would provoke such debate, because it only made it difficult for those who are still struggling with their sexual identities, still trying to live on the outside as they live on the inside. Terry Duran could have been a shining beacon for those still struggling, if only she hadn't chosen a dark and deadly path as a means to an end.

I spent the ensuing weeks following the end of my ordeal reconnecting with my boyfriend and avoiding the harsh glare of the media spotlight. I knew the attention would eventually die down and my life would resume with some modicum of normalcy. Charlie and I had not gone hiking in the neighborhood since that fateful night because I hadn't been able to get over my close brush with that irate rattlesnake. But finally, on a gorgeous sunny Sunday afternoon, we set out with Snickers on a three-mile trek up to the Hollywood sign and back.

I found some closure once Terry's body was found, and I was finally able to cry for Willard. It hadn't occurred to me that from the moment I found his body floating in the pool to the moment I unmasked his killer, I had been so focused, so obsessed in uncovering the facts, that I never had time to properly mourn the loss, to shed some hearty, gut-twisting tears. And when Charlie's captain called with the news that Terry's body had been recovered, a grief swept over me that was so strong and overpowering, I wept for two days. Charlie gave me plenty of space, because in so many respects, he is the perfect boyfriend.

Charlie had been right all along about my lingering feelings for Willard. He knew it the night when we fought over Laurette and I breaking into Willard's Brentwood home. We both knew at the time our conflict had nothing to do with my trespassing charge. It was about me refusing to be honest about why I was so persistent. Had I told him from the get-go, he may not have been happy about it, but he would have understood. Instead, I stormed out of the house rather than confront the issue head on. In some ways, Charlie knew me better than I knew myself.

We gripped hands as we climbed the hill towards the Hollywood sign.

"I think I'm going to give up acting," I said matter-of-factly.

Charlie arched an eyebrow. He had heard this before. "Really?"

"I want to be like Dominick Dunne."

"Who?"

Charlie didn't read *Vanity Fair* with the fervor and rabid passion that I did, so I had to fill in a few blanks. "Famous writer. He lost a daughter in the eighties. Her boyfriend murdered her. Dunne became a seeker of justice, a purveyor of truth. He was a fixture at the O.J. trial."

"You want to be a spectator in the courtroom?"

"No. He does a lot more than that. He investigates all sorts of high profile crimes where he believes justice isn't being served."

"Oh. Okay. Whatever you want to do, I support you."

Charlie wasn't quite getting it. He was a cop. Every day he was inundated with human pain and suffering, such horrifying acts of violence and chilling stories of betrayal and perversion. He could never understand why I would actively seek out such misery.

But Willard Ray Hornsby's murder had had a profound effect on me, and I needed to channel that experience into a new endeavor. I was going to expose the underbelly of Hollywood, the smarmy, self-satisfied element that thought they were smart enough to hurt other people and get away with it. Yes, I thought, this was my new calling. Acting was no longer a priority.

Charlie and I, both sweating, our legs aching from the steep up-hill climb, reached the top of the mountain. We were above the massive letters that stretched across the hillside, forming the world famous Hollywood sign. The city was nestled in a basin before us. The sky was free of smog and a few clouds wafted through the crystal blue horizon. I put my arm around Charlie and we stood there, gazing out at the magnificent view, while Snickers took a dump in the brush a few feet away. Oh well. No scene is perfect.

The cell phone in my fanny pack rang, and I reached in to answer it. Charlie smirked. He knew I hated lugging my cell phone around, but ever since it saved my life, I felt obligated to include it in my life more.

I flipped it open. "Hello?"

"Jarrod, it's Laurette." She sounded out of breath, excited.

"Hi. What's up?"

"You got it."

"What?"

"The NBC pilot. Without an audition. Can you believe it?"

"That was weeks ago. I thought the whole show would've been shot by now."

"When you refused to come in, they hired another actor. Some cast off from this weird cult soap *Passions*. Anyway, it didn't work out. They wanted someone funny and he thought he was doing *Saving Private Ryan*."

"But I told you, Laurette, I'm giving up acting. We had a whole lunch at the Cheesecake Factory about this."

"I know, and I thought it was a good idea. But that's when you couldn't get arrested. This is a network pilot."

Charlie folded his arms and smiled at me. He knew exactly what was transpiring and he loved every minute of it.

Laurette was practically having an orgasm on the other end of the phone. "Your call is tomorrow morning at nine a.m. You'd be an idiot to say no. What do I tell them?

I turned away from Charlie and whispered frantically into the phone, "Tell them I'll be there." Then I nonchalantly closed the phone and popped it back inside my fanny pack.

"So what was that all about?" Charlie said, grinning from ear to ear.

"Oh. They want me for a pilot. On NBC. Thursday nights."

"Uh huh. And what did you tell them?"

He was enjoying this far too much. I whipped around and said, "It's a pilot, Charlie. Of course I said I'd take it."

He nodded. "I just thought your career wasn't a priority anymore. That helping those in need was your new calling."

"Ever hear of multi-tasking?" I said. "Who says I can't seek justice for the disenfranchised while starring in my own network prime time TV series?"

Charlie hooked an arm around my neck and pulled me close. With his free hand he rubbed the top of my head with his knuckles in a playful gesture. "Sounds like a plan, babe."

And then together we headed back down the mountain towards home, Snickers scampering behind at our heels.